PRAISE FOR

DEATH AT THE

"Move over, Walt Longmire. There'............................ton is the kind of character that comes along maybe once a decade— a classic Western hero and so much more. When you're done with Frank Hayes's stellar debut, *Death at the Black Bull*, you'll smell the sagebrush in the air and have to clean the dust off your boots. An absolute must-read for fans of Craig Johnson and Tony Hillerman."

—Reed Farrel Coleman,
Shamus Award–winning author of *The Hollow Girl*

"This is one of the most impressive debut crime novels I've ever read. There's such depth and humanity in the characters, such tension in the story itself, and the sense of place is as good as it gets. I know I'll be reading every book in this series!"

—Steve Hamilton,
Edgar® Award–winning author of *Let It Burn*

"Virgil Dalton takes no prisoners in Hayes's satisfying debut novel, and fans of Craig Johnson's Walt Longmire will cheer the sheriff's desire to protect his town. With its strong sense of place, this series launch will also keep fans of Western mysteries enthralled." —*Library Journal*

"Hayes's strong debut introduces a complex and likable lawman . . . Readers will want to see a lot more of Virgil and friends."

—*Publishers Weekly*

"Hayes is a skillful storyteller and a deft hand at witty dialogue."

—*Booklist*

continued . . .

"Modern with the flavor of the Old West blended in smoothly for a mesmerizing story . . . Hang up your hat, prop up your boots, and grab a copy of *Death at the Black Bull* for a rip-roaring good read."

—Thoughts in Progress

"Hayes has created not only a nicely plotted story, but major and minor characters who are truly memorable . . . All indeed is well done. Highly recommended."   —I Love a Mystery

"Hayes is a terrific storyteller . . . The final twist was a real shocker, too! . . . He is definitely an author to watch."

—Escape with Dollycas into a Good Book

Berkley Prime Crime titles by Frank Hayes

DEATH AT THE BLACK BULL
DEATH ON THE HIGH LONESOME

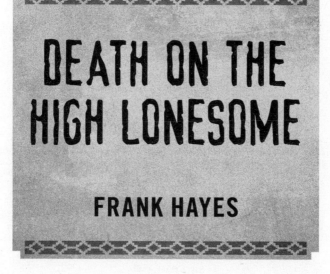

DEATH ON THE HIGH LONESOME

FRANK HAYES

BERKLEY PRIME CRIME, NEW YORK

An imprint of Penguin Random House LLC
375 Hudson Street, New York, New York 10014

This book is an original publication of Penguin Random House LLC.

Library of Congress Cataloging-in-Publication Data

Hayes, Frank, 1940–
Death on the high lonesome / Frank Hayes.—Berkley Prime Crime trade paperback edition.
    pages ; cm
    ISBN 978-0-425-27430-9
    I. Title.
PS3608.A924D44 2014
813'.6—dc23
2015017245

PUBLISHING HISTORY
Berkley Prime Crime trade paperback edition / October 2015

PRINTED IN THE UNITED STATES OF AMERICA

10 9 8 7 6 5 4 3 2 1

Cover design by Jason Gill.
Interior text design by Tiffany Estreicher.

Penguin
Random
House

1043874

To Elizabeth and John Pappas,
who have modeled for all to witness strength of character
in the face of adversity during the last two years.

ACKNOWLEDGMENTS

To all who have supported my efforts: Steve Hamilton and Bill Keller who have always kept me on course. A host of family and friends, particularly Sheila and Jerry Hayes, who hosted a great launch party. And last but not least, Ann Godoff, who opened a door and invited me to walk through.

1

Jimmy Tillman hardly ever went on the interstate. As a deputy sheriff from the town and county of Hayward, it was out of his jurisdiction. It was under state authority, patrolled by state police. However, during nightly patrols, he would pass under it. This night was no exception. He had already done so twice. The nearest interchange was down near Redbud, almost twenty miles away. The law enforcement for that part of the county was covered by Dave Brand and Alex Rankin, who staffed the substation there. Dave was Rosita's husband. She was the glue that kept the sheriff's office in Hayward together. There was talk of adding another interchange, closer to Hayward, if the town kept up its slow but steady growth.

Jimmy had time to think about all of this as he made his nightly rounds. He thought, too, about the unspoken change in his status as recognized by the town council in approving his 24/7 use of the patrol car. He knew this was in no small way due to Virgil Dalton, sheriff, the closest thing to a father Jimmy ever had. When he was younger, long before he actually reached the rank of deputy, he had often fantasized about Virgil actually being his father. That had lasted until his real father had turned up again, staying around just long enough to give Jimmy a sister, Abby, twelve years younger. Shortly thereafter his mother said Jimmy's father heard the sound of the outward bound. He left in the middle of the night like a bad dream. They'd had no word of him ever since.

It was a little after two in the a.m. when Jimmy pulled into the parking lot in back of the sheriff's office. There had been some talk recently about paving the lot, but at present it was as it had always been. Once a year, usually in the spring, some Item 4 mixed with some half-inch stone was dumped and spread, so that by now clumps of weed had managed to get a foothold. There was even a small cactus growing by the door. Dif was snoozing at the desk by the radio, but sat up quickly when the door slammed in back of Jimmy. Dif had been a deputy under Virgil's father, Sam Dalton. Now semiretired, he was a part-timer.

"Sorry," Jimmy said.

"No, jist gotta get some java. You didn't call in. Guess I kinda dozed off."

"There was nothing to report. Dark and quiet out there. Summer's done, kids are back in school. Guess they won't get crazy till that first home game."

"Yeah, football frenzy." Dif poured two coffees and was carrying them to the small yard-sale table that sat against the far wall when Jimmy came out of the bathroom. "There's a couple of doughnuts if you want to grab that box on the desk," he said.

"No. Just think I'll have my sandwich and a yogurt later when I take a break."

"Eating healthy these days."

"Trying to. Don't get much exercise in the cruiser."

"Yeah. Back in the day we made our rounds on foot. Course we could throw a rock from one end of town to the other. Only went out of town when we actually got a call. Coupla times a week Sam would do the perimeter on horseback. Think he liked it better than the patrol car. Me, never liked horses. They didn't like me, either. Still got a half-moon scar on my ass from that piebald Sam used to ride. Virgil's jist like Sam. He jist fits a horse."

Jimmy, his mouth filled with sandwich, nodded at different points in Dif's narrative. He was really happy that the town council went along with keeping Dif on part-time. Whenever Dif worked, Jimmy always made it a point to stop back at the office to eat and listen to Dif's stories. He especially liked when Dif talked about the personal stuff. He had seen Virgil many times on horseback, but now he could see Sam Dalton astride, making his rounds. There was something mythic about it, introducing Jimmy to a life, a time, and a place he could only know from the mouths of people who had been around long before he came on the scene. Jimmy didn't realize it, but he had become a student of history.

"Guess I'd better get back on my horse," Jimmy said as he took a last swallow from his cup. He started to pick up his leavings.

"Let it go, Jimmy. I'll clean up—got plenty of time. You like all those horses under the hood, don't you?"

Jimmy smiled.

"Your first car, got all the bells and whistles and the town pays for it. My first car was a '56 Bel Air Chevy, turquoise and white, best car I ever owned. Bought it secondhand of course. Drove that car everywhere. Across creeks during spring runoff, out in the desert, even took Edna on our honeymoon in it. Stayed in one of those cabins outside of Kingman up in the Hualapai. We jist about wore each other out—almost didn't make it to the Grand Canyon. Yeah, had some good times with that car. Then, after I put near two hundred thousand miles on it, I sold it for almost as much as I paid for it to a college kid who wanted to restore it. Turns out it was a classic. Hell, that car is probably still driving around West Texas somewhere." When Dif paused, Jimmy grabbed his Stetson off the table. He knew he didn't have time for another reverie.

"Well, duty calls, Dif. Gotta get back out there and look for some criminals." He opened the door. As he stepped through, he heard Dif's last words.

"Take care, Jimmy. Them lawbreakers ain't got a chance with you on the job."

It was still black as pitch when Jimmy left for his last go-round. No moon, just dark. He thought about what Dif had said about only patrolling the town back when. Times had changed. It was not unusual for him to ring up over two hundred miles on the odometer. This night he decided to make his last run east of town, then north along the saddleback, the high ground on the other side of the interstate, then under the interstate for the last time, and home. He passed by the Black Bull. It was closed, no cars in the lot. He still got a hit of adrenaline when he thought about Buddy Hinton and what had happened to him there. Then he passed the grain silos by the railroad tracks, crossed over the tracks, went by a couple of houses, all but one unlit, and turned north.

When he got up on the saddleback high over the interstate he turned west. He knew even if he could see, there wasn't much to see. The land up here was rough desert interspersed with stands of piñons, other conifers, and a lot of rock. Because of the altitude, it did have the payoff on a clear day of an expansive view of the valley.

He rarely took this route. He hit the brake lightly as an armadillo scooted across the road, again a little later for a mule deer. The land rose toward the mountains as he climbed. He rode along the ridgeline for about ten miles. Nothing, no sign of a light in the valley below. He was thinking a person could get swallowed up by the landscape out here.

He banked the cruiser to the left as he started his descent toward the underpass, which was less than a half mile away. For the first time, he saw headlights on the interstate. Truckers, most likely. Twenty minutes from now, he'd be shucking his boots, sitting on the edge of his bed. He braked as he came down the hill, slowing even more as the road started a sharp descent. The windows of the car were down. He could hear the traffic above—a couple of semis, he figured.

Emerging from the tunnel, he glimpsed something falling through the night sky. There was a deep, hollow thud. The wheel jumped out of his hand, the car veered to the left. Something crashed into the windshield, spraying him with shards of glass. He got his right hand on the wheel as the car slipped off the hard surface onto the shoulder. Trying to regain control, he yanked the wheel to the right, pulling harder then he should have. The vehicle spun, lurching across the road. He tried the brake to slow the downward momentum, but he was too late. The cruiser leaped off the embankment on the other side. He felt the sudden quiet when the rubber no longer met the road. There was a fleeting moment of expectation, then he heard the ripping of branches as the car carved out its path till it slammed into a tree at the bottom of the ravine. Jimmy's last thought was that he had never known a night as dark as this one.

*   *   *

High sun managed to find ravines and depressions that a morning sun never could. The searching brightness fell on Jimmy's car. The hood, smashed beyond repair, had just enough flat surface to bounce reflected light through the broken windshield onto Jimmy's face. Jimmy squinted in its glare, then finally opened his eyes. Minutes passed. The light that brought him back to the world moved on. He fought to comprehend. Bits and pieces started to come together. No pain. Discomfort, yes, but no pain. There was a tightness, a cramped feeling, a deflated white balloon in his lap. He tried pushing it off to the side, but his left arm wouldn't work. His right arm was free. It wasn't a balloon, it was an air bag.

An accident. It all came flooding back. Something had fallen on him. What was it? His vision was partially obscured by of all things the branch of a piñon tree. He felt hot. There was also sweat running into his eyes, which he tried to wipe away with his free hand. When he took away his hand, he realized it wasn't sweat. His hand was covered in blood. He looked down on the seat. He saw that it was saturated with crimson. There was a moment of near panic. He looked at the tree limb, then put his hand to the side of his head. He could feel the gash, a slice that ran from the tip of his forehead all the way back across his scalp to the back of his head. He knew that if he wanted to, he could lift the slice like a flap to expose his skull. Blood ran freely from the wound. He knew that scalp wounds bled profusely, but there was a lot of blood. He was literally sitting in a puddle. Hours, he realized, must have passed. How many? He knew he had to act before he passed out from the blood loss or he might never wake up. He couldn't move anything but his right arm. The side of the car had jammed his left arm tight while his legs were held by the crushed front end. He managed to get a pen out of his shirt pocket. He stabbed at the air bag till he ripped it away. The dashboard was obliterated along with the radio. If he could reach the glove box, he knew his cell phone would be there, but the branch that scalped him blocked his effort. He could feel weakness starting to creep over him.

"No, no," he said as he attacked the piñon, breaking off the shoots from the main limb. It took time. His fingers were cut by the sharp bark, but he didn't stop. At last he could see an opening. He wasn't able to see the glove box, but reaching across the console with his face buried in the still-attached branches he could feel the glove box. The impact of the crash had popped the door open, a bonus, he thought as he reached in and found his cell phone. The exertion had cost him. He knew he was fading. He punched in the number to the office, holding his breath hoping for service. Then the sweetest sound he ever heard. Rosita's voice.

"Jimmy, where the hell are you?"

2

He felt like a stranger in his own world. Clouds of dust obscured the last of the trucks as he stood watching in the driveway. They would not be back. Virgil looked on till they reached the hard road, then stood even longer while the dust settled. When he moved at last, he turned to the two newly built barns that stood in the footprints of their predecessors. Bigger, gleaming, evidence of the latest in structural technology, they did nothing for him but confirm his displacement.

Almost reluctantly, he walked toward them. When he got close he could smell the sawn wood siding. He reached a side door, but before entering, he ran his fingers over the splintered roughness that butted the doorframe. Cesar had asked him the afternoon before, as one of the workers was putting the finishing touches on some trim, if he had thought of a color or if he just wanted to seal the wood, keeping it natural. Virgil's lack of response caused him to repeat his question.

"Whatever we're going to do to the outside, we maybe want

to get done before winter. On the other hand, maybe we should just let the wood season till next year. What do you think?"

Virgil looked at Cesar like he was speaking in tongues. "I don't know. Let me think on it."

Cesar got up from his usual seat on the front porch. As he passed by Virgil's chair, he reached out and lightly touched his shoulder.

"No rush," he said. "It'll keep."

Virgil knew that if there was one person in the world who had a clue as to how he felt, it was Cesar. Now as he stood with his hand on the brand-new doorknob, he felt that when he pushed it open, a chunk of his past would disappear. The scab had to fall from the wound, in the process of healing. In the deepest part of his brain there was the realization that he had to move forward. He clenched his teeth and pushed. The door swung open so easily it surprised him. He could recall the hundreds of times when the wood in the old barns would swell and resist entry until a foot or shoulder was brought into play.

The barns were pretty much mirror images of each other in terms of their exterior dimensions. This one however had a separate tack room along with two rooms that were set aside for Cesar's living quarters. Virgil had made sure they were a significant upgrade from Cesar's previous room. He was pleased when he checked out the two finished rooms and saw that Cesar had already left his imprint. A few colorful scenes hung on one wall in the bedroom, framed with a gaucho's bolo. In the adjoining room, which served as a kitchen and living room area, there were terra-cotta plates sitting on a tablecloth with a Southwestern motif of mixed desert flowers, along with all-new appliances, which reminded him how dated the kitchen was in the main house. He did not miss the half-filled bottle of tequila sitting on the counter next to the refrigerator. When he left the living area after checking out the modern bathroom, his mood had lightened.

By the time he got to the second barn, it was again becoming a struggle to not look for the pleasant ghosts of his past. They had been so alive to him in the old barns that had been reduced to ashes. There was not the full-throated laughter of his father in response to the gentle teasing of his mother. He did not hear her singing as she curried Star. He did not see himself as a boy unsuccessfully trying to lasso one of the chickens as it pecked aimlessly along the dirt corridor between the stalls, or see his father easily do the exact same thing.

By the time he got to the second hayloft upstairs, a huge empty space, he was feeling just as empty. He came down the stairs, an improvement over the ladders in the old barns, as Cesar had readily pointed out. When he reached the bottom, he gripped the handrail tight, then sunk slowly to the second step, sinking in a sea of remembrance. There was nothing of his past in this place. He lowered his head. His hat fell to the floor. He bent down to pick it up to dust it off.

"Not even dust here," he said to the empty space.

He looked down the length of the barn to the opened double doors that led into the corral. The wide expanse of light was divided in two by an unrecognizable figure. Doubting the evidence of his own senses, he rubbed his eyes before he looked again. The figure started moving down the passageway toward him. He saw the golden red hair catching the last of the sun outside. The figure stopped less than twenty feet from him and his heart skipped a beat. A name jumped from his past into his mouth.

"Rusty."

"No, Virginia," she answered. "I thought maybe we should talk."

"Let's go up to the house." He nodded in that direction, then stepped ahead of her.

Virginia followed him wordlessly back down the walkway between the vacant stalls out into the corral. Before he could open the gate for her, she slipped effortlessly through the rails. He did the same. When he stood up on the other side, she was facing him. She was taller than he'd realized.

The house, sitting on a knoll on the opposite side of the driveway, was catching the late-afternoon sun. The glare of reflected light on the facing windows made it seem larger than it was. The cottonwood, to the left of the kitchen entrance, defied the light, shading about a third of the porch that ran across the front of the house. Virgil instinctively stopped at the bootjack outside the door and slipped off his boots.

"You were well trained." She then bent down to untie her sneakers. Virgil put out his hand.

"No, no," he said. "That's not necessary. It's just force of habit for me. My boots aren't even dirty. The barns are brand-new, just been built."

She stood up. "That's not a bad habit."

"I should have brought you in the main door. I just hardly ever use it."

"Do you often talk to yourself?"

"Oh, I guess I do sometimes. Some of my best conversations, but I get kinda concerned when I start arguing with myself, especially when I lose the argument." He half smiled.

"You should do that more often."

"What?"

"Smile. It looks good on you."

He held open the door and she stepped inside.

"Nice. Comfortable." She looked about the kitchen.

Virgil saw only the dirty dishes piled in the sink. "I didn't get to the dishes yet. I wasn't expecting . . ." He didn't finish. "Would you like something? A drink maybe? A glass of iced tea?"

"Iced tea would be great." With her own half smile. "But if you don't have any made a beer would be great, too."

Virgil took off his hat and put it on the counter, then he got two glasses and put them alongside. He reached into the fridge and brought out a nearly full pitcher of iced tea. He set it next to the glasses.

"The real deal," she said when she saw actual lemons floating in the pitcher.

"Yeah, sometimes the old-fashioned way is best." Virgil filled two glasses and handed one to Virginia. "Maybe you'd like to sit in the living room."

Before she could respond, he left the kitchen. She followed, glancing to her left at the stairs that led to the second floor. They crossed through the hall to the dining room, then through the arched opening that led from the dining room to the living room, which ran across the entire back of the house. A huge picture window centered on the rear wall looked out on a broad, grassy area. Clusters of wildflowers broke up the green. To the right, she could see the ever-running creek that twisted in back of the barns, making its way toward the road. It emptied into a substantial pond, alongside of which stood a white summerhouse with a trellised-rose entryway. The living room itself was sparsely furnished. A couple of leather chairs faced a stone fireplace. In front of the picture window was a long sofa covered in a fabric of light earth tones. On either side of the sofa were rustic end tables while on the floor was a vivid hooked rug. The only other pieces of furniture in the room were a trestle desk and chair on the half wall to the right of the entryway. Western prints hung on all the walls.

"This is really nice," she said as she sat down in the sofa opposite the picture window. "It feels like a real home."

Virgil sat at the other end. "Not quite as imposing as Crow's Nest."

"True, but also not as pretentious. I think Crow's Nest was built to make a statement. This house was built to be lived in."

Virgil nodded.

"It's so green." She gestured toward the expanse on the other side of the picture window.

"Bottomland."

"Bottomland?"

"When my great-grandfather came to this country he knew how important water was and he let that inform his choice of where to homestead. Turns out he probably got the best parcel of land in this part of the country. We're green when in the dry a lot of other people are eating dust. We do irrigate some, but that's mostly BLM lease land, not part of the deeded property."

"Interesting."

They sipped from their glasses. They each started to speak, then stopped. They smiled while the awkward moment passed.

"I thought maybe you might stop by Hilltop, but then I thought the house, Crow's Nest, wasn't the place for this conversation. I actually stopped by here last week. I met your foreman, Cesar. He was very nice."

"I'm sorry I missed you, but I'm glad you met Cesar. He's much more to me than a foreman."

"I know. I could tell by the last thing he said to me." She took another sip from her glass, then set it on the wood table next to her.

"What was that last thing that Cesar said to you?"

Virginia angled her body so she was looking directly at Virgil.

"He said it was good for me to come and talk to my father now that he is feeling alone."

Virgil said nothing as the silence in the room became almost painful. Finally, he stood up and walked to the window. The shadow of the house crept up toward the meadow in back as the sun started its journey toward evening. The demarcation line between light and dark was very clear. There was no gray, only the light and the dark. Virgil turned and looked at the girl. She sat on the edge of the sofa while he tried to understand the look in her eyes. Unexpected emotions battered him. He took a step toward her. He reached out his hand. Her fingers tentatively touched his.

"I guess we don't have to worry about the elephant in the room anymore. Cesar took care of that." His smile broadened when he saw the relief come into her eyes. "When did you find out?"

"My grandmother Audrey. She left me a letter when she died. How did you find out?"

"From Audrey. The day she died. There's a woman who pretty much runs my office. Rosita. Rosie. You'd probably like her. Everybody does. Anyway, she made a comment after Audrey's funeral about her seeming to go out with a whimper. A surprise to anyone who knew her, considering she wore the name of the town. Well, I guess as far as you and I are concerned, Rosie for once was wrong. I'd say she went out with a bang, wouldn't you?"

Virginia could only nod her agreement. Her eyes were glistening. Her fingers tightened in Virgil's hand. He gently tugged and she rose to her feet. They stood as close to each other as they ever had. In a voice barely above a whisper, Virgil was the first to speak. "Would you mind if I gave you a hug?"

"No," she answered. "I think I'd like that."

Virgil wrapped his arms around her, drawing her close. They stood like that a long time.

3

The phone was ringing when he stepped back into the kitchen after she had gone. He had been planning on driving into Hayward, figuring he'd stop by the office by way of routine. The idea of routine ended when he picked up the phone and heard Rosie's voice.

"Virgil, Jimmy's been in an accident. He was coming off the saddleback last night. Something went bad. He's been at the bottom of a crevasse for the last eight or ten hours pinned in his car. The ambulance is on its way with Toby Sweets's wrecker. Doesn't look too good."

Virgil's ranch was closest so he got to the scene before the ambulance or the tow truck. He came up toward the saddleback from the south. When he saw the interstate overhead he pulled off onto the right shoulder. He knew that if Jimmy had been on his way down, he would have lost it somewhere on the other side of the road. He also knew there was very little shoulder on that side before the drop-off. He crossed the road, looking for some indication of where the cruiser had left the road. The only evidence was some spread gravel on the hard surface. When he first glanced down the embankment he saw nothing. The sides were sheer and it was a long way to the bottom. He realized that the car must have gone airborne, so he immediately started down the slope. It was at least thirty feet of treacherous slip sliding, holding on to saplings or anything else he could grab before he hit level ground. Then he saw the first sign. Tops of woody brush had been flattened or ripped off. He followed the trajectory they offered. It was another forty to fifty feet of bushwhacking before he saw the rear end of the car. He heard sirens up above. Help had come. Whatever he was about to find, he would not have to deal with it alone. Instead of yelling, he drew his sidearm and fired off two rounds. The roar echoed along the crevasse. When he looked up, he saw two or three EMTs at the top of the ridge.

"Down here! Down here!" He waved his Stetson till he got a wave back. In moments he was at Jimmy's cruiser. There was no way he was getting in on the driver's side so he climbed over the trunk to get to the other side. The passenger's door had actually popped open on impact. He saw Jimmy's body, but the view of his head was obscured by a tree limb that had smashed through the windshield. Virgil climbed onto the car's hood. Reaching through the broken windshield, he grabbed the limb and started pulling it back. The muscles in his back tightened as the tree resisted his efforts. Two EMTs reached the car. One of them, seeing what he was attempting, jumped up onto the hood. Together they strained until the branch started to come toward them. When they felt it starting to give, they redoubled their efforts. Suddenly, it snapped as it came free. Both men reeled back with the release till they fell off either side of the car.

Virgil was lying on his back in a tangle of undergrowth when he heard the other EMT.

"He's alive, Roscoe. Get over here. We've got to get a line into him before we get him out of the car. He's lost a lot of blood."

Virgil started to get up by rolling over to the passenger's side of the hood. Through the shattered windshield, he came face-to-face with a girl who looked oddly familiar, but who was now clearly dead.

Later, slouched in a chair in a waiting room at the hospital, Virgil reflected on the suddenness of life. It was not new to him. His mother and father had left the ranch on a routine errand one day, only to drive out of his life forever. Since that day, rolling with the punches had been one of his strengths, but this day had him reaching for the ropes. He was exhausted and it must have showed.

"Don't get up, Virgil. I'll join you. You look like you've had a rough day."

Virgil looked at the doctor, who was also his friend. "You could say that, Sam. Guess you're going to tell me whether it's about to get rougher."

"Breathe easy, Virgil. I know you're heavily invested in that boy. He's going to be fine. Got two things working for him. He's young and he's got the constitution of a bull rider. Left arm is broke. So is his nose. But by and large his good looks are intact. Girls will still give him a second look. He's probably going to have a permanent part in his hair where that tree tried to scalp him. On top of that, a three-day headache to go along with that cut. What beats me is there is no evidence of a skull fracture or even a hint of a concussion. When they talk about hardheaded, they must be talking about that boy. Couple of ribs are cracked. That will only hurt him when he breathes, but that's a habit he ought to try to keep up. We got him pretty doped up, but if you want to see him before you leave, don't expect him to make too much sense."

Sam stood up, taking off his surgical cap as he did. "Now I'm going to get my supper. I'll look in on him later before I leave the hospital. By the way, he won't be much use to you for a couple of weeks."

Virgil rose from his seat. "Did you speak with Jimmy's mom and sister?"

"No. I thought maybe it'd be better coming from you. Some folks get faint seeing a doctor walking toward them in scrubs. Might be a little less upsetting seeing you walk through the door."

Virgil spent the better part of a half hour with Abby and Jimmy's mother. He was glad to give them good news, see the relief in their faces. Then he looked in on Jimmy, who would never know he had been there. He reached out and touched the side of Jimmy's cheek before he stepped away from the bed. A deep breath escaped him. It had been a close call. Anyone passing by might not have noticed the slight sag to Virgil's shoulders.

When he stepped outside into the night, he felt a slight chill in the air. It felt good. Before he got into his car, he looked up at a sky that couldn't hold another star. It was good to see they were all where they belonged.

It was past nine. He wasn't surprised when he pulled into the parking lot in back of his office to see a few extra cars there. Bob Jamison's red SUV he recognized. "Ears," as he was well known, always kept a high profile. Pretty near everyone within the town limits of Hayward knew the mayor's car. The other cars he did not recognize, with the exception of Dif Taylor's pickup, which on any ordinary night would have been the only car there. Virgil had a hunch that this night was not quite over for him. Before he turned the doorknob to his office, he took in a slightly deeper breath.

He was tired. It had been a long day. He could have done without this final chapter but he knew if he didn't give an accounting tonight, it would only be facing him in the morning.

There were four of them beside Dif and the mayor, all members of the town council. The only missing member was Harriet Kleman. Harriet and her husband, Karl, ran a florist business. Karl liked seeing the Kleman's Florist truck parked prominently in front of city hall. Harriet's absence tonight, Virgil knew, was not for a lack of concern, but due to the fact that she was getting ready to give birth. Karl was nearly forty-seven and Harriet was forty-five. They'd been married for twenty-five years and were childless. They pretty much figured that ship had left the dock for them after years of trying and thousands spent on fertility treatments. They'd even toyed with the idea of adoption or using a surrogate, but had finally resigned themselves to the notion that it just wasn't meant to be. That's when Harriet decided to run for a seat on the city council. Shortly after winning, a couple of severe bouts of indigestion and some missed periods along with a kind of bloated feeling sent her to a doctor. They were expecting a diagnosis of gallstones and menopause onset. Instead, it was a set of twins. Karl had been practically catatonic ever since. The joke around town was that these would be the first gallstones enrolled in preschool. Dif was the first one to get to Virgil when he stepped inside the door.

"How is he, Virgil?"

"He's good, Dif. I just left him. Doc says he'll be down awhile, but that he'll be good as new." Bob Jamison had joined Virgil and Dif.

"I'm so glad to hear that, Virgil. I know how much you like that boy."

Virgil heard similar positive comments coming from the table where three of the council members were sitting.

"Yeah, well I'm not so glad," Lester Smoot said as he stood by Virgil's desk. "We got a cruiser lying in Toby Sweets's junkyard, smashed to bits and only good for parts. I hear that kid you like so much had a girl with him in the cruiser. Trailer park trash, that's all he is, and Bob, you talked us into giving that loser use of the car, twenty-four/seven."

Dif moved so quickly even Virgil was taken off guard. His fist hit Lester Smoot's nose dead center. The crack of bone sounded like a rifle shot. Blood shot out like lava from a volcano. Lester went down. Dif stood over him as he started to moan.

"You sorry son of a bitch. That boy is worth ten of you. Before you get up off that floor, you better think twice about what you're going to say next or by God you'll be sleeping in the hospital bed next to him tonight."

Virgil came alongside Dif. "Take it easy, old-timer. I think you made your point."

Dif stepped back. Lester managed to get to his feet holding on to the desk.

"You . . . you broke my nose. He broke my nose. You all seen it. That old bastard. He broke my nose."

Dif took a step forward. Lester scrambled to the far side of the desk, slipping in a blood puddle.

"You all seen it."

Bob Jamison stepped forward. "Well, I must have got distracted, Lester. But if you say so, it must be true. Because I know you wouldn't lie about such a thing. I don't know if any of the others here saw anything, but I'm sure they'd all pretty much agree, you wouldn't want us talking about something like this in public if it weren't true."

"What are you talking about?"

"Here, Lester." One of the council members had left the table and brought a towel to Lester, who was dripping blood like a leaky faucet.

"Well, Lester," Bob Jamison continued, "you wouldn't want the story told around town that Dif here, a seventy-five-year-old, had busted you, a thirty-something-year-old man, in the nose and had come away from the incident without a scratch. You being held in such high regard and all. No, we know you wouldn't want a story like that being spread around in places like Margie's or the Branding Iron, a place I know you like to frequent. No . . . no, you wouldn't want that told unless it was absolutely true. So, that's just the way we'll make sure to tell it. Old Dif here just got the better of you. Now, since I'm mayor and Virgil here is sheriff, we'd be more than happy to follow up on your complaint if you want to make one. That is, unless you think you're mistaken and just got a little light-headed and maybe walked into a door or some other protrusion you just didn't see, because you were so happy to hear how one of our deputies who was seriously injured in the performance of his duty is going to be all right."

A loud silence followed Bob "Ears" Jamison's narrative. Dif Taylor sat down in a nearby chair and appeared to be breathing heavily.

"Jesus H. Christ. Jesus H. Christ." Lester Smoot held the towel soaked in blood to his nose and walked unsteadily to the door.

"Marvin, maybe you could drive Lester over to the hospital

and get his injury looked at. Tell them it happened while he was doing town business and the town insurance will take care of any bills."

Marvin Lewis, the man who had brought Lester the towel, stood by the table where he had been sitting. "C'mon, Lester, let's get you fixed up so the girls will still smile at you."

The two of them stepped out into the night. After a brief silence, Virgil turned to Dif Taylor.

"Man, I hope you never get pissed off at me, Dif."

Virgil stayed till the last of the council members left. It was just him and Bob Jamison. Dif was going outside to clear his head, he told Virgil.

"I haven't popped anyone in twenty years," Dif said as he stepped through the door. "I thought those days were behind me. Lester jist hit a nerve."

"That was a close one. I'm glad Lester's ego is more fragile than his nose," Bob said.

"Got to give it to you, Bob. You handled that like a politician."

"Yeah, well, I'll feel a lot better when Jimmy wakes up and can tell us something about what happened and where that girl came from."

All the way back to the ranch, Virgil thought about what Bob "Ears" Jamison had said. What kept him awake, though, was her face and the nagging thought that he had seen that face before.

4

Virgil stepped onto the porch with his second cup of coffee in his hand. The steam swirled above the rim in the cool morning air, a reminder of the change that was coming. He sucked in a deep breath. The chilled air told him all he needed to know about the new season. He was ready for it. The previous spring, along with the summer that followed, had been gut-wrenching. Three bodies, a grim enough statistic, but their lives were much more than that. His own vulnerability exposed and the shocking revelation that he had a daughter. It was that last revelation that had him now trying to regain his footing. He put the still-steaming cup to his lips and looked at the newly built barns through different eyes. Moving forward, in the words of his newly discovered daughter . . . Starting over. Starting fresh. He was ready for the new day, whatever it would bring.

"Feels good, doesn't it?"

The words jolted him. "Jesus!" He almost spilled his coffee.

"No, that was my father. I'm still Cesar and we pronounce it 'He-sus.'" Virgil watched the man who had been in his life longer than any other step over the side rail of the porch.

"Where are you coming from?"

"The holding pens. Wanted to check what shape they were in before we bring any of the cattle down. The loading ramps need a little work. Thought I'd put Pete and Joe on it today, so we're ready. Weather's changing."

Virgil nodded. "There's some coffee in the pot. Get a cup and we'll talk."

"I'll get the coffee, but there's not that much to talk about. All we have to do is come up with a number. Bottom line is we're heading toward winter without feed."

He left Virgil with that thought. The slap of the screen door sounded like an exclamation mark. When he returned, he sat in one of the porch chairs. Virgil pulled a chair from the other side of the door so he could sit next to him.

"I'm not trying to ignore reality, but I don't want to decimate the herd if we can avoid it. We'll spend years trying to build it back up."

"*Comprende*," Cesar said. "But we lost most all our hay when the barns burned down. Maybe got fifteen, sixteen hundred bales in that old place across the road, but that'll be just enough to take care of the horses. Virgil, most of this part of the country is dealing with drought. A lot of beef's going to market for the same reason this fall."

"That's what I'm thinking. If we send them to market now, we'll take a big hit."

"Can't argue with that, but whatever we keep, we've got to feed. At least we've still got graze—many other places don't. Your granddaddy chose well when he came here. The cattle are still doing well on the grass. No weight loss. But fall grass isn't spring grass and it doesn't grow back near as quick."

Virgil got to his feet. "Let me think on it a bit. We've still got some time. Maybe something will come up. Anyhow, I'm outta here. Got to check on Jimmy." He didn't go into detail about the incident. Past experience told him Cesar probably knew the whole story.

"Hope he's okay. He's young, he'll bounce back, *muy pronto.* Too bad about the girl."

Instead of going directly to the hospital, Virgil stopped by the office. The door was open. He had to jump out of the way to avoid the dust storm that blew out of the opening. Following it was Rosie on the end of a broom.

"Did you have the whole town in here last night? You know, I'm going to be looking for something extra in my paycheck, to cover these janitorial duties."

"Guess it don't hurt to look." He slipped past as the last of the sweepings ended up in the parking lot from which they had come.

"Guess you'll want me to get you a cup of coffee now."

"No. I had two cups before I left home. It is nice to know that you can multitask, however. Should include that on your résumé, along with those janitorial skills. I'll bet that fast-food place over in Redbud would hire you in a minute. Then you and Dave could commute together and share daily fast-food lunches. It'll be just like when you were teenagers and couldn't get enough of each other."

For once, Rosie had no comeback. Then the phones on both desks started ringing simultaneously.

"It isn't even eight thirty," Rosita said as she reached for the phone on her desk. Virgil walked to his, following her lead. Each spoke for a couple of minutes, then hung up. They looked at each other. Rosie spoke first.

"That was Velma Thompson. Seems Charlie's gone missing. She said he went to check on some strays up in that high country that they might have missed in the last roundup. I said you'd get out there as soon as you could. Your turn."

"That was a trucker named Wilbur Anderson. He wants to come by in an hour or so. He says he thinks maybe he killed somebody."

Rosie looked up at the wall clock that had been marking time for the last forty-some years. "Guess we won't be collecting moss today," she said.

"Don't look like it. Guess I'd better get to the hospital before Mr. Anderson shows up. If I'm a little late, give him a cup of coffee."

"Maybe I should run around the corner and buy him some doughnuts. After all, while I'm sitting here alone with a possible murderer, I should probably try to keep him happy."

"That's not such a bad idea, but if I think I'm going to get hung up, I'll call Dif. He's still feisty enough to give you some protection. He busted Lester Smoot pretty good last night."

"I figured something like that happened after mopping up the blood this morning. Guess old Dif's still got some gas in the tank. Knowing Lester, he probably got no more than he deserved. Send Dif on over."

By the time Virgil pulled into the hospital parking lot, he had already called Dif. He explained the situation.

"Don't worry, Virgil, I'll head right over. Woke up feeling a lot better than Lester. Called him and apologized for being a little quick on the trigger."

"Good move, Dif. How did he take your apology?"

"Real good. Said to forget about it, but did ask me not to mention it around town. Said he didn't want people to get the wrong idea."

"Yeah, I suppose he didn't want that little incident exaggerated in the retelling and have the locals thinking their elected officials are not acting in a professional manner. Just let it go, Dif."

"Okay, Virgil. Edna says I should start acting my age. I said I was."

It was a little after nine when Virgil walked into Hayward Memorial. He was thinking he'd spent more time there in the last six months than he had in all the other years since its construction almost fifty years before. He knew exactly where to go, somewhat of an accomplishment since it had gone from a small local hospital to a very large regional one. When he got off the elevator on the fourth floor, he bumped into Chet Harris, the intern, finishing up his time as the coroner's assistant.

"Hey, Sheriff."

"Chet, good to see you in the world of the living."

"Well, I've got to get out of the basement once in a while. Too quiet down there."

"Yeah, but some people are dying to get in there."

"Sorry, Sheriff, that joke is so old it's got legs. Now, if you really want to hear some good ones, go out for a beer some night with Dr. Kincaid."

"You're kidding me. Ark has a sense of humor?"

"Oh, yes. That weak offering of yours, he wouldn't waste on a five-year-old."

"Wow. So all those years drinking formaldehyde haven't made him stiff. Unless a good-looking woman walks by."

"Now, that's better. He'd have a good comeback for that." A nurse pushing a cart full of meds passed by. She smiled at Chet.

"Hello, Karen," Virgil said.

"Oh, hi, Sheriff. I didn't realize it was you."

"Yeah, wearing a uniform with a loaded hogleg strapped to my hip I'm practically invisible."

She kept on walking.

"I'm beginning to understand why you came out of the basement. Karen's a good reason. How long have you been a two-some?"

"Sheriff, you are a detective in uniform. I'm impressed."

"Like a lot of suspects, you didn't answer the question."

"Six months." Chet smiled.

"Does that mean you're likely to stay around after your internship is up?"

"Well, let's say for right now, it's more of a possibility."

"I'm glad to hear it," Virgil said. "By the way, how's the new eye?"

"I thought you'd never ask. So far so good. No irritation."

"Which one is it?"

"That's funny. You're about the tenth person to ask that question."

Chet pointed to his right eye. Virgil took a step closer.

"Perfect match. Guess it's time to sell the parrot."

Chet laughed. "No, I'll keep the patch and the parrot. Halloween's just around the corner and everyone loves a pirate. Worked for Johnny Depp."

"Listen, I've got to go check on my deputy. Do me a favor and tell Ark I'll be downstairs in about half an hour."

"Will do. Good talking to you, Sheriff."

"We're past that, Chet. My name is Virgil."

Chet nodded, then stepped into the elevator.

Virgil walked down the hall toward Jimmy's room. Sam Harris was talking with Jimmy's mom in the hallway.

"Hello, Mrs. Tillman. How's he doing, Sam?"

"Like I said last night. He's strong and young. He'll heal quick, but he's going to need some PT for that arm. Probably be here for the better part of a week. We'll start the physical therapy before he leaves, then he'll just come in as an outpatient. I was just going over everything with Mrs. Tillman. You can go on in, Virgil."

Virgil said his good-byes to both of them and stepped into Jimmy's room. Jimmy was sitting up in bed watching the television. As soon as he saw Virgil, he clicked it off.

"Hey, Sheriff."

"Hope I didn't come in the middle of a good show."

"No. I was just trying to get some baseball scores."

"Oh, yeah. It's getting toward crunch time. Do you think the Rangers are going to be in it this year?"

"Outside chance, but the Cardinals, Dodgers, and Tigers are looking real good."

"No East Coast teams?"

"Boston for sure, maybe Tampa, but the Yankees and Orioles at this point are real long shots."

Virgil pulled up a chair. "You're looking real good, Jimmy. A lot better than last night."

"Yeah, I guess, but I don't remember too much about that."

"You up to trying to replay the tape for me? I'd like to get what happened straight from you."

"It's all kinda jumbled. I tried thinking about it last night, but they insisted on giving me something to make me sleep. From then on it was all bits and pieces."

"Well, do the best you can. Let's see if we can put some of those pieces together." Virgil listened while Jimmy walked him through his tour the night before.

"I remember how dark it was. Thinking how up on the ridge I couldn't see a light. Then I did."

"What do you mean?" Virgil asked.

"Well, I was coming down, heading toward the underpass, then I saw some lights on the interstate. I remember thinking, seeing them made me feel good. You know it was so dark, it was kind of like I wasn't alone. Guess it sounds kind of weird."

Virgil shook his head.

"Then I went into the underpass. It was even darker. After that everything is mixed up in my head. As I was coming out there was some kind of explosion. The windshield . . . the glass . . . something hit it hard. I remember trying to hold on to the steering wheel. The car was out of my control. I yanked on the wheel. I think the tires were off the road, on the shoulder. I think I remember tires screeching on the hard surface. Then I felt like I was flying. That's the last thing I remember."

"Anything else, Jimmy? Anything at all? Do you remember what hit you? What crashed into the car?"

"You mean the tree? The doctor told me a tree limb came through the windshield and sliced open the side of my head."

"No. I mean the woman."

Jimmy sat up a little more in the bed. "The woman? What are you talking about, Sheriff? What woman?"

Virgil spent the next few minutes explaining to Jimmy that it was a woman coming off the overpass that landed on his vehicle, shattering his windshield, partly coming through, but then thrown off the car when it crashed into the tree at the bottom of the ravine.

The look on Jimmy's face told Virgil all he needed to know. After reassuring Jimmy that he did nothing wrong, he stood up.

"Sheriff, who was the woman?"

"I don't know, but I'm hoping that Dr. Arthur Kincaid will be able to help me out with that. He's probably down in the morgue now waiting for me."

As Virgil stood by the elevator, he was hoping that he was right. That Dr. Arthur Robert Kincaid, known by all his friends as Ark, would indeed have something for him. At least enough to help him get rid of the nagging feeling that somehow he knew this woman.

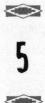

5

Virgil could see Art Kincaid through the glass in the upper part of his office door. He waved Virgil in, then pointed to one of the chairs opposite his desk.

"My least favorite part of the job." Ark pointed to a stack of folders on his desk.

"You're preaching to the choir, Ark. I'd rather muck out five stalls than sit behind a mountain of paperwork."

"At least you've got that option as an excuse. My only option is to slice open a cadaver. Not exactly on par with mucking out stalls."

"Guess I picked the wrong person to complain to."

"We all do it, Virgil. I leave here after a crazy day and want to vent. Then I get out of my car. World War III is raging as I walk through the front door. If I'm smart, I bite my tongue. Save my venting for a quieter time, take the baby off Terry's shoulder, grab a beer out of the fridge, then go referee the boys."

"Boy, my life is dull by comparison."

"Just different. But I wouldn't trade what I've got for anything. Virgil, you haven't lived till you've walked across a family room littered with toys like a minefield while an almost-two-year-old is wrapped around your leg hitching a ride."

Virgil sat back in his chair. "I don't believe it, but I think I'm envious."

"So . . . I guess we should get to the reason for your visit. Wasn't the easiest autopsy I ever performed. She was pretty banged up."

"I know. I was up close and personal."

"Yes, I heard. The EMTs told me. Maybe that was one time sitting at your desk in back of a pile of papers wouldn't have seemed so bad. Anyway, as I've told you on other occasions, this is only a partial. Tox screen won't be complete for a couple of days, along with some tissue sample tests, but here's what I've got, so far. No ID, but I think you already knew that. Age approximately thirty-five, give or take, Caucasian, maybe mixed ethnicity, Nordic with southern European, Italian, or Spanish. Five foot two, weight one thirty-five. No obvious physical problems. Those are the basics. Beyond that, I can tell you a couple of things. She was in really good condition. Strong. I don't mean gym-workout strong. I think she was day-to-day strong."

"I don't understand."

"Well, my guess is her job or whatever she did on a day-to-day basis was pretty physical. Also, she'd been doing it for a long time. This wasn't a woman who was getting a monthly manicure or a regular massage in some spa. Her body was under severe stress. There was no food in her stomach. Her dehydration was so critical that she had most likely been hallucinating. I'd venture that she was no longer capable of rational thought. She'd been on her own for at least four or five days."

"Cause of death?"

"Massive trauma to her body was the immediate cause. That's why the autopsy wasn't a walk in the park."

"Was that from the fall off the interstate?"

"No. That was from what caused her to get thrown off the highway. I'd say she was hit by a vehicle. My thought would be a truck, maybe even a semi."

"So, the truck hit her and killed her," Virgil said. "The impact threw her off the overpass. Then she landed on Jimmy's cruiser. Perfect timing."

"That's the scenario as I'd reconstruct it."

"Guess the first thing I have to do is talk to that truck driver."

"Will he be hard to find?"

"No, not really. As a matter of fact, I think he might be having a coffee and a doughnut with Rosie in my office, right now."

Ark looked surprised, so Virgil went on to explain about the early-morning phone call.

"Was there anything about her clothing," Virgil said, "that could give us a fuller picture of who she was?"

"Not really, Virgil. Outdoor wear, nothing you'd wear in an office. That's one of the aspects we're working on now. Trying to put a name with a face, but so far we've been drawing a blank. I don't think she's local. At least, I've never seen her before."

Virgil didn't respond right away.

"Listen, Ark," he finally said. "Before I leave, I'd like to take a look at her, if you don't mind."

It was so still he could hear every breath Ark took, and the throb of his pulse in his own ears. Sunlight filtering through half-drawn blinds did little to lighten the atmosphere. Ark had walked directly to the center of the room, toward the sheeted figure that lay on the examining table. Virgil followed after a momentary hesitation. He'd been in the presence of death many times, but it had never become routine for him.

"I know you think I'm well used to this," Ark said, "but I'm not. I've never been able to treat death as a clinician. I look at it as a kind of trust. Whatever has brought them to me . . . to this table . . . I can't change, but what I can learn from them can make their leaving easier for whoever they left behind. In a case like this, even more so. What is the narrative of this woman? Beyond who she is, where did she come from? Why did this happen to her?"

"I guess in a way we're both doing the same thing, Ark."

"Why did you want to see her, Virgil?"

"I know you said you didn't think she was local, but somehow she seemed familiar. I need to confirm, so I can put that notion to rest or . . ."

He didn't finish the thought. Dr. Arthur R. Kincaid stepped to the head of the table, reached over, and drew back the sheet, exposing the face of the woman lying there. He folded the sheet slightly below the top of her shoulders, then took a step back. Virgil moved to stand alongside of him.

Her face looked thin. She had prominent cheekbones, which were more accentuated by the thinness. Virgil remembered what he'd been told about her not having any food in her stomach. Her hair reached her shoulders. Brown with a few streaks of gray. He was surprised that her skin showed evidence of her life outdoors. Most of the bodies he'd seen in this room, even darker ethnic types, had a lighter pallor. Some almost looked ivory.

"Do you know her, Virgil?"

Virgil took a step closer, leaning slightly over the still form.

"I don't know her, but I've seen her before. Now I've just got to figure out where."

Ark replaced the covering over her face. They both stepped back from the table, then turned and walked to the door.

Virgil paused there, then looked back. "The silence is deafening."

"That's because you're listening for life," Ark said.

6

Rosita sat across from the man she was trying to see in the role of murderer. She was failing miserably. He looked like most every other stranger she had met for the first time. When he came into the office, he politely introduced himself. Despite her earlier comment to Virgil, she wasn't the least bit nervous. After a polite exchange, she offered her visitor a cup of coffee. There were no doughnuts. Wilbur Anderson, as he had introduced himself, was so generic he could have been selling vacuum cleaners. Dif came through the door about ten minutes later. Rosita was anxious to get the lowdown on the Lester Smoot incident. She knew Virgil was so tight-lipped she'd never get the details from him, but Dif was another breed of cat. He loved talking about his past escapades and he was good at it, even though the embellishments were rampant. No one really minded them.

Dif always had a willing audience. He was well into his narrative when Virgil arrived. Virgil could pretty much get the lay of the land a few seconds after he came into the office. Rosita and Dif had their heads together, so entranced with the details of the previous night, Rosie hadn't even realized Virgil had come in until Dif lowered his voice to almost a whisper. It must have been a good retelling, Virgil figured. Even the alleged murderer was sitting on the edge of his chair hanging on Dif's every word.

"Sorry to interrupt the flow of conversation, folks. I'm assuming you're Wilbur Anderson."

"Yes, sir. I am."

"Well, Mr. Anderson, why don't you come over to my desk? Then we won't interfere with *Tales from the Darkside*."

Rosita shot Virgil a look as Wilbur Anderson came over to the desk, almost reluctantly.

"Guess it was kind of exciting here last night."

"Yes, we have our moments," Virgil said. "Now, why don't you tell me why you might have killed someone."

For the next few minutes, Wilbur Anderson explained that he was an independent trucker working generally out of Albuquerque, where he lived.

"I do long hauls or short, whatever I can to keep that truck on the road. Don't make any money if it's sitting in the driveway. Anyway, I got a shot at a white glove job. That's usually electronics or something real technical, usually government work. I don't care, but they're usually small loads, sometimes like this one from White Sands, highly classified. It's real good money. When you get a crack at that kind of freight, you don't want to pass that up. You know, one can lead to another. That's a good list to get your name on—didn't want to miss the opportunity. But I'll be honest with you, Sheriff. I was really beat. I'd just come off a quick turnaround from a run to Fresno. But I didn't mean to do no harm."

"Okay, Mr. Anderson. Just tell me what happened."

"I had left the weigh station, was really rolling because that mile-grade uphill was ahead of me. Just crested the top, started the descent. That's a long way to the bottom. You know where I'm talking about?"

Virgil nodded.

"Well, I started downshifting. A lot of forward gears in that truck. Even though I wasn't packing a heavy load, I try to be real careful. Don't want to burn out the brakes. Brake jobs are expensive. It was real dark. I remember: no moon, just black. Think it was about two in the a.m. Nothing else on the road. Gets kinda lonely, especially on long runs at night. Anyway, I was downshifting, like I said. Got a call on the CB. Reached over—that's when it happened. Barely saw, thought it was a muley. Felt the thud, saw it fly off to the side outta the corner of my eye into the dark. Honest to God, Sheriff, I don't want to hit anything alive. I done it. More than a few times. Makes me sick in the pit of my stomach. Hate hearing that thump. Thought for sure it was a muley. You gotta understand, one second it was there, then gone. Happened so fast. Took me a quarter mile to bring the truck to the side. I know some truckers don't. They just keep right on, let the kangaroo catcher do its job and keep right on. I never been able to do that. I got a gun in the cab for just that reason. Used it a couple of times. It's registered. Don't want to see anything suffer. If Smokey's near, I call him, let him do the job. It's not that I want to. Anyway, I went back. So dark, took a light. Nothing. No deer, no muley, nothing. Walked a good half mile, couldn't find any sign. I was beginning to think I imagined it all. After about a half hour of looking, I finally give up, got back on the road. Went on to Houston. It was when I was heading back when a CBer told me somebody had been hit during the night. I swear, Sheriff, I looked and looked. Never meant for anything to happen."

Virgil looked at Wilbur Anderson. He had the gut feeling

that he was looking at an honest man. Wilbur was no killer. Just someone who had been caught between the crosshairs of fate and coincidence.

"Think you can rest easy, Mr. Anderson. This wasn't your fault. The medical examiner cleared you. They'll be no charges. Just leave a phone number with Rosita. She'll make a copy of your driver's license for our records in case we need to follow up. She'll also take a statement from you and have you sign it. Then you can get on your way. I really appreciate you coming in—you made my job a lot easier."

Virgil saw relief come into Wilbur Anderson's eyes. "By the way," Virgil said, "if you'd like to stop at Margie's place around the corner for lunch before you get on home, just tell her to put it on my tab."

He was standing outside the door enjoying the late-morning sun when Wilbur Anderson left. The nights were definitely cooling off and the sun had become a lot more tolerable during the day. Rosita soon joined him.

"You're sure about this, Virgil? No charges?"

"Yes. Ark told me that woman was hallucinating when she ran out onto the interstate. He said she was severely dehydrated. Probably hadn't had water in three or four days. Forty-eight hours without water, you're in trouble. Ninety-six, it's amazing she was still on her feet, much less having any idea where she was or what she was doing. If Mr. Anderson's truck hadn't hit her, she'd probably be lying dead out there alongside of the road in some cholla. Maybe wouldn't have been found before the scavengers did their job and there was nothing left but bones. No, Mr. Anderson didn't kill her. But I think somebody did."

"Who, Virgil? Who do you think killed her?"

Virgil took off his Stetson, slapping the dust off it against his leg. "The person she was running away from. That's who I think killed her."

It was a little after one when Virgil walked through the door of Margie's place. Margie's had been the go-to place for good food at a reasonable price in Hayward for over thirty years. Virgil liked Margie. They had been in school together, but the connection didn't end there. Years later they had shared their common story. They had both gone to out-of-state colleges, and neither had ever figured to spend their future in Hayward. Both of their lives had done a one-eighty because of events beyond their control. In Virgil's case, it was the death of his parents in a car crash on the new interstate. For Margie, on the other hand, it was her father's sudden death that changed everything.

One day, Howard had decided because it was slow in the restaurant to go across the street to get a haircut. In the way people get careless doing everyday things, when he stepped outside he saw the ancestor of the yellow dog that presently but not as frequently would lie down in the middle of Main Street, undisturbed sometimes for hours. He took it as a sign of the absence of traffic. As far as automotive traffic was concerned, he was right. What he didn't know was a quarter mile away on a cross street a trailer loaded with steers heading for Luther's Livestock Auction down in Redbud had been rear-ended by a pickup. The cattle, seeing the gaping hole rendered by the pickup, saw an opportunity to not end up on someone's plate in the immediate future. They turned the corner and bolted down Main Street. Howard froze in the face of the unexpected. He was not the first person in Hayward to die in a stampede, but he was the first person to have it happen in the middle of Main Street.

After the funeral Margie decided to stop by the restaurant for something, only to find a couple of the regulars standing outside. She opened it up, managed to serve them, and had been there ever since. Virgil, the staff at the office, along with others who had been going there for years, christened it Margie's place. It had worn the name ever since. The key to its success was Margie's understanding of what her customers liked to eat. Obviously, a restaurant that offers as one of its signature dishes chicken-fried steak and biscuits smothered in brown gravy has few illusions of haute cuisine.

It was going on three when Virgil left, loosening his belt a notch, before heading back to the office. Dif had gone. Rosie was sitting at her desk.

"Guess I'd better get out to the Thompson place. See where Charlie got to before Velma gets too antsy. Charlie probably used that 'looking for missed strays' notion just to get out of the house."

"Virgil, about that. I think you're going to have to change your plans. Got a call a half hour ago from Kyle Harrison. Says he needs to see you. He'll be here within the hour."

"What's this about? Couldn't we discuss it on the phone?"

"I asked him. Told him we got off to a flying start around here today. But he was like a bulldog with a bone. Wouldn't give an inch or a hint. He's a nice guy, but he is a federal agent. They all take that course on sharing only on a need-to-know basis. Guess I don't qualify."

"Well, I guess you better call Velma. Maybe I can get out there later. Better yet, maybe Charlie's showed up—save me the trip."

"Virgil, I wouldn't mind getting out of the office for a few hours. Since you're going to be here, I thought maybe I could take a ride out to Thompson's."

Virgil pushed back his chair. "So what am I looking at now, a closet deputy?"

"C'mon, Virgil, the personal touch. Like you said, Charlie will probably be there. If not, it'll at least let Velma know we haven't forgotten about her."

"Okay. Take my car. If you need me for any reason, I'm as close as the radio. Don't do anything stupid. I can always get another deputy. Good office managers are an endangered species."

"You got that right. I'll leave stupid to the boys."

The ride to the Thompson ranch was a good half hour. It was one of those crisp, clear days with a sky so blue that it hurt to look at it. Rosita rolled down the two front windows. The breeze was like a scent-filled tonic. The sun-warmed air layered over her. She basically followed the same route that Jimmy had followed two nights before. The Thompson ranch was on the far side of the interstate, which actually ran along the property's border. The ride in daylight would make a photographer's mouth water. Twice she stopped to take in the view. Some said that on top of the saddleback, on a clear day, you could see all the way to Mexico. Rosita just knew it was one of her favorite places. She and Dave had driven to the top on one of their first dates. She remembered it as the first time she took him to be a serious prospect. Twenty-some-odd years later, they still made the occasional trip. It had turned out to be a good choice for each of them. They had reared three nearly normal kids but more important, they still liked each other. The fact that Dave spent quite a bit of time down in the substation at Redbud didn't hurt the relationship, either. A little distance, Rosie came to think, was not necessarily a bad thing. It gave them each a little breathing room.

By the time she entered the road into the Thompson ranch, the sun had reached its midpoint. Its downward slide was just enough for her to break out her sunglasses. It was the only thing about coming winter she didn't like. She didn't so much mind the cold or occasional snow which white capped the mountains. In this part of the country, winter didn't generally hang around long enough to become a nuisance. What she minded was losing the light. She had come over time to the conclusion that she was one of those people who were definitely light-affected. She had even joked that she was also one of those people who, if she lived in Alaska, would become a drunk or a homicide. Not a suicide, she said, but a homicide. Dave, in turn, said he most likely wouldn't be living with her under those circumstances.

The Thompson ranch was one of the largest in area. It also had been in the same family for over a hundred and fifty years. Unfortunately, it had fallen on hard times. Charlie and Velma were each closing in on eighty. They had two sons and a daughter. Each of whom had left the place as soon as they could. Ranching, they discovered growing up, was hard work. Rosita noticed the absence of cattle as she drove the long road in. She had heard that most had been sold off the last few years. When she got within sight of the ranch house, she saw a couple of horses in a nearby corral. The house was a long, low adobe, looking so much a part of the landscape that with a quick glance it could have blended in with the sandstone ridge that met the far horizon.

As she pulled up to the corral fence, she could see that Velma Thompson was sitting on the covered porch that ran across the front of the house. There was no sign of anybody else around, although Velma had mentioned to Rosita in their last face-to-face, which had taken place in town six months earlier, that Manuel and Lorenzo, two of their long-term hands, were still on the ranch. She explained that Charlie wanted to keep them on the payroll to help with general maintenance. He also kept a small herd of Red Angus, as a nucleus, in case one of the children decided on a midlife career change.

"Charlie always was a wishful thinker," Velma said.

As she stepped out of the cruiser, Rosie looked around again for a sign of either Manuel or Lorenzo. She got a whinny of acknowledgement for her efforts from an old bay gelding standing with his head over the corral fence, near where she parked the car. He called again. She gave a quick wave to Velma, then moved toward him.

"Okay, I guess we all need some attention from time to time." She took the few steps to the fence, then reached out to him. She stroked his muzzle lightly, then ran her fingers down his neck, picking a strand of hay out of his mane as she did. He gave a soft nicker in response. "My, my, you men are all alike. Just never get enough attention, no matter how old you are."

Looking him over, she concluded he was of great age. "My guess is you're on the yonder side of thirty."

His eyes closed under her stroking. He shifted his weight. She saw his hip bones stick out. The sway in his back was deep. He was thin throughout.

"I'm thinking this is probably going to be your last winter, old-timer, but it was a pleasure to meet you before you go."

She pressed her face against him, gave him a light kiss on his nose, then stepped back.

"Velma probably thinks I'm getting ready to become a horse thief, I spent so much time with you and haven't even said howdy to her."

Rosita turned toward the house. The sun had warmed her. She could smell the horse scent on her hands. It was not unpleasant.

She waved again to Velma as she stepped onto the first flagstone on the long walk, amid abundant sprays of flowers on either side of her.

"The flowers are still beautiful, Velma," she shouted. "It'll be a pure shame when the first cold breath of winter gets them. But you haven't lost that green thumb of yours."

Velma didn't respond. Her chair sat in the shade of the porch overhang. Rosita bent down to admire some lupine. She continued to admire the flourishing gardens up to the point when she stepped up onto the porch.

"So has Charlie come back from rambling?"

Rosita felt the light breeze that eddied across the porch. She saw it whisper through Velma's white hair. Then Rosie put her hand to her mouth.

"Oh, no, Velma. Oh, no."

When the phone rang on his desk, Virgil figured it was Kyle Harrison telling him he was running late. He was surprised to hear Rosie's voice.

"Where are you? I know you're not in the cruiser."

"I'm in Velma's living room on the home phone."

"What's up?" Virgil asked. "Isn't Velma there?"

"Virgil, she's here, sitting on her chair on the front porch. But Virgil, she's dead. Velma's dead."

7

Virgil had barely hung up the phone when Kyle Harrison walked through the door.

"Hey, Virgil. You look like a man who needs someone to throw him a lifesaver."

"Yeah, well, it hasn't reached critical mass yet, but this day that started off gangbusters doesn't look like it's going to get much better."

"Well, if it's any consolation, I've had more than a couple of those days in my life, too."

Virgil smiled broadly.

"Did I say something to cause that reaction?" Kyle asked.

"That's the second time today that I've wasted my sad tale on people who can match me stroke for stroke. I've got to find someone other than a county coroner who spends a good part of his time cutting up dead people and a narc who's lucky if he can get through a day without someone trying to hand him off to that coroner."

"Yeah. I guess that old saw about being judged by the company you keep places us on the list of untouchables for most social invites. But it does keep the adrenaline flowing through our veins, doesn't it?"

Virgil winced. "Is that what we are? Adrenaline junkies? Waiting for our next fix?"

"I don't know, but my wife says my eyes light up every time I get one of those calls in the middle of the night."

"That's pathetic," Virgil said.

"Yeah, it is, but I gotta admit she's right."

"Okay, before I kick you out the door so I can deal with the latest thing that just got dropped in my lap, what's so important that we couldn't deal with it in a phone call?"

Kyle got up from the chair he had sat in next to Virgil's desk. He walked over to the small table against the far wall and poured himself a cup of coffee. After he took a swallow, he turned toward Virgil.

"You always have the best coffee."

"That's because I forbid anyone to make it except Rosie. But you didn't come all this way to compliment us on our coffee-brewing skills. What's up?"

Kyle walked back to sit in the seat next to Virgil's desk. "Two things," he said. "The first, we could have talked about on the phone. U.S. marshal. I told you after that huge bust a couple of months ago, you'd get on the radar. So here it is. I've been asked to feel you out on the idea of becoming one of us. Before you say anything, I want you to take some time and think it through. We don't need an answer right now. Actually, it's kind of an open-ended invitation, so if the timing isn't good now, maybe sometime down the road. Think about it. If you have any questions or concerns just ask."

Virgil didn't respond right away. Instead, he got up, walked around the office, looking at it like it was the first time he'd ever seen it.

"You know, my mom told me I took my first steps here. That chair I sit in was my dad's. One way or another, I've been tied to this place my whole life. When I graduated from college, then was accepted into law school . . . Well, if anybody told me then that I'd be here twenty-some-odd years later, I'd have said they were drinking the Kool-Aid. But here I am, still sitting in my daddy's chair. Back then I would have jumped at that offer or pretty much any other, just to put this place in my rearview mirror."

"Timing is everything, I know, Virgil, but things change. I guess like they say, change is the only constant in life. You're still a young man. You've got a lot of life ahead of you. I know you've got deep roots here, but sometimes it's good to shake things up."

Virgil retuned to sit in his chair. "Well, thanks for the offer. It's good to be wanted. For now I'll put it on the back burner and let it simmer. Now, what about that second thing?"

"That's something a little more unusual, and for that I'll need you physically for a couple of hours."

"Afraid that's not happening today. Got something that just jumped to the top of my list. Matter of fact, I should be on the road now. I put in a call to Dif, my part-timer, but he hasn't called back."

"Virgil, I'm off the clock now. I'll sit in for a couple of hours. That's the least I can do. You know, that bust didn't hurt my stock any, so I figure I owe you."

Virgil grabbed his hat off the desk. "That's great. Drink all the coffee you want. I'm out of here, before you change your mind. Dif shows up, tell him I'm on my way to the Thompson ranch. He can reach me there."

"Virgil, I'm going to try to set up the other thing for tomorrow."

"Okay. Do you want to give me a hint?"

"No. I think it's better if you don't know till then, especially if you've got a situation now that needs your focus."

Virgil gave a slight wave, then was out the door. All the way to the Thompson ranch, he puzzled over Kyle's reticence. He even passed the turnoff because he was so preoccupied.

"Damn, missed the turn." He backed up Rosie's car a full quarter of a mile before he saw the marker.

"Charlie sure likes his privacy." The only indication of the ranch was a sign proclaiming the name HIGH LONESOME and an arrow below pointing down the dirt road with the notation 8 MILES. The sign hadn't been refreshed in at least twenty years, Virgil figured. Sagebrush along with cactus had grown up around it.

"If you didn't know it was here, you'd never find it," he said to the empty car. The road in was rough. Dust clouds trailed in his wake while more than a couple of times loose stones bounced off the underside of the car. Like Rosita, he was aware of the emptiness. He hadn't been here in a few years, but remembered clusters of cattle dotting the now-vacant landscape. He saw a couple of mule deer, but no livestock. There were a couple of places where the fencing was in serious need of attention. The earlier preoccupation with Kyle's last comment had slipped away, then vanished completely when he saw Rosie standing by a corral fence, stroking a horse that looked like it belonged in a cartoon. He pulled alongside the cruiser that she had driven. Rosita was still stroking the old horse when he got out of the car.

"That sway is so deep, I think I could jump over that horse's back from a standstill," Virgil said as he got out of the car. "Wonder why Charlie hasn't put him down? His time has come and gone."

"Not always easy to say good-bye, Virgil. You know that. I think this old guy was something special in his day."

Virgil took a step back, eyeing the horse.

"I can't believe it. Rosie, I think you're right. I do believe this is the horse Charlie rode in his last rodeo years. If I'm right, he took a first, his last year in bulldogging on this guy. This old-timer's got to be at least thirty-five."

Rosie patted him once more, then stepped away. "I called the EMTs. Thought maybe they'd get here before you."

"Good," Virgil said. "Where's Velma?"

Rosita nodded toward the house. Virgil could see the figure sitting in the porch chair even though the late-day shadows were creeping across the front yard.

"She's where I found her. I called from the house, but it didn't feel right staying there. I felt like a trespasser. That's why I decided to come out here and hang out with this old guy till you or the EMTs showed up."

"Any sign of the help?"

"No one. Nothing."

"They must be around here somewhere. There must be somebody besides Charlie and Velma on this place."

"Well, Velma told me some time back that Manuel is still here. She also mentioned Lorenzo. I don't think I know him, but Manuel has been here a long time."

"Manuel and Cesar are good friends. I've met him a bunch of times. I've run into him at the feed store with another fella. That must be Lorenzo. Daylight's slipping away, so wherever they are on the place, they should be heading in before long."

"Virgil, I think I hear something."

Virgil looked back down the ranch road he had just traveled. "From that dust cloud, I'd say the ambulance is about a mile off. Rosie, why don't you go in the house while they take care of Velma? See if you can find an address book so we can call Velma and Charlie's family."

"All right, I can do that."

"Rosie, you okay? I mean, I know you weren't expecting any of this."

"I'm all right, Virgil. Just trying to get my balance back. Like you say, I wasn't expecting this, but then I guess neither was Velma. Now, I wonder what became of Charlie? Maybe his horse threw him. He could be lying out there in the mesquite wondering why no one is coming to help him."

"That ain't likely, Rosie. The last time a horse threw Charlie Thompson, he still had his baby teeth. I'm not saying you're wrong. He might be lying out there, but it's not because his horse came out from under him. More 'n likely, it's because of something he never saw coming."

The last of the sunlight was ringing the horizon by the time Virgil was heading back down the Thompson ranch road toward the asphalt. He had sent Rosie back over an hour earlier. As expected, Manuel and Lorenzo had showed up. They said they had been out running fence. Virgil mentioned the couple of spots he'd seen on his way in that needed attention, but Manuel told him what was left of the herd had no access to that area. In any event, they had it on their list. He broke the news to them about Velma.

"Miss Velma, no. She was good this morning. No."

Virgil could see they were both shaken by the news. He asked if they had any word from Charlie. They both shook their heads.

"Do you have any idea where he might be?"

"*Quién sabe*, no can say," Manuel replied. "Mr. Thompson, he rode off into the high country two, three days ago."

Virgil could see the worry come into his dark eyes.

"High Lonesome," Lorenzo added. Virgil looked at the younger, smaller man. His face still lacked the deep chiseling effects of wind and rain that grooved Manuel's face.

"The High Lonesome?" Virgil said.

"Señor Thompson always call the *montañas*," Manuel said. "The High Lonesome. He always say that's where the ranchero begins, up in the High Lonesome. That's where the name of the ranch comes from. The *montañas*. The mountains."

Virgil mulled over Manuel's words on his way back to town. He was surprised when he pulled into the lot to see Rosita's car there.

"What are you doing here? I told you to go home."

"I was going to but Dave is down in Redbud. Won't be home till late, if at all. Alex's wife is due anytime. Dave is covering for him so he can be available. I understand, but the house is empty. Dave junior is away in college and since Harlan discovered girls, between them and football he's a ghost. I just didn't feel like being there by myself. Here at least there's stuff for me to do. Kyle was here when I came. Dif will be coming in soon. Keeps my mind occupied."

"I guess you got a little more than you bargained for today. I'm sorry about that."

"It's not your fault. There was no way of knowing. It was just that I didn't expect to find Velma like that. We still don't know what became of Charlie."

Virgil lowered himself into his chair, throwing his hat onto the desk. "I got a strange feeling about all of this."

"What do you mean, Virgil?"

"Well, that woman that's lying over there in the morgue. It struck me when I was riding back, something Manuel had said. She actually came out onto the interstate from Thompson land. That's too much coincidence for me."

8

Dif came in the office door a little after six. Virgil hadn't wanted to leave Rosita sitting in the empty office alone, so he had stayed.

"Rosita told me about Velma," Dif said. "Kinda give me a cold chill. Happens every time, when someone I grew up with passes. Velma and I were in the same class."

"Guess it does get your attention when it hits a little closer to home. Were you and her an item back then?" Virgil asked.

"Well, I don't know about an item. I think she kinda used me to get to Charlie. Your daddy and Charlie were bigger than life. Cowboying together, both of them crazier than a rabid dog. Charlie would gallop down Main Street, sitting backward in the saddle, rolling a cigarette. Hell, even I was impressed. The girls, well, they just went nuts. How do you compete with that?"

"My dad never told me about those days."

"Most dads don't tell their offspring about the crazy-ass things they did when they were young. Kinda diminishes the authority of an authority figure to see them with their pants down."

"I just don't believe what I am hearing," Rosita said, "with the vocabulary of a philosophy teacher to go along with it. Diminishes? Authority figure? Dif, you been taking night classes or just reading those *JAMA* articles in Doc Hicks's office?"

"Why, Rosita, didn't you know I'm chock-full of superfluous knowledge?"

Virgil broke out into a laugh. "I always knew you were chockfull of something, but all along I figured it was something that'd pass naturally through your system. I was going to suggest a dose of Miralax to help with that."

More laughter filled the room. Night had fallen. The darkness inside had been displaced by a little humor, along with the sharing of past history. The three sat together for almost an hour. The conversation covered everything from the World Series to the federal deficit and a lot of other things they didn't agree on, but that didn't matter because it was more about the sharing than anything else.

Finally, Virgil got to his feet. He looked at the relic of a clock that hung on the wall. "My stomach and that clock are reminding me that I haven't eaten in over twelve hours."

"That's a bad habit I've managed to avoid," Dif said as he patted the overlap on his belt.

"What about you, Rosie?" Virgil asked.

"No. I figured to have a bite with Velma." A hint of something came into her eyes as she said it.

"C'mon then," Virgil said, coming to her rescue. "Let's you and me grab something. It'll be like a date. Then you can tell Dave about it. Stir his interest."

"After twenty-four years, I think I'd need a backhoe for that."

A little more prodding and Virgil got Rosie headed toward the door. When they stepped outside, Virgil immediately went toward the cruiser.

"Virgil, it's a nice night. Why don't we just walk to Margie's?"

"Just get in the vehicle." He held the door open. Rosie gave him a puzzled look as he slid in on the other side. They drove in silence for the next couple of minutes until they crossed over the bridge that Jimmy and his sister, Abby, regularly fished from, then headed west along the river for a mile, until they saw the red glow that announced their destination.

"The Branding Iron. Guess this is going to be a steak night," Rosie said.

"Figured we needed something a little different. A little step up from Margie's."

They passed some empty outside tables on their way to the front door. "Guess it's a little too cool for folks to be sitting out here looking at the river now," Virgil said. "Probably be putting them away soon till spring."

The long, low building was built of logs so dark that at night it was hard to distinguish its actual dimensions, but on the side of each window that looked out on the parking lot, red and white checkered curtains framed the light from within. When Rosie and Virgil stepped inside, a young hostess greeted them, then led them to one of the tables by a window.

A waitress placed a beer in front of Virgil and a margarita in front of Rosie. "This is a nice change," Rosie said.

"I figured after today we both needed a break." For the next half hour, they enjoyed their meal and each other's company, avoiding any talk of the day's events. They were sitting over coffee when Virgil's eyes widened in recognition of someone who had just entered the room. Their eyes locked. Then Virgil gestured to the young woman to come over.

"Hello," the girl said tentatively as she stood by the table.

Virgil smiled at her, then turned toward Rosita. "I'd like you to meet Rosita Brand. I told you Rosita pretty much runs the sheriff's office and tries to keep me on the straight and narrow. Rosita, I'd like to introduce you to my daughter."

The girl smiled. "Nice to meet you. I'm Virginia. Virginia Dalton."

Rosita looked at Virgil, then at the young woman. "This has become the best part of my day," Rosita said. "I am so happy to finally meet you."

Virgil walked Rosita to her front door. The air was crisp, the night sky filled with stars.

"Virgil, I'm so happy for you. We all need some special people in our lives. I think you've been shortchanged in that area."

"Oh, I don't know. I've always got you and Cesar. You're special."

"Virgil, you've got to do better than an old Mexican and someone who's trying to keep you on the straight and narrow."

"That's odd. I don't think of you as old. I didn't even know you were Mexican."

Rosita shook her head. "I'm serious, Virgil. Build a relationship with that girl. That'll be good for you both."

On the way back to the ranch, the words stuck with him. He had become a father, but the knowledge of it did not come with a set of instructions. It was new ground for him. By the time he pulled off the driveway alongside of the corral, he was feeling the effects of a long day. He looked toward the near barn to see if there was any sign of life coming from Cesar's rooms. All was in darkness. The moon was full, casting a silvery glow over his world. A slight shiver rippled through him. There was no doubt that a new season had come. There was a slight glaze on the roof and the hood of the pickup that was parked nearby. He remembered what Kyle said, about change being the only constant.

As he went toward the house, he wondered what the new season would bring.

9

"**A**re you going to join us for the white man's feast?" It was the only message on the answering machine.

Virgil recognized his cousin Billy Three Hats's voice right off. Virgil glanced at the calendar as he sat over his second cup of coffee. Thanksgiving, only a little over a week away. He was still staring at the calendar when Cesar came into the kitchen.

"Watching your life pass by?" Cesar said as he reached for the coffeepot.

"You read my mind."

"Yeah, well don't dwell on it, take it one day at a time. That's what works best. Live in the moment. The future will take care of itself."

Virgil set his empty cup on the table, sat back, a look of mock astonishment on his face, and crossed his legs. "Have you been hanging out with Dif lately?"

"Not that you'd notice. Why?"

"I mean, you two are turning into a couple of regular sages. In any event, before you ask, I think I might have gotten a line on a pretty good hay source, so maybe we won't have to decimate the herd. Manuel told me they have a lot more hay up at the Thompson ranch than they need."

"I heard about Mrs. Thompson."

"Guess you've been talking to Manuel, also."

Cesar reached into his pocket.

"I don't believe it," Virgil said. "A cell phone? You've actually decided to live in the twenty-first century?"

"Maybe partway," Cesar said. "I want to be able to reach out and touch somebody."

Virgil laughed. "Never thought I'd see this day. Guess that means I don't have to put a landline in the new barn like I did in the old one."

Cesar held up the phone. "I'm connected," he said. "Now about that hay."

Kyle Harrison was waiting for Virgil at the office.

"He's usually here by now," Rosita said as she glanced at the clock. "Maybe he stopped by the hospital to see Jimmy."

"Well, I've got some things I've got to take care of, so tell him I'll be back a little after one to pick him up."

"Does he know what this is about?"

"No, and I want to keep it that way."

"Anything you want to share?"

Kyle looked at Rosie as he stood to leave. "I know you two are close. I will say that today is going to resurrect something that I think Virgil's been working hard these last couple of months to put behind him. Maybe your relationship can help him process today's revelations."

"Are we talking about something or someone?"

"Well, I guess you could say it's a bit of a mixed bag. He and I are going to take a short trip back in time and place. The place is going to be the Black Bull."

Rosita realized after Kyle left that she had somehow risen to the level of "need to know" in Kyle's eyes. Now she was beginning to wonder if that was a good thing. Virgil, meanwhile, unaware of what the day before him held, had just stepped out of the elevator in Hayward Memorial Hospital.

Jimmy's bed was empty, so he checked with the nurse's station. One of the nurses told him Jimmy was having a physical therapy session, but would return shortly. Rather than sit in the empty room, he decided to touch base with Art Kincaid. He got back on the elevator. As he stepped out of it, he saw Ark go into his office. He tapped lightly on the glass window. Ark waved him in as he sat down behind his desk.

"We've gotta stop meeting like this, Virgil."

"Yeah, but I understand if I really want a fun night out, we should go out for a beer sometime. Then you can tell me some of those grisly jokes I've been hearing about."

"Let me guess—you've been talking to Chet, my intern. He told me he ran into you yesterday. He's a good guy."

"Yes he is. Hope he sticks around," Virgil said.

"I think there's a good chance."

"Sex is a good lure."

"None better. Besides, Karen is a nice girl. But you know that, Virgil. She was one of the nurses that took care of you a few months back when you needed some TLC."

"She was. Hope he doesn't let her slip away."

"Yeah, we all need somebody," Ark said. "Except maybe you."

"Don't know about that. Kinda feel lately like I'm missing out. Rosie's already suggested that I should cultivate some special person in my life."

"Like maybe that young girl?"

"You know about Virginia?"

"Virgil, this is still a small town. I've known for a while."

Virgil stood up from the seat he had taken. "Well, I'd better get upstairs," he said. "Want to check on Jimmy before I get on with my day. Thought I'd stop by in case you had anything for me. So, let's do that beer some night. Like to hear some of those cadaver jokes."

"You got it."

Virgil opened the door.

"Oh, Virgil, by the way. We got Velma Thompson last night. I've only had time to give her a cursory look."

"Anything?"

"Not yet. But I've known Velma a long time. I'd have never expected her to slip away in a chair on her front porch while she was sipping tea. I mean, she was one of those people I thought would bury all of us. I don't surprise easily, but this one threw me."

Virgil hesitated in the doorway a moment. "Thanks, Doc. We'll talk." Then he stepped out into the hallway.

It was after eleven when he left Jimmy. His empty stomach was gnawing at him. The morning jolt without food had him feeling like a hollow drum.

"Hey, Virgil."

"Margie."

He looked around, finally settling on a booth that looked out on Main Street. It was late for breakfast, too early for lunch. There was only one other table with customers and Virgil could see they were getting ready to leave. Main Street was quiet. He saw a woman go into Talbot's hardware, an old man walking a dog, two or three cars go by, then an empty stock trailer. He figured the stock trailer might be heading down to Redbud. Luther's Livestock Auction had become the largest feedlot in the area. It had started out as a purely local auction over forty years before, but with the construction of the interstate, and then the opening of the interchange a little over ten years later, the area had experienced a little boom. Luther's was one of the recipients. It had developed into a kind of hub, reaching beyond the county. A lot of cattle were brought there, not only for sale, but for fattening after coming off the range and being a little down in weight. The interstate and train lines converged, so it became a logical center for the livestock industry.

Margie brought over a plate along with a glass of orange juice, setting them in front of Virgil.

"Don't I even get a chance to check out a menu?"

"You can if you want, but you won't do any better."

He looked at the steaming plateful of pancakes covered with sliced strawberries, edged on each side with a couple of sunny-side eggs sitting on crisp bacon. Virgil wasn't about to argue. Margie left, returned with two cups of coffee, then slid into the booth opposite Virgil. She poured a little half-and-half into each cup, sliding Virgil's across the table after adding a half teaspoonful of sugar to his.

"Am I that predictable?"

"Virgil, I've been feeding you for twenty years. If I don't know what you like by now, I should be looking for another line of work."

"Don't even consider that, Margie. You're good at what you do."

"So are you, Virgil. Which reminds me, I heard about Velma. Never figured Velma to go like that. She was tough right down to the bone. And Charlie's gone missing?"

"So far."

"Good people. I'll miss them. Last coupla years since things got quiet on the ranch, they used to stop by more often. I guess they were in a kind of semiretirement mode. Back in the day that ranch was some operation. Kinda sad to see it go downhill."

"Guess none of the kids were interested."

"It's an old story, Virgil. Hand something to somebody on a silver platter, they don't appreciate it. I remember an interview I saw with Michael Landon. You remember him, Little Joe on *Bonanza*."

Virgil nodded.

"Well anyway, he told how one of his kids asked him to buy him a new car, then got pissed at him when he refused. I remember him saying that if he did, he was robbing him of the experience of the thrill of working for that first car, then the satisfaction of achieving that goal as the reward for that work. He went on to say he had a garage full of new high-priced cars, but none pleased him as much as the first car he ever owned, which he had bought for six hundred dollars and was six years old when he bought it."

"Do you think his boy got it?"

"Probably not, any more than those Thompson kids."

"I didn't really know them," Virgil said. "Guess we moved in different circles."

"Well, they were also older than us, Virgil. Velma would talk about them sometimes. They didn't come back often. That bothered her. The girl, Marian, turned out all right. She lives near San Francisco, has two or three children. The boys were another story. A couple of marriages, gambling, some other stuff. The youngest, Vernon, has come around the last couple of months a few times. I think Charlie was hoping he'd come back to the ranch. Maybe help Charlie to bring it back. But Velma told me it wasn't going to happen."

"What about the other son?"

"I'm not sure, but I remember Velma saying he was working on some deal with Vernon. She said it had to do with some company he worked for. She mentioned the name, but I can't remember it. Anyway, I don't think the Thompson ranch is ever going to be a going concern again."

Virgil put the rest of his pancake in his mouth, then drained his orange juice.

"Yeah, I guess, but as someone said to me recently, times change, nothing stays the same."

Rosita was on the phone when he came into the office. He walked through the door that joined the office to the annex where the holding cells were located. At the moment there were no occupants. He'd talked to Alex, who was driving up from Redbud with two prisoners. One Alex had caught after he stabbed another guy in a knife fight. The other had stolen a car outside of the new motel that had recently opened by the interstate. He checked each cell to make sure they would be ready for their new occupants, then he returned to the office. Rosita had just hung up the phone.

"You know Alex is coming up from Redbud, right?" Virgil said.

"Yes, sir. That was Dave on the phone, telling me why he won't be home tonight. Alex is bringing them up because his wife had the baby yesterday. This way, after he drops them off here, he can go visit his wife, then stay overnight at his mom's. She's taking care of the three-year-old."

"Call Dif. Make sure he knows about our two guests. Maybe he'll come in a little early. Give you a break."

"Don't worry, Virgil. I'm fine."

"Well, hopefully, they won't be here long. I'd like to get them processed quickly, then get them over to the detention center. It'd be good if we could keep the cells available for the locals who get a little carried away during the holidays."

"Yes. I remember, last year we had a full house till after New Year. We had enough hangovers to start a new AA group."

"Thank God for Bill W. Otherwise we'd have to build an addition."

"Amen to that," Rosie said.

"By the way, were you able to get in touch with the Thompsons?"

"The daughter, Marian, will be here tomorrow. She said she would get ahold of her brothers."

"Good. Listen, I want to make another run out to High Lonesome before they get here. I'd like you to go with me."

"Why do you want me to go with you?"

"I know you're not anxious to go back there, but I want to check the scene out before anyone gets in there and starts moving things around."

"What are you looking for?"

"I'm not sure myself. Guess I just want to make sure that there isn't more to this than what it appears to be. You were there, the first person on the scene. I want to get your recollection while the place is untouched. I don't know, maybe I'm overthinking this whole thing, but the fact that Charlie hasn't showed up, then Velma dies in a way that surprises most people, makes me wonder. I'm not sure, but I wonder if I'm missing something. It won't hurt to take a look. You don't miss much. That's why I'd like you with me."

"Okay. And add me to that list of people who are shocked at Velma going while she was sitting in a chair having a cup of tea."

10

Kyle Harrison showed up right after Rosie came back from lunch.

"Ready to go, Virgil?"

"As ready as I can be, not knowing where I'm going or why. Can you at least tell me how long this is going to take?"

"That's going to depend on you and the dynamic of the moment."

"This is sounding stranger and stranger."

Kyle merely shrugged his shoulders, then headed toward the door. Virgil got up somewhat reluctantly and followed him.

"Don't worry," Rosie said as they headed toward the door. "Everything here is covered. Dif will be in soon. Tomorrow we'll get out to High Lonesome before anyone else gets there."

"Okay." Virgil gave a half wave, then stepped out into the parking lot. Kyle was standing by Virgil's car.

"Looks like I'm driving," Virgil said.

"Actually, I'm going to ride with you to our destination, but another agent will take me back."

"Well, I've got to know where we're going."

"We're going to the Black Bull," Kyle said as he got in on the passenger's side.

Virgil braked the car, then looked at Kyle, who avoided his eyes. For the next ten minutes they rode in absolute silence.

"I don't get it," Virgil finally said. "Why are we doing this?"

"For the time being, let's just say I'm keeping a promise."

"A promise. To who? What does this have to do with me?"

"It has to do more with you than anyone."

"Kyle, I don't like riddles. Lately, it seems like I've had more than my share. My gut's full. I don't need another thing to ruin my night's sleep."

Before Kyle could respond, his cell phone rang. Virgil caught most of the conversation. It was clear there had been some kind of a complication.

"Okay, okay. Tonight. It has to be tonight. We can't be here much longer. Everything is set for tomorrow. Don't forget."

Virgil had turned off the county road into the parking lot of the Black Bull. He had gone out of his way the last couple of months to avoid where he now found himself. The crunch of stone beneath his tires was a too-familiar sound. Although the day was sun filled, the closed-up building looked dark to him. He pulled up to within a couple of feet of the stairs that led up to the covered porch in front of the building, which on a hot summer night held almost as many people outside as could be found within. The memory of the nights he had spent there made the building seem more derelict. Kyle's conversation on the phone had ended, but Virgil was all but oblivious to that fact.

"Virgil . . ." Kyle's insistent voice seemed somehow far away.

"Yes." The car was still idling, so he turned the key in the ignition.

"I'm sorry, Virgil. There's been a change of plans."

Virgil didn't answer, but looked at him, not understanding.

"We've got to reshuffle the deck. Things aren't working out as I planned. Here." He took out a key from his pocket. Then he handed it to Virgil. Before Virgil could frame the question, Kyle said, "It's to the front door."

"Why are you giving this to me?"

"You'll get the answer tonight."

"Tonight?"

"Yes. Something's come up. So you're going to have to come back here tonight to get your answers. I'd like to tell you more, but I can't. Like I said, I made a promise. All I can say is that things are not always what they seem."

"I don't get it."

"You will tonight. Now, I've got to ask you to take me back. Sorry I wasted your time."

Virgil put the key in his shirt pocket. Then he started the car. He drove slowly out of the lot. When he reached the hard surface, before he pulled out, he looked in his rearview mirror. Through the dust of the parking lot, he could see the Black Bull on the roof of the building, looking down.

11

"What are you doing here?" Rosita asked. "I thought you and Kyle Harrison had something going on that was going to eat up the rest of your day."

"So did I. So did I."

Rosita could tell by Virgil's tone that he was not a happy camper, so she didn't push.

He threw his Stetson onto his desk, sat down, riffled through some papers, picked up a pen to sign some invoices, threw the pen down a minute later, stood up, and did a lap around the office. He paused at the window, looking mutely for a long minute at nothing.

"Goddamn it." His voice startled Rosie, who did not startle easily. When he turned away from the window, she saw a look in his eyes that evidenced a level of turmoil she hadn't seen in a long time.

"Did Alex show up?" he asked.

"We got a couple of lawbreakers back there feeling sorry for themselves. Of course, it's the old story, they're not sorry for what they did, but that they got caught."

"They'll feel a lot sorrier if they end up in front of Judge Harrison. Alongside of her, that TV judge is a fairy godmother."

As Virgil was saying those words, Dif walked through the door. "Did I hear somebody comparing Myra Harrison to a fairy godmother?"

"Not likely," Rosie said. "That woman would send her own mother to jail without a tear."

"So would I. Have you ever met her mother? Anyhow, that's what we call strict law enforcement around here. Must be why the crime rate in Hayward is so low."

"Well, speaking of that low crime rate," Virgil said, "since there's an unexpected gap in my day, Rosie, how about that trip out to the Thompson ranch?"

"If it'll settle you some, okay. Anything to get that burr out from under your saddle."

A few minutes later, Rosie and Virgil were on their way to High Lonesome. They were climbing the saddleback when she spoke next. "Virgil, you've got a bit of a lead foot today. You want to tell me what's gnawing on you or do you want to keep it penned up inside while you drive us off the rimrock? I don't mind dying, but I'd like to think that they could find enough of me to bury. We go off this ridge, that's probably not going to be the case. Jimmy only went down fifty or so feet. We go off here we ain't gonna hit bottom until tomorrow and we ain't gonna look pretty."

"Sorry," Virgil said as he eased off the accelerator. "Guess I don't like pulling the scabs off healing wounds."

"You talking about Ruby and the Black Bull?"

Virgil nodded. Then he explained about the aborted trip with Kyle.

"Virgil, you are one of the few people I know who can meet life head-on. Don't go back on me now. Whatever it is you're going to find out tonight, take it as it comes."

"Guess I don't like mysteries," he said.

"Hell, Virgil, you're in the mystery-solving business. That's why we're going where we're going. You just don't like those mysteries when they're about you."

"You sure don't give me much slack."

"You want that, find a stranger. We've got too much history together."

"Well, speaking of mysteries, let's take a hard look at this one." He had turned off onto the High Lonesome ranch road. Though everything looked the same, each knew in the quiet on the ride in, it was different. Arriving at the end of the road, the tableau was changeless. The same horses in the same corral, even down to the old horse who greeted them as they exited the car, his head hanging over the fence, waiting for some acknowledgement.

"Hold on a sec, Virgil." Rosita reached into a bag she had brought with her, taking out a couple of apples. She quickly walked to the old horse. Virgil could hear the crunch as the horse bit into the apple sitting in the palm of Rosita's extended hand. The sound immediately brought the other two horses to the fence. Rosita had an apple for each one. When she returned, Virgil held out a clean rag that he had gotten from the car.

"There's a lot of slobber from a horse eating a juicy apple, particularly one that's lost most of his teeth."

Rosie took the rag. "My fingers are sticky."

"Price of a good deed. Next time, toss them on the ground or . . ."

He pointed toward the horse trough in the corner of the

corral. Rosita went over, dipped part of the rag in, then wiped her fingers.

"That's better," she said. Virgil had already started toward the house. Rosie quickly caught up to him. Together, they walked along the path that led up to the porch. "I feel like I'm in a time warp."

The flowers were still as bright and vivid as they were the day before. Sunlight splashed the garden, while a light breeze had the flower heads casually waving. She looked toward the porch, doing a double take when she saw the chair. The light no longer invaded the covered area. In the back of her mind, she realized that she had been in the same spot at almost the exact same time the day before. She looked again, half expecting to see Velma in the chair. She had stopped walking. Virgil turned around then, reached out his hand to her.

"It's all right, Rosie. Velma's moved on." The touch of his hand encircling hers brought her back.

"I'm okay. It was just for a minute . . ." The thought was left incomplete.

"I know. Come on, let's get this done." He led her a few steps forward until they stepped up onto the porch. For the next few minutes, he walked her through the timeline of the previous day.

"Let's do it again," he said. "This time I want you to look more closely at the details. How Velma looked, the house inside, anything that seemed out of place or didn't fit. Walk through like you did yesterday."

After she stepped off the porch, Rosita closed her eyes for an instant. Then she opened them as she stepped back up. She saw Velma in her blue print dress with the tiny white flowers. She even saw the yellow hearts in the center of each flower. A whisper of a breeze touched the white hair on Velma's head, which was slightly turned. She saw the empty teacup on the small table that stood next to Velma's chair. Then she went through the door to the interior of the house. The open living area was to her right. She saw the step down, the fireplace on the far wall faced by the sectional sofa, and she saw the two rocking chairs near the picture window, each flanked by an end table. To the left, she saw the counter that separated the living area from the kitchen and dining areas. Everything looked as it had on the previous day.

"Well, anything?" Virgil asked.

Rosie took one last look around the room before she answered. "Exactly the same, Virgil. Nothing's changed."

"Is there anything odd? Out of place?"

"No. No, I don't think so."

"Take your time. Anything. The slightest thing."

Rosita walked to the front door, looked out on the front porch, then turned, letting her gaze once again roam the interior.

"I don't see anything different from yesterday, but . . ."

"But what?"

"Well, I hadn't thought about it before. It's not that it's out of place or odd. I mean, it definitely does belong." She hesitated.

"What are you talking about?"

Rosita pointed to the counter. "The cup."

"What about the cup?"

"It's dirty," she said. "You can see the stains inside of it. It's dirty."

"I don't follow," Virgil said.

"Well someone must have been here drinking from it. Velma's cup is outside on the table. Somebody else was drinking from this cup. They must have spent some time here with her. I wonder who it was."

"That is a very good question," Virgil said.

* * *

It was a little after five when Virgil pulled into the parking lot at Hayward Memorial Hospital. He had dropped Rosie off at her car. He found Art Kincaid in his office.

"It's too early to get out of here for beer and gallows humor if that's what you're after."

Virgil held up a plastic bag with a cup inside.

"Oh, you're here for afternoon tea."

"Not quite," Virgil said. "Can you run a test of some kind to determine what was in this cup?"

"It's possible, if there's some residue. What are we looking for?"

"I don't know. Velma Thompson was drinking from this cup. It was on the table next to her. I sealed it with plastic wrap. There's maybe half a teaspoon of liquid in there."

"That should be enough. Let's see what we can find out for you, Virgil. I'll get it to the lab. We should have something for you by tomorrow."

"Thanks, Ark. Maybe it's nothing, but I just want to make sure."

When Virgil left the hospital there was a breeze blowing leaves around the parking lot. Virgil turned up his collar. He glanced at the sky. Scudding clouds bumped into one another. He could taste the change that was coming. He had thought about stopping by the office, but changed his mind after talking to Dif and finding out that Alex was there. Instead, he stopped by Kleman's Florist to send flowers to Alex and his wife on the birth of their baby. Karl Kleman was in the store, looking like an astronaut getting ready for liftoff.

"How's Harriet?" Virgil asked.

"Huge," was Karl's reply. "She looks like she's going to explode. I don't know, Virgil. All these years we've wanted kids and now . . ."

"She'll be fine, Karl."

"Oh, I know. She's sitting in the living room amidst all the stuff we got for the babies, smiling like Buddha. It's me, Virgil. I'm gonna be forty-seven on my next birthday. I don't know how to be a father. I mean, what do I know about babies? Oh, why am I complaining to you? You've no idea what I'm talking about. You've never been a father."

Karl's words changed Virgil's plans for the rest of the day.

The pecan harvest was done. He saw that the trees, which only a few weeks earlier were sagging with their burden, had regained their stature. The leaves were losing their vibrant color. There was no activity that he could see in row after row on the long drive up to Crow's Nest. The last time he had actually been in the house, Audrey Hayward was still alive. The irony was that it was only then, on the last day of her life, that there existed a kind of positive respect for each other. They had always been adversaries, but deep in his bones he knew that her love for her daughter and his love for Rusty had been at the heart of their conflict. Now that Audrey was gone, in an odd way he realized she had left him in her debt, with the disclosure that Virginia was his and Rusty's child. It was a secret she had kept for twenty years. She could have gone to her grave with the knowledge, but she chose to pass it on to him. When he left Crow's Nest that day, it was after finding out that he was a father and had been, even if in name only.

As he pulled to a stop in front of the house, he thought to himself that maybe he should have called first.

"She's probably not even here." When he knocked, Audrey's son Micah opened the door.

"Virgil, good to see you. How's everything?"

"About everything, I don't know. All I can handle is our corner of the world. Sometimes, even that's too much."

"Yes, sometimes we get overloaded. Guess you know more about that than most."

"Like they say, it's part of the job description. By the way, how did you make out with this year's harvest? I noticed the trees were all empty as I drove in."

"It was a fair harvest. Trees could have used more rain. We irrigate, but we count on a little help from Mother Nature. This year she was pretty stingy. Guess in the long run, it all balances out. Anyhow, Virgil, what can I do for you?"

"I was wondering if Virginia was here."

"Let me run upstairs. Just got in ahead of you. Been down at the office in Redbud." Micah started for the stairs, then hesitated. "I'm glad you know, Virgil. It was a hard secret to keep all those years."

Virgil didn't reply. Micah turned and went upstairs.

Virgil stepped into the living room, which was just off the center hall. He saw little had changed since his last visit. He walked to the mantel over the fireplace. He was looking at a photograph of Rusty when Virginia found him.

"You know," he said, "she was about your age when this was taken."

"Yes. I know."

"You are very much like her."

"Am I?"

"Oh, yes," Virgil answered.

Virginia started to say something, then stopped.

"I should have called before I came," Virgil continued. "But it was a whim."

"That's not necessarily a bad thing. Why did you want to see me?"

"I'm not quite sure. I think it had to do with getting to know how we fit together. I mean, where? How to begin?"

"Yes. I understand. I've thought about that myself. I'm not too sure."

They both looked at each other while an unexpected silence invaded the room. After the moment passed, Virgil spoke. "Would you like to take a ride? If you have the time, there's someone I'd like you to meet. It's a nice day."

Virginia glanced out the window. "It is a nice day. Yes, I'd like to take a ride with you."

"Good." Virgil smiled. After she ran up the stairs and told Micah, they left the house. They drove straight through Hayward, following the route that led to Redbud.

"This will be my second trip to Redbud today. I just got back with my uncle only a half hour or so before you came."

"Oh, he told me he had been down there, but he didn't mention you were with him."

"Probably because he didn't know what you wanted. He's been very good at protecting me."

"I guess like a father."

"He's been the only father I've had."

"Yes. Micah is a good man. I've always thought that."

"I'm glad you feel that way. By the way, who is it that you want me to meet?"

"Another good man," Virgil said.

They were a little over ten miles from Hayward on a stretch of road so straight the pavement looked like it disappeared at the horizon. Desert landscape bordered the road on either side, broken up only by the saguaro cactus, standing tall, like silent witnesses to the passage of time. Virgil slowed the car, then pulled off to the right onto the barest hint of a road. If you didn't know it was there, it easily blended into the colors of the earth. Virgil cut the engine and the car rolled to a stop.

"I thought we were going to Redbud," Virginia said.

"No, but before we go farther, I should tell you something."

Virginia looked genuinely puzzled.

"Do you know anything of my background or ancestry?" Virgil asked.

"No, not really. I know that your parents are dead. I think I heard something about a car accident years ago. You live alone. Your father was the sheriff. You've been the sheriff for about fifteen years. Not much else."

"Do you know that I'm half native? That my mother was full-blooded?"

"No. I didn't know anything about that."

"That means you are quarter-blood. How do you feel about that?"

"I . . . I don't know."

"Some people even today, around here, have racial attitudes about Hispanics, Native Americans. Indians, if you will. Those attitudes aren't always positive."

Virginia looked at Virgil, a slightly mocking look on her face. "I think those people are the same people who are homophobic and anti anyone who isn't exactly like them," she said. "Those people aren't just here. They're everywhere. Thankfully, I don't think there are as many of them as there used to be. But why are you telling me this?"

"Because, I realized maybe you might have a problem meeting the man I was bringing you to. You see, he is my grandfather and your great-grandfather and he is a full-blooded White Mountain Apache. So what do you think?"

Virginia glanced out the window at the desert landscape. "I think you should start the car. I would very much like to meet my great-grandfather."

Virgil turned the key in the ignition. Slanting sunlight creased the terrain as they headed toward a distant plateau. Deeper crevasses were already in darkness.

"There he is," Virgil said as they topped the last rise.

Virginia followed the direction of his outstretched hand. She saw a figure drive a small flock of sheep into a makeshift corral, then draw a gate to seal the enclosure. She noted how the sides of the structure were reinforced with mesquite. A young dog was barking at the last of the flock that had gone through. Virgil pulled the car to a stop alongside of the double-wide trailer. A tall butte at some distance in back of the trailer blocked the stirring breeze that caught their dust trail as they had made their way to the top of the ridge.

"This is stunning," Virginia said as she exited the vehicle, looking out on the desert trail they had traveled to reach the high point where they now stood. The sepia shades from light tan to dark brown broken by reds and occasional blue crisscrossed the vista below. It was an artist's palette that stretched the limits of the naked eye. They stood there while the lone figure made his way toward them, the young dog trotting at his heels.

"Hello, Grandfather. I've brought someone to meet you."

"Good. I always enjoy company."

"I'm Virginia. Virginia Hayward." She looked into the dark face etched by a long life to find a growing smile and bright eyes.

"Yes. Of course you are. It is good to finally meet you. I am your grandfather, but maybe you should be calling yourself Virginia Dalton. You have your mother's red hair, but I see much of your father in your face."

"But how did you know?" Virgil asked.

"After your mother and father were buried, I went one day a short time later to offer a blessing on them. That day I met a beautiful girl with flaming hair who had also come to pay her respects. We spent some time together sitting on a bench. She was delightful. She told me her name along with the name of a boy she loved. That boy stands before me now with his and her daughter."

"Grandfather, you amaze me."

"That is good, to be able to surprise someone at my age. I would never want to be thought of as boring."

Virgil's laughter echoed off the cliffs. "I don't think you will ever have to worry about that," he said.

"Let us go inside. I would like to celebrate this meeting. I have a nice cold bottle of Chardonnay."

Once inside, he went to a cabinet that stood at the end of the wall that led into the dining room. He took three wine-glasses and set them on the kitchen table.

"Virgil, there's a bottle chilling on the door in the refriger-ator. Would you get it?"

Virgil did as he was asked. "Grandfather, are these new glasses?" Virgil asked as he poured.

"No. I have had them a long time, but I only like to use them for special occasions."

In the quiet silence, the three sat for a long time talking while they enjoyed their wine.

"I love the location of your home," Virginia said at one point.

"Yes. I chose it for the beautiful sunsets. In warmer weather, I like to sit and watch the close of day. Sometimes, I think on my past, but mostly I prefer thinking about tomorrow. I do not live in the past. Every sunset is different. It is like watching an artist at work. Sometimes, we miss the beauty in the world because we get caught up in our lives. I've been guilty of that especially when I was younger. Now, I think I look with different eyes."

"Yes," Virginia said. "I think I've been guilty of that, too."

The old man smiled. "Do not beat yourself up over that. You will see many sunsets. I can't afford to waste any. I'm running out of them."

He reached across the table and covered her hand with his. Her eyes brightened and a smile grew on her face. Virgil watched the interaction. He liked what he saw. A little while later they stepped outside the trailer.

"See what I mean?" Grandfather swept his hand in the arc of a magician. They stood looking off the mesa. The only sound was a hint of wind along with an occasional bleat coming from the makeshift corral. The young dog was curled up in a ball by the two steps that led up to the trailer. The last shards of light struck the earth at random, filtering through some low-lying clouds. They watched until there was only a sliver on the horizon.

"It's getting cold. You better get inside, Grandfather."

"Yes. If I catch a cold, Mrs. Hoya will not be happy."

"Mrs. Hoya?"

"Grandfather's significant other," Virgil said.

"There you go, blowing my bachelor image, Virgil."

Virginia laughed. "Well, Grandfather, I'm glad a man like you, so handsome and full of life, is not going to waste. I hope Mrs. Hoya realizes what a good catch you are."

"Granddaughter, I will tell her. I'm sure she will appreciate your words. Remember, my door will always be open to you."

Virginia kissed the old man and gave him a serious hug. His face lit up.

"I think you made a great hit with Grandfather."

"I'm so glad you took me to meet him. He was not at all what I expected. Chardonnay. He drinks Chardonnay. I really like him." They had been on the county road awhile. "I'm really glad you asked me to come with you. Another piece of the puzzle."

"Guess maybe we've both been missing some pieces."

By the time Virgil turned off the road heading up to Crow's Nest, it was dark. Somehow the house that stood at the highest point on Hilltop Ranch was even more imposing on a dark night. The lights from within seemed like beacons. Virgil pulled up directly in front of the house.

"I'm pretty busy right now, but I hope we can find more time to spend together."

"I'd like that. Hopefully, before I leave."

"Leave?" Virgil said.

"Yes, after the holidays. Going back to school. I still have one more semester. Then I'll have my degree and like Grandfather said I can begin concentrating on tomorrow."

"I didn't know. Maybe we'll have a lot more time after that."

"I'm not so sure. We'll have to see."

"What do you mean?"

Virginia took a deep breath, angling herself in the seat so that they were face-to-face. "I don't know, but I'll try to explain. Virgil, I like you. But when I found out about you I was angry. Really angry. Not at you. I didn't even know you then. I knew logically it wasn't your fault. But I felt cheated. First by my mother, then by you. Maybe it doesn't make sense to you, but I grew up thinking I was one person to find out later I was someone completely different. I guess it's hard for you to understand. I mean we have no shared memories or experience. No Christmas mornings, no birthdays, no learning to ride a bike while you held on to the back of the seat. Nothing. I don't even know what your favorite foods are or how you like your coffee or even if you drink coffee. We can never go back to recapture that. You can't rewind the clock. Remember some more of Grandfather's wisdom. We live in the present. I've got to come to grips with who I am, then figure out how I'm going to get on with my life. In a way, I almost wish my grandmother never told me about you. On the other hand, I'm beginning to understand why my mother fell in love with you. I'm so confused."

Virgil could see tears freely streaming down Virginia's cheeks. He didn't say anything right away. He reached out his hand, lightly touching a tear, then laid his palm against Virginia's cheek.

"I don't know if this helps," he said, "but I'd like you to know that I also feel cheated. All those things you missed, I missed also. I would've liked to have been there, but like you said, we can't go back. So, I guess the only thing we can do is go forward. Like Grandfather, I prefer to think about tomorrow, whatever it will bring. But I want you to know that I want you in all of my tomorrows. By the way, I like my coffee with just a hint of half-and-half . . . a little sugar."

Virginia smiled, took his hand, gave it a light kiss, opened the car door, then ran up the stairs to the porch without looking back.

12

Except for the motion-sensitive lights triggered by his car as he parked near the barn, along with the overhead light on the front porch, which Cesar had turned on for him, the place was in darkness. There was no sign of life. He vaguely remembered Cesar having said something about checking with Manuel about a quantity of hay they could buy from the Thompson ranch. He knew the quality might be questionable, but he also knew that Cesar would make the right call. He never worried about the day-to-day operation of the ranch. Virgil had always known that Cesar made it possible, like he had for Virgil's father, to function as sheriff. Virgil also knew that this role in Hayward had changed significantly from his father's time. Hayward was growing. Three full-time deputies along with Dif were no longer enough, especially when one was down, as was the case with Jimmy. It was something Virgil knew he would have to address, but for now all he wanted was a little downtime. It had been a long day and he was beat.

He threw the switch as he stepped into the kitchen. Glancing at the clock on the wall, he realized he'd been gone almost twelve hours. He opened the refrigerator, standing for a long minute, trying to find something quick to throw into his stomach, which felt like a hollow drum. His search was not rewarded. Finally, he grabbed a couple of slices of white cheese, ripped the cellophane off, and stuffed them in his mouth. Then he grabbed a can of soda and washed the cheese down while he stood there with the door open. He remembered getting yelled at by his mother for doing the exact same thing. It was the kind of flashback that occurred not infrequently. He closed the door, stood in the quiet, listening for the sounds of past ghosts, then moved toward the stairs. Ten minutes later, he was standing in a hot shower, trying to wash away the day. His clothes lay in a pile by the bed where he had dropped them. When he came back into the room, he picked them up. He threw everything but his pants into the bathroom hamper. He picked those up, folded them, and placed them on a hanger. During this process, something fell out of one of the pockets, landing noiselessly at his feet. He reached down to the hooked rug. Even in the dim light, he recognized the key.

"Damn, I forgot."

It was the key to the front door of the Black Bull. He laid it on the night table by the bed, picked up the clock next to it, set it for 8 P.M., then stretched out on the bed. His mind was racing. He had little hope of sleeping, even as tired as he was, so he awoke with a start when the alarm went off just over an hour later. He was groggy from the deep sleep, so he sat on the side of the bed a couple of minutes. Then he got to his feet. It had not been that long ago when the prospect of a trip to the Black Bull would have been the high point of his day. She would be there waiting for him. Now it was just a sad reminder of dashed hopes and expectations. It had been a long time since Virgil's underside had been so exposed. Even now, the thought of her was an opened wound. For an instant, he toyed with the idea of not going. Why should he care about Kyle's unfinished business, whatever it was, or what promises he had to keep? Besides, he had made it a point the last few months to go nowhere near the Black Bull, and he didn't want to go now. Going to meet Kyle, in a long list of things he didn't want to do, was close to the bottom. The hurt was still fresh.

When he stepped outside, he saw a light coming from Cesar's rooms in the barn. He was tempted to step over, but he knew it would just be a weak attempt to avoid the inevitable. A buck with a full rack streaked across the driveway in front of him as he headed toward the county road.

"I know what's on his mind," Virgil said to the empty truck. "Rutting season's in full swing."

He pulled out onto the hard surface, gunning the engine. It was a black, cold night. There were no other vehicles.

"Guess I'm the only one heading to a dark, empty road-house. Need to have my head examined." Then he gave a soft laugh. "Gotta stop talking to myself. Or get a dog."

The next ten minutes were spent in silence until he rounded a bend in the road. Then he caught his first glimpse of the Black Bull.

"Looks like somebody's home," he said, seeing a light coming from the vacant building. The familiar crunch of tires as he pulled into the parking lot did little to lessen his reluctance at being there. When he stepped out of the truck, he looked around for Kyle's vehicle, but came up empty. He thought about walk-ing around back to see if it was parked there, but reckoned that was not such a smart move without a flashlight so he stood for a short time by the truck. He thought about the light coming from inside, but chalked that up to security. He saw no movement there.

"Well, maybe I'm early or he's late."

He fingered the key in his pocket while he stood next to his truck. The chill in the night air was making its presence felt. His first inclination was to get back into the warm cab and wait, but he changed his mind and walked up the stairs to the porch. When he reached the top, he took one last look around. Not a sign of a car or pretty much anything else, so he took the key from his pocket and walked to the front door. He slipped the key easily into the lock. When he stepped into the semidark room, he was surprised at the warmth. Glancing to his left, he could see the black bull waiting in silence for his next victim. A quick look around the rest of the room told him everything else was as he remembered. The unlit fireplace centered the far wall, while empty tables and chairs circled the dance floor in front of it. High-backed chairs lined the long horseshoe bar, in quiet anticipation. It gave him an uneasy feeling. Small wall lights on either side of the bar and on the wall midway up the stairs that led to the top floor were the only illumination. Darkness that hugged the corners and recesses in the room blunted any sharp edges, heightening the emptiness. The murmur of the wind outside was the only sound he heard beyond his own heartbeat and the pulse in his ears. He felt unsure, almost like an intruder to a forbidden place. There was no music, no twang from a guitar or a soulful voice wrenching emotion from the lyrics of a song. No "Yahoo!" from a wannabe bull rider or even the subtle laughter that flowed from discreet conversation at the scattered tables. It was only him, standing in the half-light, feeling the presence of departed ghosts from nights not so long ago.

He moved across the room toward the end of the bar. He paused to see the initials he had carved so long ago during another life, at the invitation of the owner. A thousand or more hieroglyphs covered the surface, shellacked and preserved for the amusement of the patrons who would one day sit at this bar. His carving testified to the last twenty years of his life and the love he had shared with Rusty. As he stood there, his fingers tracing the long-ago declaration, the distant sound of music found his ear. At first he doubted what he heard, then, looking about the huge empty space, he turned his head toward the stairs. He walked to the first step. He started to climb, paused at the landing, then climbed the rest of the flight. He opened the door at the top, stepping into the small, empty room that he knew had always served as an office. He did not stop. Instead, he crossed to the far wall, to the door that led into the living area. As he stood before it, the plaintive voice of the Prairie Rose froze him in his tracks. His hand rested on the doorknob while K.D. Lang's voice pierced his consciousness. He had held Ruby close, moving in slow unison, when they had danced to that voice and that song. He was thrown back to another time and place. Inexplicably, the doorknob turned in his hand, then was plucked from his grip as the door opened from the other side. Transfixed, he looked at her like she was a mirage and he had been lost in a terrible wasteland. He wasn't conscious of his own breath or anything that might have connected him to some kind of reality. There was only the sudden vision that filled his gaze. A vision that he had lost.

He saw her reach out to him. He drew back. He could not give in. He could not surrender, knowing what he knew. He felt the softness of her hand as it reached out, touching his cheek, tracing the scar that had morphed into an age line. He felt her drawing him inside, drawing him close. The room was spinning. K.D.'s persistent, mournful wail filled his ears as she came nearer. He tried to resist. They swayed together. He was lost in remembrance. Finally, as the voice ebbed then faded away, she broke the spell.

"Virgil, I missed you. I longed for you." She reached up, drawing his lips to hers. He drowned in the sweetness of her taste. He didn't care about anything but her. There was no time for rational thought or explanation, just the hunger of the moment and the yearning for what had been. He crushed her to him, wrapped himself in her essence, devouring her like he was a starving man. By the time they were filled with each other to the point where they could hold no more, hours had passed. They had slipped away into the embrace of a long, dark night.

Cold sunlight slipped into the room as Ruby looked over at Virgil. She didn't want to break the spell, but there was no denying the sunlight pouring through the windows. No denying the world. She reached over. He stirred under her touch.

"No," he said.

"Yes," she said with a smile.

He opened one eye and looked at her.

"We have to talk," she said. "Kyle will be coming for me soon. I only have a little time."

He rolled over, turning away from her. She ran her fingers over his back.

"Your back is smooth. All of the burns from the barn fire are gone. Come on. Get dressed. I'll see if I can scrounge up something for us to eat. I know there's coffee. I brought in a few things yesterday."

"Yesterday," he said. "Only now counts." He rolled back over, caught her, and gave her a long, soulful kiss. "I don't want this to end."

"Neither do I," she said. Then she kissed him back and jumped out of bed.

They had finished a fairly meager breakfast. Each held a cup of coffee, waiting for the other to address the elephant in the room.

"I don't understand," Virgil said.

"I know. That day when you came with Kyle and the other agents, I couldn't tell you. I had to play out a role. When the cartel set me up as the owner of the Black Bull, I jumped at the chance as a way of escaping them. I had virtually no idea what their game plan was, only that I was to function as a kind of watchdog or intermediary. They don't trust anyone. I was to keep tabs on Wade Travis, their connection. I tried to tell you that day, I knew nothing about the killings. I only found out about them and the contraband at the very end. But I knew I was just a pawn from the very beginning. They would have never let me go. As soon as I was able, I made contact with the DEA. They determined the role I was to play until I could find out what the cartel was planning. But you found out before me, about everything. I had no choice but to act complicit. Even now, to save my life, I have to continue playing the part of an apprehended felon. Tonight Kyle has arranged for me to be flown out. The cartel believes I'm going to be tried in a federal court, then sent to a federal prison. I've given a lot of information to federal officials. If the organization ever found out, I wouldn't last a day. I had no choice but to go into some kind of witness protection, but I don't know how this is going to work. Kyle told me they have a plan, but I couldn't leave without seeing you. Kyle promised me. He kept his promise. That's why it had to happen like this."

"But then what about us? You and me?"

"I know. I had to see you. Now I've got to finish what we started. Before we left, I wanted you to know that what we had was real. I was supposed to keep tabs on you. That was the plan before we actually met. Once that happened I knew I was in way over my head. I wanted to tell you, but I couldn't. So many times I had to bite my tongue. Then, when everything came to a head, I knew I couldn't go into any kind of program without you knowing. The last couple of months have been hell for me."

Virgil reached across to clasp Ruby's hands in his.

"One last thing, Virgil. What we had meant so much, but I know a possibility of a future for us is just that, only a possibility. So I want us to separate knowing that we both have to move forward without looking back. I wouldn't change a moment of what we had. But neither of us can live on what might be. I will always love you, even if I never see you again."

Virgil loosened his hold on her hands. She saw his eyes glisten. He said nothing. Instead, he came around the table, wrapped her in his arms. They stood that way a long time. The distant sound of a horn finally separated them.

"That's Kyle," she said. "I've got to get ready."

Only then did Virgil speak. "Before you, I was drifting through life. You made me realize that. When we separated, the way we separated, left me with an open wound. I don't feel that way now."

Ruby nodded, then kissed him. "Virgil, it will be easier for me if you leave first."

She saw the resignation in his eyes. Then he took the key from his pocket, dropping it on the table.

"Here," he said. "When you leave, you're going to have to lock that door. I'll be here when you come back to unlock it. After all, the Black Bull is legally yours. When you reopen, I might even take a chance riding that bull to celebrate."

Ruby picked up the key from the table, then watched as Virgil went out the door.

When he stepped outside, she watched him from the window, walking to his truck. She saw him wave to Kyle, who was standing next to his car.

Virgil sat in his truck. He didn't feel like talking to Kyle or anybody. He looked up at the building. He saw a curtain in an upstairs window flutter as if someone had just brushed against it. He looked at the black bull perched on top of the roof, still missing that part of its ear that had been shot off. It almost seemed to him like a metaphor. No one is truly whole. He was no exception. We're all broken, he thought, just in different ways. Then he turned the key in the ignition.

13

"Hey, Rosie, where's Virgil?" It was almost four when Dif came through the door.

"I'm not sure. He didn't come in, never even called. I tried him on the landline when I couldn't get him on the cruiser's radio. Nothing—like he dropped off the planet. It's not like him to not call or just not show up all day."

"Sounds to me like a man who don't want to be found," Dif said. "Maybe he got lucky last night. Could happen."

"Yeah, when pigs fly. Virgil got the wind knocked out of him by Ruby. Don't think he's quite ready to get back on that horse."

"Wouldn't worry. Everything seems pretty quiet around here, from what I can see."

"You're right, Dif. Doc Kincaid wanted to talk to him. Other than that, it has been pretty quiet. Hope it holds through Thanksgiving."

"Me, too. Edna's got a million coming to dinner. Ain't hard to get a crowd when you're passing out free food and drink."

"Never was, never will be," Rosie said. "Well, if he calls or checks in, tell him to call Doc Kincaid. Oh, and tell him there was a head-on outside of town. Since Alex Rankin was still here to take his wife and new baby back home, he went to the accident scene and made out a report. No serious injuries, but the EMTs took one driver to the hospital."

"Okay, I'll pass that along if he shows up."

Rosie had been gone only a few minutes when Virgil walked through the door.

"Hey, buddy, Rosie gave you up for dead."

"Yeah. I should have called. Got tied up."

"Hope you mean that in a good way. Don't worry. I calmed her down, told her maybe you got lucky. But I didn't tell her that I happened to see you come out of the Black Bull, then wave to that federal guy, Kyle, or that I saw that pretty lady watching from that upstairs window as you drove away."

"Damn, like living in a fishbowl."

"Well, you know small-town life would be pretty boring without the gossip."

Virgil winced. "Dif, keep it under your hat, will you?"

"What are you talking about, Virgil? Didn't see nothing except that gobbler I picked out from Sam Dixon's flock, the one that's going to be the centerpiece on our table this Thursday."

"Thanks, Dif. Thursday? Oh, Thanksgiving!"

"Anyway, Virgil, Rosie told me to tell you Doc Kincaid called."

Virgil picked up his Stetson, which he had only a minute before laid on his desk. "Listen, Dif. If you're all right here, maybe I'll run over to the hospital, look in on Jimmy and see Ark."

"Hell, this place is as quiet as a tomb. Don't reckon there's gonna be a crime spree break out in Hayward this late in the day. Quitting time. Everybody wants to get home to a hot meal and a cold drink. Go ahead, Virgil. Oh, when you're over to the hospital, you might want to check on that injured party they brought in. Forgot to tell you, Rosie said Alex took the accident report. It's on your desk."

Virgil walked back over to his desk, picked up a folder, opened it, read the report, then placed it back on the desk. "Vernon," he said. "Vernon Thompson."

"What's that, Virgil?"

"That injured party, Vernon Thompson. Gotta be Velma and Charlie's boy. That's a coincidence. I was wondering when I was going to meet up with them."

"Well, it looks like today, at least for one of them," Dif said.

Virgil turned and retraced his steps to the door. "See ya, Dif. If you need me, holler. Thanks for not remembering that other thing. Rosie gets wind of that, my life will turn into a soap opera."

"Already has, Virgil. By the way, since I planted that cover story, don't be surprised if, when she sees you, she asks if there's any salt left in that shaker. You know Rosie, she suspects anything, she goes right for the jugular."

Jimmy wasn't in his room, so Virgil went to the nurse's station.

"You just missed him, Sheriff. He was discharged about twenty minutes ago."

"Discharged?"

"When they're young, they bounce back pretty quick."

Virgil shook his head. "I figured he'd be here at least another three or four days."

"Well, he will be coming in for PT through next week. But he's looking real good."

"Okay. What about number two on my list, Vernon Thompson?"

"Let me check." The nurse scanned the computer, then picked up the phone. "Just wanted to double-check what the screen showed me. Sorry, Sheriff, looks like you're digging a dry well there, too. He was never admitted. Looked at in the ER and sent on his way. Anybody else?"

"Guess you wouldn't know if Doc Kincaid is around?"

"Matter of fact I do. He's downstairs. Sent him one of our less successful outcomes a little over an hour ago. He's probably finished. Should be in his office by now."

"Thanks."

Five minutes later Virgil was pulling up a chair opposite Art Kincaid in his office. "So, what have you got for me, Ark?"

"Nothing conclusive as far as cause of death, but some questions that need some answers. Preliminary tox results indicate Velma had barbiturates in her system."

"Enough to kill her?"

"No, but the fact that there was enough to show up in her system suggests it was more than a minimum dose which would barely register. Probably enough to put her to sleep."

"So what are you saying?"

"I'm not sure myself. Maybe she was asleep from the drug, then something else killed her. Or someone."

"But why? Why would anyone kill Velma Thompson? It makes no sense. No sense at all."

"I'm just the coroner, Virgil. You're the sheriff. I think this puts the ball in your court now. I still haven't found out what actually killed her, but I guess maybe you have to look into her death also. We're still nowhere with the woman who came off the overpass. No ID. Nothing."

"No doubt, but where to start?"

"Maybe finding Charlie Thompson might provide some answers, Virgil."

"Or more questions," Virgil said as he walked to, then opened, the door.

"Yep, I guess that's why they call these things mysteries," Ark said.

Virgil recognized the truck, so he wasn't too surprised to see his cousin Billy Three Hats, also known as Captain William Lightfoot of the reservation police, sitting on his front porch.

"Billy, what are you doing sitting out here in the cold?"

"Hell, it's going to get a lot colder than this, Virgil. I been in the truck all day, running around trying to chase down a lead on the whereabouts of a meth supplier. The fresh air feels good to me."

"Any luck with your search?"

"Nothing definite, other than a couple of leads from some users on the rez. Not too many years ago, we thought alcohol was our biggest problem. Then along came meth, the escape for the new generation."

Virgil nodded. "So come on inside before that cold really starts to set in. I'll fix us some dinner. Got a couple of rib eyes—I'll throw them on the grill. Probably the last time I'll use it before the snow flies." Virgil looked up at the sky as he said it. Cobalt blue, not a cloud. The wind was picking up, blowing from the northwest. Swirls of fallen leaves were dancing in the driveway while Jack was in the corral, snorting at some dry chaff that was blowing around his hooves.

"That's the best invitation I've gotten today," Billy said.

Just then, Cesar came out of the barn. When he saw Billy and Virgil, he waved.

"You about done?" Virgil yelled over.

"Pretty near," Cesar yelled back. "Just got to let the horses in to feed."

"Well, finish up. Billy's staying and I'm throwing some steaks on the grill."

"Sounds good," Cesar said, waving in reply.

"Boy, them steaks didn't suck," Billy said as he sat back from the table, patting his stomach.

"No, they didn't," Virgil said.

Cesar still had a mouthful and nodded in agreement.

"You work out something for that extra hay from the Thompson place?" Virgil asked him.

"All done," Cesar said as he set down his fork. "Gonna get close to ten thousand bales starting tomorrow. There will be more if we need it. Pretty decent, got good color. Guess Charlie figured it was there so he might as well bale it. Lucky for us. Hope to get it all in the barn by the end of the week."

"So we've got something to be thankful for after all this Thanksgiving," Virgil said. "We won't have to decimate the herd."

"That's right," Billy said. "You lost all your hay when the barns burned down."

"Well, not all. We had some in that old barn across the road, but not near enough. If we didn't get a reliable outside source, we would have had to sell off over sixty percent of the herd. Because of the dry in these parts, a lot of beef is being sold off, so the going price isn't much of an inducement. We're fortunate, we've got pretty good water for graze most of the year, but we've got to have feed for the winter. I hated the idea of cutting the herd that much. Now I won't have to."

"By the way, Virgil, I'm going to need a check for that hay for Miss Thompson."

"She's at the ranch?"

"Came yesterday. Seems like a nice lady. She says she can act for her father since she has power of attorney. She explained that to me."

"I heard about Mrs. Thompson," Billy said. "What about Charlie? How long has he been gone now?"

"Four days and counting," Virgil said.

"What are you thinking, Virgil?"

Virgil didn't answer right away. He took a sip from his coffee, then looked out the kitchen window at the dark night. "I'm thinking tomorrow I'm going to head out to the Thompson place. Then I think I might be taking a ride on Jack up into that High Lonesome country the next day or so, see if Charlie's up there. I sure would like to find him."

"That's a lot of country to try and cover on horseback," Billy said. "Might be like trying to find a needle in a haystack."

"You know that country, Billy. I mean, the rez has a common border with the Thompson ranch for quite a ways, doesn't it?"

"About twenty miles, Virgil. I've been up in that area. High plateau, most of it. Good hunting, a mix of high desert and grassland. Years ago when the Thompson ranch was going full bore, a lot of the cattle up there would get real rangy. I mean, spring roundup was like watching an old western. Them cattle were as wild as them ten-point mule deer that call that country home. Charlie was real decent. When some of those strays crossed the line onto the rez, he and his hands would round them up, but always leave a few for the folks on the rez. I guess it was his way of being neighborly. He also didn't mind if we crossed the line when we were hunting. Trying to find someone in that country, well, that's gonna take a lot of looking and more than a little luck. Hell, just to get up there is going to take half a day. Maybe you'd be better off looking from the air. From a helicopter."

"I thought of that, but I reckon the council would throw a collective fit when I submit the bill. I'm trying to walk the line with them because I'm going to be telling them real soon that we need another full-timer. So I decided to go have a look for Charlie myself. Maybe I'll get lucky."

"You want me to tag along?" Cesar asked the question while he and Virgil stood on the front porch watching Billy Three Hats heading down the driveway toward the county road.

"No. You got enough to do with Pedro and José getting that hay. It's going to take you a couple of days. We want to get that into the barn before the weather turns."

"Well, Virgil, you better be careful in that high country. I don't much like the idea of you going up there alone."

Virgil looked at Cesar standing partially in shadow where the porch light didn't reach. "I've been going out on my own for a while now, old-timer. Don't worry. I run into trouble I'll send up a smoke signal."

"I don't read smoke. That's for those relatives of yours on the reservation. Just make sure you have your cell."

Virgil stood on the porch after Cesar had gone down to his apartment in one of the new barns. Billy Three Hats was right, the air did feel good. Chilled on the heels of a light wind, it had swept away the last of the summer heat once and for all. He pulled up his collar, saw stars twinkling in the night sky, and reckoned it had been a good day. Thoughts of Ruby swept over him like the soft breeze. He couldn't read tea leaves, but he knew the future looked better now. The hint of the winter that was coming, because of her, held a promise that he couldn't have foreseen. He turned his back on the night, then stepped into the kitchen. The cleanup didn't take long, so when he was done he went into the living room to check the weather for the next couple of days. He didn't know what he would find in his search up in the high country, but at least he could be prepared. The late news was ending so he knew he was in time for the weather report.

"So before we move on to the weather, again that late-breaking story. A small, private plane seems to have crashed in the Superstition Mountains. Preliminary reports are that there were three occupants, the pilot, a federal marshal, and a prisoner who was being transported to an undisclosed location. A search has begun. Further details are unknown at this time. Now for the weather."

Virgil sat in the quiet a long time. He could hear the ticking of the clock on the mantel over the fireplace, the creaking noises as the night air found entry into the tiniest gaps in the old house. Twice, he started to rise from the cozy grasp of the comfortable chair, only to sink back down. When at last he struggled to his feet, his world view had changed. He put in a call to Kyle Harrison but got no response.

Later, he lay wrapped in a fog, sifting through the words he had heard, trying to make sense of it all.

14

He stood with his foot on the lowest rail of the corral. The cold sun had come up, doing little to warm him as his expired breath condensed in small clouds. He was still the sheriff of Hayward County and he knew two things. First, he had never given in to self-recrimination. Second, he was not about to start now. Virgil was hardwired in the school of suck it up. He remembered an incident from his youth, before he'd even made it to double figures. A particularly rank gelding had chosen on a morning not unlike this to make him part of the landscape. As he lay in the dirt looking for some kind of comfort, his father stood over him.

"You know that ground's not going to get any softer the longer you lie there." Now, all these years later, the lesson still held.

A pickup came rolling down the driveway. It was probably older than most of the population of Hayward. Two men got out. Virgil took his foot from the bottom rail, pushed the brim of his hat a little higher on his forehead, nodding as they exited the pickup, whose engine continued to sputter even after the ignition key was withdrawn. Finally, it gave a little pop and went silent.

"Good morning, señor."

"Morning, Pete," Virgil said. "You and Joe are going to put in a long day. Hope the old man doesn't kill you."

They each smiled broadly. Virgil didn't know whether it was his reference to Cesar or the fact that he had Americanized them. They were brothers, but could have been twins, they looked so much alike. Dark eyes in darker faces, straight black hair that rarely saw a comb, perpetual smiles showing gleaming white teeth. Virgil hired them at Cesar's request over ten years before when they were still wet from the river. They were, according to Cesar, his cousins. Virgil's response to that was that he had never met anyone from the other side of the river who wasn't a cousin. Nevertheless, they had turned out to be as steady as a spring rain. The more Virgil's job as sheriff grew, the more he realized how crucial they had become. They all turned at the opening of the barn door. Jack came busting out into the corral, snorted, dropped his head, and bucked.

"He feeling good," José said. They watched as he did two laps around the corral, then came to a stop in front of Virgil. Virgil's arms were resting on the second rail of the four-rail fence. Jack started to nibble on his sleeve. Virgil reached his hand in to stroke his face. Jack dropped his head under Virgil's touch, becoming a different horse.

"He loves you," Pedro said.

"Yeah," Virgil said, "we kinda appreciate one another."

Just then Cesar came out from one of the other barn doors. Virgil stepped back from the corral fence. "Don't work these boys too hard today. Remember, they got to be able to eat that Thanksgiving dinner tomorrow."

"Just enough to work up a good appetite," Cesar said. "You want help loading Jack? I already attached the trailer."

"I saw. Did you secure the lock on the ball along with the umbilical chain?"

Cesar winced. "Make one mistake, one time, haunts you forever."

"Yeah, well, we'll save that debate for another day, but if you boys will excuse me now, I'm going to load Jack and double-check the hitch. Have a nice Thanksgiving."

"*Sí*, señor," they added in unison. "And you, too."

Virgil left them standing by the corral and went into the barn. When he returned, they had already left for the Thompson ranch. He put his saddle into the cab of the truck, then got a couple of flakes of hay, placing them in the feed rack of the trailer. Last, he loaded a sack of sweet feed. Jack stepped into the trailer quickly. Cesar had hitched up the one-horse trailer, so even with Jack's thousand-plus pounds, Virgil hardly felt the pull on the heavy-duty pickup. When he pulled onto the hard surface, he glanced in the mirror. Jack was already contentedly munching on the hay.

Virgil stopped at the office to tell Rosie his plans. He could hear her in the holding cell area when he came into the office. He walked over to his desk and saw that everything was pretty much as he had left it the day before. The accident report from Alex was just where he had dropped it.

"Sorry about not checking in yesterday," Virgil said as Rosie emerged from the hallway leading to the cells.

"It's nothing. Don't worry, Virgil. You got enough on your plate right now."

It was a surprising answer. Virgil looked at Rosie. There was concern showing in her eyes.

"Kyle Harrison called," she said. "He told me about the plane. About you. Yesterday. We can talk about it if you want."

"No. Not now. Maybe sometime, but not now. I think it's best if I keep my head in the game. In a little while, I'm heading out to the Thompson place. Got Jack in the trailer. Going to stable him there, then go looking for Charlie. I might start tomorrow."

"Virgil, it's Thanksgiving."

"Yeah, I know. My grandfather's not going to be too happy. Just don't think I'd be the best company right now. Don't feel like being in a crowd. Maybe getting up in that country will help to clear my head a little, get some perspective."

He went over to his desk, looked at the accident report again, then picked up the phone. Alex answered on the second ring.

"Redbud Police Annex. How can I help you?"

"Very professional, Alex. Didn't figure you'd be back in the office so early. Thought maybe the new baby would be keeping you up."

"Actually, Virgil, so far, so good. Looks like we got a keeper, practically slept through. What can I do for you? Oh, by the way, my wife said to tell you thanks for the flowers."

"Alex, I just wanted to get a little background on that accident you covered yesterday. Good report, but I was hoping you could give me a little more."

"Not too much to tell. One car drifted over the line, caught the other, then they each spun out. The drifter's driver was the only one that got physically banged up. They brought him to the hospital to check him out. That's where I caught up with him. Virgil, I didn't ticket him. It was Vernon Thompson, Velma and Charlie's son. Knew about his mom. Just didn't have the heart there and then. He seemed pretty off."

"How do you mean, Alex? Upset or something else?"

"Kinda hard to say. Didn't smell alcohol, but I figured maybe he was on some kind of meds. You know, because of his mother's death. Had kind of a glazed look. Hope I didn't make a mistake, but I chalked it up. Figured insurance would take care of the vehicle damage. There wasn't any damage to anyone except Vernon."

"Okay. I'm heading out there today. If he's there, I'll check him out. By the way, tell Dave when he gets in, I'm going to look for Charlie. Be out of touch for a couple of days."

"Will do. You're not going up into that backcountry by yourself? You'd better be careful. After all, Charlie ain't come back yet and he knows that country better 'n anybody."

Virgil hung up the phone, mulling over Alex's words. He was right—it didn't bode well that Charlie hadn't come back by now. Then the office door opened. Virgil got an unexpected greeting.

"Hey, Sheriff."

"Jimmy, what are you doing here? You just got out of the hospital."

"The doctors said I could resume normal activity as long as it wasn't physically strenuous. I figure coming down here, sitting behind a desk qualifies. Rosie told me what you were going to be up to, so I figured you might be a little shorthanded, what with Thanksgiving and all. I could ride the desk rather than sit home watching football. Here I could do both, along with giving Rosie and Dif some downtime. They could probably use it."

"Can't argue that. They both been putting in extra hours."

"Wish I could go with you looking for Mr. Thompson, but riding a chair is one thing, a horse, something else."

Virgil glanced over at Rosita, who had been unusually quiet during the exchange.

"So you know about that. One step at a time, Jimmy. Okay, if you're up to it, call Dif, tell him he can stay home. Put an edge on that knife he's going to use to carve up that bird tomorrow."

Virgil turned to Rosie, who was still sitting quietly at her desk. "So, since you dragged this poor kid out of his hospital bed to get some time off, you might as well get out of here also. Guess you got a little prep for tomorrow, too."

"Thank you. I do have a lot to do. Virgil, why don't you wait another day or two on Charlie? Then maybe you can get someone to go with you."

"No, Rosie. I already waited too long, considering how Velma ended up."

"You think there's a connection?"

"I don't know, but you know how I feel about coincidences. Charlie's away, Velma ends up dead, and Charlie hasn't come back. Sure is odd. On top of that we got a poor girl who dropped out of the sky on top of Jimmy here. We still don't know anything about her other than she came out onto that highway from High Lonesome ranch. That just makes it even stranger to me."

Virgil stood up from his desk. "Anyhow, now that my top hand is back, I'm going to take off."

"If he's your top hand, what does that make me?" Rosie said.

Virgil looked hard at Rosie, then headed for the door.

"You know," he said, "all these years, I'm still trying to figure that out." He didn't wait for the response.

The ride out to the Thompson ranch was uneventful. It was a little after ten by the time he got there. The foreman, Manuel, was closing the door to the largest of the three barns as he pulled up.

"You just missed Cesar. They say they're going to try to make two more hay runs today. He told me about you going to look for Mr. Charlie."

"Is anybody in the house?" Virgil asked.

"Miss Marian is there. She came the night before last. If you want, I'll unload your horse while you go see her."

"Thanks, but Jack and I have a long-standing relationship. It might go a little more smoothly if I handle it. I'm going to put him in that corral, then maybe you can point me to an empty stall I can use."

"In this barn, you can take your pick. There's plenty of empty ones. Not like the old days."

"Yeah, so I hear. Guess Charlie was hoping one of the boys would show some interest."

Virgil did not miss the subtle change in Manuel's body language. When he did not respond, Virgil's interest was piqued.

"Too bad," Virgil said. "This ranch really had a reputation. You know, my dad and Charlie were real close. Back in the day, they used to rodeo together. He always said Charlie was fearless. He'd ride anything they could saddle. Worked hard on this place, too. Sure is a shame."

"Those boys want no part of this," Manuel said, gesturing at the whole ranch around him. "All they want is to take, give nothing back. Mr. Thompson was a hard man, but good. Never ask someone to do something he wouldn't do himself. Give those boys a great life, but they throw it away. *¿Quién sabe?*"

"Some people don't appreciate when they're given something they never earned. But like you said, who knows?"

Virgil watched as Manuel walked toward the barn, then he moved to the back of the trailer. He let the ramp down. Jack snorted, then began stomping his feet in place and shaking his head in the cross ties.

"Don't get your shorts in a knot. I'm running as fast as I can." He went around to the side door, then stepped up into the trailer. Jack was still tossing his head. Virgil reached over the bar, clipped a lead rope on Jack's halter, and undid the cross ties. He slipped under the bar, then gently put a finger to Jack's chest. He gave a slight nudge. Jack immediately started backing up and down the ramp. Virgil followed until they were both on solid ground.

"Good boy." Virgil stood at Jack's head while he looked him over, then encouraged him to take a few steps. Jack stepped gingerly forward, away from the confinement of the trailer. Virgil led him to the empty corral, opened the gate, then led him through. Once inside, he unclipped the lead rope. Jack snorted again, threw his head from side to side, then pranced around the corral while Virgil walked back to the open gate. A woman was waiting there.

Marian Thompson was all angles, lean and ramrod straight. Her hair had a peculiar streak of white that ran left of center until it disappeared in the auburn lock that reached her shoulders. She had clear, blue eyes along with a smile that showed a row of even white teeth. She would have stood out in any crowd.

"I'm guessing you're Sheriff Virgil Dalton."

"Guilty as charged, ma'am."

"Don't ma'am me, Virgil. I'm Marian. Marian Davies, formerly Thompson. Don't know that we're that many years apart, but I can't say that I ever remember meeting you."

"Same here, Marian, but if I ever met you, I'd remember."

"Well, that's a lot better than ma'am, Virgil. Almost makes me feel desirable. A smart man knows that it's important to make a woman feel that way and I judge you to be a smart man."

"I try," Virgil said. "Sometimes I come up short."

"Oh, my. Smart, modest, and easy to look at. That's a lethal combination."

"Real sorry about your mom, Marian."

"I appreciate that, Virgil. I loved my mom. It's tough to let go. Just wasn't expecting it."

"I understand. Guess you're wondering why I'm here and why I brought Jack."

"Just a little bit. That's a lot of horse you put in the corral. I was watching from the porch. Big gelding."

"He is big, but if you were a little closer than the porch, you would have seen that he's intact."

She stepped to the side to get a better look at Jack, who was still stretching his legs.

"My, my, so he is. Bet the girls are eager to make his acquaintance. Stunning."

"Tomorrow morning, at first light, I'm going up on that tableland to see if I can find your father."

"You think something's happened to him?"

"Well, I believe tomorrow's the fifth day he's been gone. Aren't you concerned?"

"I wish he was here, because of what happened to Mom. It's going to be tough on him, but as far as being concerned, well . . . You have to understand, my dad has always been the toughest man I've ever known. He's gone up on that plateau hundreds of times, most of the time branding, riding herd on some of the meanest critters God ever saw fit to cover with cowhide. He's been gored, kicked, and stomped on, been down more times than I can count, but he's never been out. So no, I haven't been concerned. Do you have a reason to be, besides how long he's been gone? Because he's been gone many times longer than this."

For the next few minutes, Virgil told Marian about the

recent events that ended with him bringing Jack up to High Lonesome ranch. When he finished, Marian reached out and ran her hand along one of the rails of the corral, then looked toward the unbroken stretch of land that ended at the far horizon. She didn't say anything right away. Her teeth were clenched so that the skin on her face was so tight her cheekbones became even more prominent.

"Damn barbiturates," she said. "You'd have to just about hog-tie her to get her to take an aspirin. So, what you're saying here is, Mom didn't go naturally."

"That seems to be the case, but Ark, I mean Dr. Kincaid, is still looking."

"But this makes no sense. Why would someone do this? To a seventy-five-year-old woman who never did harm to anyone?"

"That's the question I'm trying to answer. Maybe if I find Charlie that will give me a piece of the puzzle that I'm missing."

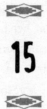

15

Virgil stood alone in the huge, empty barn. It was an eerie feeling. He set his saddle on the top rail of the closest stall. He had already hung Jack's bridle on the hook of a corner post. Now he started down the center walkway, which ran the length of the barn. Every stall was empty. When he had walked into his newly built barns the day they were completed, he had felt the loss of past remembrance. Here the feeling was more of abandonment. Perfectly good buildings that no longer had a purpose. It seemed like such a waste. An orange cat came out from one of the empty stalls. She came over to him, brushing up against his leg. He bent down, stroked her, then picked her up.

"Got the whole place to yourself. Probably even the rats have left."

She purred contentedly. He set her back down, then walked back out to his truck. He grabbed a bale of hay from the bed of the pickup, brought it back into the barn, then set it down outside the stall. He put his knee into the center, pushing it into a

V shape so he could pop the hay cords. Then he took three flakes, opened the stall door, and dropped them into the hay rack. All of the wood had the rich, dark patina of age and use. He rubbed his hand over the edge of the top trim of the hay rack. From the decades of animals rubbing their necks on it as they reached in for hay, it showed no wood grain and was as smooth as marble.

Virgil went back outside and unhitched the horse trailer. Jack was still in the corral. Finally, he walked down toward the house. Marian Davies was outside in the flower garden. When she saw him coming, she stood up. He saw a profusion of flowers lying in neat piles at her feet.

"Mom loved her gardens and her flowers. Some of them have already been nipped by the frost. I figured I'd gather up what I could. The mums look okay. The white and yellow will look good with a mix of the blue asters. See if I can keep them fresh enough to bring to Simpson's when we can get Mom there for a last good-bye."

"That's a real nice idea," Virgil said. "Rosita . . . Rosie, who found your mom, loves her gardens."

"I don't remember her, but Dave Brand, her husband, was in school with me. Really nice guy."

"Still is," Virgil said. "He's one of my deputies. Actually, he's in charge of the annex down in Redbud."

"Redbud? Why down there? Nothing but cactus and armadillos."

"Guess it's been a while for you. Since the interstate interchange was completed, there's a motel, a Quik and Easy, and the headquarters of Hayward Trucking."

"Micah Hayward running the operation down there? Heard about Audrey. She was a piece of work."

Virgil couldn't stifle a smile at the reference. "I guess you could say Audrey was one of a kind. As far as your question, Caleb, Micah's son, handles most of the operation down in Redbud while Micah, now that Audrey's gone, oversees everything at Crow's Nest."

"Guess when you're out of the loop, the wheels keep turning. People die, children grow up."

"Yes. The past is the past." Virgil glanced back at the empty corrals and barns.

Marian followed his gaze. "So, what can I do for you, Virgil?"

"Was wondering if I could ask a favor. I've decided to go visit my grandfather. Then I'll either stay there tonight or head back to my place. If you could ask my foreman, Cesar, before he's leaving with his last load of hay to put Jack in that first stall in the large barn, I'd appreciate it. He'll see it's set up for him. This way I won't have to stop back, but I'll be here to get an early start in the morning."

"No problem, Virgil. But if you don't know that country up there, how do you figure you're going to be able to find Dad?"

"Well, I'm hoping to get lucky."

It was a little after noon when he started up to the mesa. His stomach was growling. He'd worked hard to keep the plane crash in the Superstitions on the back burner, but it hadn't been easy. Real-time images of him and Ruby together or her alone kept randomly popping into his mind. There was some comfort in going to see a man who had been an anchor point in his life. He had buried two wives and all of his children, none of whom had made it past forty. Now he was presiding over third and fourth generations. He gunned the engine at the last rise, then pulled his truck next to his grandfather's double-wide. When he got out, he saw no signs of life, so he went inside. He had just sat down at the kitchen table with a sandwich and a soda when the door opened and his grandfather came in carrying some packages. Virgil got up and took them from him.

"There's more outside, Virgil." He went outside and saw Mrs. Hoya struggling with a case of soda she was trying to get out of the back of the pickup.

"Here. You go inside. I'll take care of the rest of this."

"Thank you, Virgil." She insisted on carrying one of the bags. By the time he finished his last trip, they had already put away most of the groceries.

"Seems like you got enough here to last a month."

"Oh, most of this is for tomorrow," Mrs. Hoya said.

Virgil sat down to eat the sandwich he had made.

"We didn't expect you today," his grandfather said.

Virgil spent the next few minutes explaining why he would not be able to make his customary Thanksgiving visit.

"Well, we will miss you," his grandfather said. "I understand, but I am concerned. That's rugged country. You will be alone."

Virgil sat quietly, listening to yet another person telling him to be careful, but this was his grandfather, who knew well the dangers of the world. He spent a couple of hours visiting with both his grandfather and Mrs. Hoya. They brought him up to speed on all the reservation gossip. A couple of times as she was speaking, he saw his grandfather roll his eyes. Finally, he stood to leave.

"You are welcome to spend the night."

"I know, but I thought maybe I'd get home before Cesar and the boys finish their last hay run. I'll be there to help them and I can take care of the barn chores tonight. Cesar still thinks he's a young man."

"Only in his head," Grandfather said. "When he gets out of bed tomorrow, his body will tell him otherwise and tomorrow you will be a pilgrim."

"A pilgrim?"

"Yes, you know the story of the Pilgrims and the first Thanksgiving. One time, long ago, I looked that word up in the dictionary. I think it was after an argument with my brother. He didn't want to celebrate Thanksgiving. I think he said it should be a day of mourning for all Indians."

Virgil sat back down. "You didn't agree, Grandfather?"

"Well, I wasn't sure. But my brother was so adamant, he got me angry. He did that a lot. You know what people today say: pissed off. He used to piss me off a lot. So I looked up that word, 'pilgrim.' A pilgrim is a seeker, someone who is looking for something. It didn't say what they were looking for, but I think a pilgrim is looking for answers because he doesn't know. You are looking for answers, too. That's why tomorrow you will be a pilgrim."

"Did your brother change his mind?"

"No. He was hardheaded. He was one of those people who think they know everything."

"How do you feel about Thanksgiving now? Billy Three Hats calls it the white man's feast."

The old man looked about the trailer and at Mrs. Hoya before he responded. "I think it was a good thing for those people. They had come through some hard times and survived. Everybody goes through hard times in their life. My brother said that they killed Indians and the others that came after them did the same. He was right, but they weren't the first to do that. Indians had been killing one another, long before those people came. I think it is a good thing to be thankful, especially after you've lived through difficulties. Anyhow, I am thankful."

He reached across the table, covering Virgil's hand with his. When he withdrew it, he covered Mrs. Hoya's hand in the same way. She was beaming.

"Grandfather, I hope someday to be as wise as you."

"When I first saw you today, Virgil, there was sadness in your eyes. I don't know why. You don't have to tell me. But you are a seeker. Someone who seeks answers is already wise."

Virgil carried the conversation with him when he left.

He had just passed through Hayward, a couple of miles to go before the turnoff to the ranch. As he rounded a curve, he came upon a pickup off on the shoulder. He slowed, then pulled up in back of the vehicle. He got out and walked around the passenger's side of the truck to the front. He saw a young woman was talking on a cell phone. When she saw him, she quickly ended her call. Virgil thought she looked familiar.

"What's the problem?" Virgil asked.

"I ran out of gas. Meant to get some before I left town, but with shopping for tomorrow, I forgot. I was hoping, when I realized I was almost out, that I could make it home, but . . ." She raised both hands in dismay.

"Well, we've all done it. Don't worry, I've got gas in the truck. Give me a minute and you'll be on your way."

Virgil got his five-gallon gas can from the bed of his pickup, then poured it into the empty tank.

"You're all set," he said.

"Aren't you the sheriff?"

"Yes, I am."

"I didn't recognize you at first, out of the uniform. I'm Hayley, the nurse from the hospital. I remember when you came looking for Jimmy Tillman."

"Oh, yes. I knew you looked familiar, but you're also out of uniform."

"Yeah, well, I guess we've both got to pass for civilians once in a while. Otherwise, we just become vaguely familiar faces. Sheriff, wait till I get my wallet. For the gas."

Virgil waved no, shaking his head. "Gas is on me. Better get home with your groceries. Glad I could help. I'll wait to make sure she starts right up."

Hayley climbed into the cab. The first time she turned the key, the engine came alive.

"Thanks, Sheriff. Happy Thanksgiving."

Virgil watched as she pulled off the shoulder onto the hard surface. A small dust cloud stirred up as the back tires dug into the shoulder before catching the hard surface.

"Damn. Damn, that's it." He pulled out his cell, then speed-dialed Art Kincaid's number.

"Ark."

"What's up, Virgil?"

"That girl, Ark. That poor girl who hit Jimmy's cruiser. Remember, I said she looked familiar. Coupla months back, she had a blowout. I came upon her alongside the road. I stopped and changed the tire for her. I knew I had seen her before. She was wearing a kind of uniform with a logo on the pocket. You know the kind of outfit, work clothes, same color, maybe olive green, khaki. The pickup had a logo on the door also."

"What was it, Virgil?"

There was a long pause.

"I can't remember," Virgil said. "I'm trying to picture it, but I'm drawing a blank."

"Well, without it, your recall doesn't give us that much more."

"Yeah, I know. At least I know I'm not cracking up. I mean, I've been looking at that woman's face a lot of nights when I was trying to get to sleep. Now at least I know where I met her."

"True, but like we talked about when you were in the office . . . now you've only got more questions. What was she doing? Where was she going or coming from? What company did she work for? Maybe if you get answers to some of those questions, then we can figure out who she is."

Virgil sat in his pickup after the conversation ended. He put his cell phone in the console, looking out at the empty, winding road. He was no closer to identifying the unnamed woman lying under a sheet in the basement of Hayward Memorial. He didn't know how, but he was going to find out her name, why she was in Hayward, and how she came to flying out of the night to land on Jimmy's cruiser.

16

Virgil had finished the last of the barn chores by the time Cesar, Pedro, and José pulled in with the final load of hay. Each of them was driving a pickup. The beds of each pickup were loaded as were the hay wagons each was pulling. Virgil waited for them as they pulled up.

"Looks like a parade," he said as they exited their respective vehicles. "I'd have hated to be driving a car in back of you guys." They all looked whipped.

"We should have thinned the herd," Cesar croaked, shaking his head as he brushed off the chaff from his pants.

"Hang on a minute," Virgil said as he turned and ran over to the house. A couple of minutes later he was back with a pitcher filled to the top, along with some plastic cups. Each of the men took a cup, filled and emptied it in one swallow, then filled it again. "That's a lot of hay. I saw what you already sent up the conveyor. Have you got it all?"

"As much as we're gonna get for now. Depending on the

weather, this should take us at least to February, I figure," Cesar said.

"That being the case, we're not going to send this all up the conveyor, only the stuff in the beds of the pickups. The hay wagons we'll line up in the walkways of the barns. Leave the hay in them, feed that first." José and Pedro each smiled at the suggestion.

"I don't know," Cesar said, wiping the smiles off their faces. "We have to get those hay wagons back along with that third pickup we borrowed."

"They won't need those hay wagons till next year. I'll square it with Marian Thompson. I mean, Davies. I'm sure she'll be fine with it. I can drive their pickup down there tomorrow. When I come back from my search for Charlie Thompson, I'll call. You can come down and get me and Jack. You and these boys are done for the day." Virgil saw the relief come into the eyes of José and Pedro, then almost reluctantly, Cesar. "Fellas, if you could just empty what's in the bed of your pickup onto the elevator, you can get out of here for your Thanksgiving holiday." Virgil didn't have to ask them twice. While they did that, he insisted Cesar go take a shower and get out of his work clothes. By the time Cesar returned, Virgil had backed the hay wagons into the barns, then sent the two pickup loads of hay up the conveyor to join what was already there.

"Looks like you're going to need a shower now," Cesar said. "By the way, I put Jack in that stall before I left. He'll be waiting for you. Be careful up in that backcountry tomorrow."

"I will, don't worry. See you in a couple of days." Cesar walked away, shaking his head.

When Virgil stepped into the kitchen, he could see the message light flashing on the phone. He drank the last of the ice water from the pitcher he had brought out to his men. It felt good going down, but was a reminder to him that he had hardly broken a sweat compared to the physical exertion of Cesar, Pedro, and José. He punched the button on the phone. He heard Kyle Harrison's voice.

"Virgil, the search continues. Nothing yet. I'll call if there's a change." The second message kicked right in. He recognized Virginia's voice.

"I stopped by your office to find out what you were doing for Thanksgiving. Your deputy Jimmy filled me in. Doesn't seem like much of a holiday for you. Maybe we can do better at Christmas. By the way, it's pretty obvious you really have two children. Me, by way of the old-fashioned method. Jimmy, by adoption. You are definitely the father he never had. See you soon." There was a brief silence. "I hope." Virgil reached over to erase the second message, but instead of deleting it, played it again. When it ended, he sat for a moment listening to the silence. Then he got up, went upstairs, and took a shower.

There wasn't even the faintest glow on the horizon when he walked to the borrowed pickup the next morning. The roosters were still fast asleep. The night was reluctant to let go. Even the pickup rebelled until the third try. It was cold. It didn't feel any warmer, sitting on the cold vinyl, waiting for the engine to catch. When it finally did, it had the raspy sound of an old man coming off a three-day drunk. He got to the end of the driveway before he realized he had left the saddlebags sitting on the kitchen table. By the time he left the house the second time, a rooster was crowing, the faintest glow showed on the horizon, and the engine was humming like a Jimmy Buffett tune.

Driving down the eight-mile driveway to High Lonesome ranch was an exercise in dodging most of the wildlife that called Hayward County home. At the end, he saw a light, surprisingly coming from the barn. He pulled up close, turned off the engine, then stepped out of the cab. He was caught off guard when he saw the figure of Marian Davies as he stepped inside.

"Morning, Virgil."

"Morning," he answered. "It wasn't really necessary for you to come out here this early. Hope it wasn't just for me."

"No. It was because of me," she answered. "I got to thinking after you left yesterday. You're giving up your holiday to go look for my dad. I'm sitting here doing what? There's something wrong with this picture. So, Virgil, you're not going alone after all. But before you go stereotype on me, you need to know two things. My dad set me on a horse long before I could even stand. So don't go looking for me over your shoulder because I won't be back there. The other thing is, I know this country, you don't. I'll be better than a GPS and you can yell at me if I make a mistake. By the way, I fed, watered, and saddled your horse for you."

"Jack let you saddle him?"

"He was a little balky at first, but when he figured out I knew what I was doing, he settled right down. I notice you got a snaffle bit on him. He must have a real light mouth."

"Yes. He's got a soft mouth, doesn't need a curb." Virgil was a little taken aback by the exchange, discussing bridle restraints with Marian in her barn at six in the morning. It didn't look like there was going to be any place for his input. "Well, I guess we'd better get this show on the road." He made the remark without a great deal of conviction. She didn't seem to notice as she opened the stall next to the one she had just led Jack from after she had placed Jack's reins in Virgil's hands.

"Meet Ringo," she said. Virgil looked at the gelding that stood alongside Jack. He had a Roman nose and a blind eye. Virgil figured he couldn't have been more than fourteen, three hands way short of Jack's sixteen-one. He was a full-on buckskin right down to the black stripe that ran down the middle of his back. "He was born where we're going. Pop found him alongside of his mother after she had snapped her leg in a hole. Put a bullet in her, then brought him home to me. Had to bottle-feed him for the first couple of months. Maybe don't have that three-bars pedigree like your horse, but he's got a heart like a locomotive, tough as nails, can turn on a dime and give you change. Won barrels on him three years running, till I got married. So like I said, you won't have to be looking over your shoulder for him or me because we'll be right alongside you." Virgil said nothing. He knew when he'd lost a fight, even one he'd never been in, so he just threw his saddlebags over the saddle and led Jack from the barn. Marian followed. When they got outside, each of them checked their girths before mounting. Virgil noted Marian kneeing the gelding's abdomen, then tightening the cinch. Virgil's saddle sat snug on Jack, so he put his left foot in the stirrup and sprang up. He watched her step up, throw her leg over, then settle into her seat with the grace of a ballet move.

"Let's go to the High Lonesome," she said.

The sun had broken through. The late autumn sky was blue and cloudless. Within ten minutes, the ranch complex had disappeared. They were leaving a dust trail along with scattering rocks as they began a gradual ascent toward the distant tabletop. For the first hour they rode side by side. When they reached any level areas they broke into a light canter, but most of the time they were climbing. The terrain was rough and broken. Mostly desert with hidden arroyos and rock outcroppings, there was little green to interrupt the earth tones. An occasional yucca or piñon could be seen, twisted into modern art by winds that, when they blew, scoured the land, sandblasting everything on it. Finally, about three hours into their trek, Marian pulled Ringo to a halt. Virgil followed her lead.

"I think we better take a break. Your horse needs it." Virgil looked down at the lather which stained Jack's neck. He didn't argue. After he dismounted, he loosened Jack's cinch.

Once he saw how wet he was, he removed the saddle, setting it on a huge rock. Then he reached into one of the saddlebags. He took out a good-sized piece of terry cloth, then started wiping Jack down. The horse stood quietly, breathing noticeably. Virgil rubbed his flanks, the saddle area, working up to his neck and finally his face. The towel was heavy with moisture. The late-morning air meeting with the wet caused a little steam to rise. When Virgil wiped Jack's face along with the area of his throat-latch, Jack gave a contented snort. Lastly, Virgil wiped the inside of his ears. He noted a tiny trace of blood on the cloth, evidence of some ear mites that had tried to find a home. When he had finished, he glanced at Marian, who was sitting on one of the boulders that were the most dominant feature of the immediate landscape. She had finished with her horse long before Virgil. Virgil walked over and sat beside her. She handed him a bottle of water. Virgil popped the cap, then took a long drink.

"That's my fault," Virgil said apologetically. "That's my fault." He pointed to Jack, who was still standing quietly where Virgil had left him. "I've not been putting in the time with him lately, like I should. He's out of shape. So am I."

"Don't beat yourself up, Virgil. We all get busy. Life inter-feres. Some things get put on the back burner. It was Jack's turn. Besides, I don't think you're out of shape from where I sit. In

Jack's defense, he's what Pop used to call a bottomland horse. Ringo here is part billy goat. The mustangs that roam this land have never seen the inside of a barn. You've got a good, solid horse there. He just needs some time to adjust. So do you. We've been riding uphill for the last three hours. We have that and more to go to reach the top. The air is starting to get thin. We've probably climbed up close to fifteen hundred feet. Takes some time getting used to."

"Guess I never thought about that," Virgil said. "Pretty rough up here. Nothing for cattle to eat but dirt."

"You'll see, it's a lot different up top," Marian replied. "Anyhow, I suggest a little break now and a lot more walking for us."

"Is this the way your dad would have come?"

"There is another route, about a third shorter, but it's three times as difficult. Dad is tough, but he's not stupid. He would never go that way alone at his age. No. He came this way." When they left their resting spot half an hour later the only thing on Jack's back was an empty saddle and the saddlebags.

Two more stops and almost six hours later found them within a quarter mile of the top of the plateau. Whatever warmth there was from the midday sun had come and gone. Nevertheless, Virgil could feel rivulets of sweat running down his back. Much of the last few hours had been on foot with both him and Marian leading their mounts.

"Virgil, I need to stop for a minute." Virgil held Jack close, not unhappy for the break, while Marian sat down on a rock, then slipped off her shoe. She withdrew a piece of shale from inside. Virgil noted the red mark on her sock. "Should have stopped sooner," she said.

"I've got something for that," Virgil said. He went to his saddlebag, took out a first aid kit, then knelt down and dressed the cut on Marian's instep.

"You must have been a Boy Scout."

"Always be prepared," he replied. "I think you better get back on Ringo. The friction of walking is only going to make that worse."

"I guess you're right," she said. "We're almost to the top. There's an old line cabin not too far away. Might be a good place to spend the night, then we can get an early start. Tomorrow, we won't have to walk. Be a lot easier on the horses, too. Then we can start looking for Dad."

"I can't believe cattle ranged up here. Nothing but scrub pine, cholla, and rock."

"Wait till we get on top. You'll see. It's a different world. I love it."

"I've always wanted to see a different world."

"Well, give me a leg up on that one-eyed horse of mine and follow me. You won't be disappointed."

17

The fatigue of the long day's trek to reach the plateau no longer mattered in the slanting sun of late afternoon. Virgil wasn't disappointed. The land was showing a different face. Huge rock cliffs, barren land broken by a mere hint of green from scrub plants and cactus that struggled to eke out existence, were replaced by solid pine and aspen golden in the setting November sun. Wild grasses held firmly to the soil. The land, more green than brown, showed gradual undulations and little of the treachery underfoot that they had earlier endured to reach it. Virgil's eyes roved the scene in genuine surprise.

"Now you know why the reward was worth the journey," Marian said.

Virgil nodded his head. They had been standing next to their horses and the slack reins they held allowed each of the horses to drop their heads for the first taste of fresh graze since the start of their trek.

"That line cabin's a little farther on," she said. "A good place to end the day."

"Why do they call it a line cabin?"

"You know, I'm not really sure. There's a couple of them up here. Maybe they got their name in the old days. Stringing line, barbwire, along boundaries. Hands had a roof overhead while they were running wire, because it wasn't efficient to head back to a bunkhouse twenty miles away at the end of each day. Besides, you couldn't always count on good weather, especially in the time of spring or fall roundups. So they probably got a lot of use. I know ours did for a lot of years."

Marian stepped up into her saddle. Virgil did the same. They rode in silence at an easy lope for the next twenty minutes in a westerly direction. The sun was in their eyes most of the way, broken occasionally only by some low-hanging branches.

"There it is." Marian pointed in the direction of a clearing up ahead.

They dropped their heels in their stirrups, squeezing them into the flanks of each horse, eager for their destination.

The cabin was built of rough-hewn logs cut from trees that had previously occupied the clearing. Virgil could see the remains of stumps scattered throughout the area. The cabin stood as a ghost, a reminder of a past that Virgil knew was rapidly disappearing. He wondered how many men had sheltered here in the last hundred years, what their stories were, how each life had played out. Alongside the cabin was a lean-to, which looked like a more recent addition or, more likely, the fourth- or fifth-generation replacement of the original part of the corral. No doubt over the years, it had offered a place out of the rain, wind, or snow to the hundreds of horses that stood under its eaves.

They dismounted by the corral gate, nothing more than rails piggybacked on one another to slide across to open or close the entrance. Marian held both sets of reins while Virgil slid the rails across to create the opening. He could tell by their resistance that they hadn't been moved in a long time. Marian led both horses through while Virgil reset the rails. Then they unsaddled the horses. The two horses, free of the strictures of their rigging, took a step or two, then lay down in the dirt to roll, sending clouds of dust skyward.

"I almost feel like doing that myself," Marian said.

"Well, if that water pump over there is still working, maybe we'll have a comparable option."

They carried the saddles and bridles over to the lean-to, where they found a couple of homemade saddle racks. After setting each one, they covered them with the saddle blankets. Grabbing the saddlebags, they then slipped through the bars of the corral and walked to the front of the cabin. After a few futile attempts, Virgil finally had to give a substantial kick to get the door open. Even then, he had to put his shoulder to it to be able to enter. The musty taste of age along with the absence of sunlight hung heavily in the air.

"Nobody has been in here in a long time," Virgil said.

"Last time I was here, I was a girl."

Virgil smiled.

"What?" Marian said. "What?"

"The way I look at it, you're still a girl."

"You say the nicest things, Virgil, but I have no illusions. The years have left their mark. When I was here last, my whole life was ahead of me. The promise of all my youthful dreams."

She paused for an instant.

"Well, enough of memory lane," she said. "Let's get this

place functioning before dark. If you'll scrounge up some wood, I'll see if I can get the mustiness out of here."

"Sounds like a plan," Virgil said, stepping back out through the door and walking away from the cabin.

By the time he returned with his second load of deadfall, Marian had swept the place out, let in some fresh air, and spread a couple of threadbare blankets she had found in a battered cedar chest. Before the shadows completely invaded the cabin, Virgil checked the fireplace, then built a good fire. He had filled the wood bin, so while Marian started getting together a meal, he went back outside. He put hobbles on the front feet of each horse, then let them out of the corral to graze. Even without the hobbles he doubted they would go far. There was a plentiful supply of mixed wild grass. For a few minutes he watched them eagerly moving from clump to clump. An almost Zen-like tranquillity pervaded the scene. There was the barest hint of a whisper moving the tips of the pines. If he stood really still he couldn't feel the nagging pain in his lower back, a memento of a long day in the saddle and an even longer day on foot. Finally, he headed back to the cabin.

Marian had packed a frozen steak, which was well thawed by the time she laid it on a rack in the fireplace alongside of a couple of potatoes and a halved butternut squash. She had washed a couple of plates and some cutlery in the outside pump. By the time they were ready to eat, Virgil had returned the horses to the corral and grained them down.

"Well, it's not turkey with all the trimmings," she said as she laid the food on the heavy plank table. "But it'll have to do."

"It's a lot more than I would have had if I'd made this trip by myself."

For the next few minutes, they attacked the meal with gusto. Marian was the first to sit back from the table.

"I can't remember the last time I ate like that," she said.

Virgil, who was finishing off the last bit of steak on his plate, nodded in reply. Marian got up, went to the fireplace, then with a ragged towel reached in to a coffeepot that had more age on it than either of them. She set it on the table with a thud.

"That must have come out here with the first wagonload of settlers," Virgil said.

"Well, it's been here since I can remember."

Marian poured the thick, dark liquid into a couple of metal mugs that had been hanging on the wall to the left of the fireplace.

"Looks like a matched set," Virgil said. "Any half-and-half?"

"Sorry, we're going to have to drink it black."

Virgil put the steaming cup to his lips, then took a sip.

"My, my, that'll take the enamel off your teeth. Let's see if we can soften the blow a little. Be right back."

Virgil got up and went outside. He was back in less than a minute.

"Here's something we can add to make it go down a little smoother without taking the lining off our stomach."

He unscrewed the cap off a pint of whiskey, then added a dose to each cup. They picked up their cups, warmed their hands on them, savoring the aroma, then finally took a sip.

"This isn't half bad," Marian said. "I might just have to drink all my coffee this way from now on. Wonder if Starbucks ought to consider getting liquor licenses?"

They sat sipping coffee, exchanging small talk in the quiet of the evening for the next half hour. Only stirring to throw another log on the fire or to retrieve the coffeepot, which had been reset on a bed of coals. By the time they were pouring out dregs, Virgil's pint bottle was half empty. Marian had just come in from the privy out back.

"I gotta say," Virgil said, "when I got off Jack, I was glad. Haven't been this achy in a long time."

"Yes. It's been a while since I spent that much time on the back of a horse myself. That medicine you brought has dulled the pain very nicely. Thank you."

"You know, I wasn't real thrilled with the idea of you coming along. But I'm glad you did. I would never have found this place. Hell, to be honest, I don't even know if I would've reached the top of this mesa. I definitely bit off a little more than I could chew."

"Well, I knew you weren't jumping for joy at the prospect of me joining you, but why did you want to make this trip alone?"

Virgil didn't answer right away. Instead, he poured a little from the bottle into his cup, which held no coffee. Then he took a long swallow.

"I'm afraid my reason was selfish. It wasn't so much about your father as it was about me trying to get away. To be by myself, to kind of sort things out. I need to be able to move on but I was kinda stuck because of things that happened. Unexpected things that turned the world upside down. I guess there are no easy answers."

"I can understand that. Life kind of jolts us when we least expect it. Like the call I got about Mom. Time stops, everything gets turned around. In the back of my mind I knew they weren't going to be there forever. Losing her was one thing, but now . . . I mean, what you've told me. Now my Dad. I'm kind of reeling, trying to not lose my grip on a world that's spinning out of my control."

"Yeah, I guess we both forgot to duck."

"The trouble is, I never saw the punch coming," Marian said.

Virgil heard the catch in Marian's throat and he looked away.

Night had overtaken the world. The fire threw broken light across the room. Shadows danced on the walls. Every time a log broke sparks flew up the chimney. Only the sounds of a light wind against the windows of the ancient cabin or the sudden hiss when flames found a pocket of moisture hidden in a log broke the silence. They sat a long time with their thoughts, staring into the fire as if it held the answers as to what would come next. Virgil reached for the bottle again, meeting Marian's hand, reaching at the same time. The touch for each was electric. It was the first time their eyes met in the dim light. Her hand closed around his. He could see tears flowing freely from her eyes. No words were spoken. When he stood, she came to him. He buried his lips in the nape of her neck, then held her close. A shudder of surrender went through her body. When he drew back, she reached up to him till their lips met. He tasted his loss and hers in that first kiss. Much later, the fire ebbed as they held close, giving the warmth that only one human being can give to another.

The world looked different, maybe a little more hopeful, when they stepped outside the next morning, each holding a hot cup of black coffee.

"I sure wasn't expecting this." Virgil was reacting to a changed landscape. Sunlight bounced off trees and grass layered in white. Billions of tiny crystals clung to leaves and blades of grass, along with anything else that could give them purchase and the chance of evading the touch of a rising sun. A natural masterpiece, which would be gone in the blink of an eye.

"It's the elevation," Marian said. "Down in Hayward, they probably woke up thinking they had a heavy dew or a sprinkle. They don't know what they're missing."

"Yep," Virgil said as he put the cup to his lips for the last time.

"I'll take that inside, Virgil." She reached out with a smile in her eyes. Virgil handed her the empty cup.

"Better check on the horses. It's going to be a long day."

He watched as she turned, then walked to the cabin. He saw the first drips off the roof as the ascending sun started to claim its first victims. By the time he had fed and hobbled the horses so they could graze till he and Marian were ready to leave, the only white left was in patches clinging to the bases of evergreens. By the time the horses were saddled and ready for the day's journey, even those reluctant patches were gone. Virgil handed Ringo's reins to Marian.

"Virgil, I just wanted to say . . ."

"Not necessary," Virgil said. "I know, last night was last night, but I don't think either one of us regrets it. I know I don't."

"Neither do I," she said.

She stepped up into the saddle, took a last look at the cabin, then neck-reined Ringo a hundred and eighty degrees in the opposite direction. They had ridden for less than a mile when Virgil suddenly pulled up.

"Your dad was here." He pointed to a dung pile. "That didn't come from a mule deer. So, why didn't he stay at the cabin?"

"Knowing Dad, if the weather was good, he'd just as soon sleep out."

"Do you have any idea why he came up here?"

"I asked Manuel. He said Mom told him he heard gunfire

when he was out checking on what was left of the herd. But Manuel also said a couple of times Dad mentioned that when they had the big roundup and sell-off last year that he was sure they missed some cattle. He wanted to get up here and see if he was right. Some of those crossbreds are pretty near feral. So I wouldn't be surprised if some of them got away from the wranglers Dad had hired for the drive. It wasn't like years past when they were regular hands and invested in their job. Some of them probably signed on, then when they got up here, saw what they were going to herd, decided they weren't going to break their necks doing the job. I've been on roundups in years past. It's no mean trick dodging these trees when you're trying to round up half-wild cattle."

"I can imagine," Virgil said. "Did your brothers help with the roundup?"

"My brothers? You've got to be kidding."

"Well, I've heard they had no interest in keeping the ranch going, but I thought . . ."

"Virgil, they broke my father's heart."

18

The air was crisp. November sun offered light, but little warmth. It would be a while before the blistering heat that dried up seasonal water holes and turned grass brown would return. That was all right with Virgil. He was ready for a change. The terrain reminded him of the Mogollon Plateau area up by the Grand Canyon. Bunch grass covering rolling hills dotted with clumps of pine, cottonwood, and aspen. It was easy riding for both him and Jack. After almost an hour, he noted Jack was showing a little lather. He wasn't blowing hard and needed little encouragement when they came to an occasional rise. Virgil and Marian had ridden mostly in silence. It was inevitable that when Virgil looked at the expanse of land riddled with gullies he thought they were on a fool's errand. There were literally hundreds of places where Charlie Thompson with or without his horse could be. They had topped a small knoll when he saw a reflected light down below. He pointed it out to Marian, then headed toward it. The steady trickle of a stream formed a small pool at the base of an arroyo. Virgil reached bottom first, dismounted, led Jack to the water's edge. It was clear, bright, and running freely. A feed showed at one end, a runoff at the other. Marian had ridden right up to the edge before she dismounted.

"I don't remember this water hole," she said. "Do you think it's safe?"

"It's running clean, not stagnant. I think it's sweet water. The fact that you don't know this spot just tells me how daunting this is going to be. There's so much ground to cover. If we only had a sense of where he was heading."

"I think our best bet would be to stay within a half mile or so of the boundary with the reservation land. There's another cabin about a half-day's ride. We could separate, then crisscross along that border, looking for signs. That's fairly level ground as I remember, with pretty good elevation. You can see pretty far. If we don't find anything, we can stay at the cabin tonight, then head back by a different route tomorrow."

"Okay. It beats anything I've got. Let's take a break here, then head toward that fence line."

Jack and the gelding had already plunged their noses into the clear water. Ringo splashed his feet, then moved out to the end of the reins Marian held. The water was over his hocks.

"If I let go, I bet he'd lie right down in it," Marian said.

"Looks that way. Better hold on to those reins or you're going to be sitting in a wet seat. Well, what do you know?"

Virgil pointed up the creek a quarter mile or so where the water flow came around a sweeping curve, then disappeared behind a rock outcropping.

"Your dad was right."

Three or four cows with large spring calves at their side had come down to the water to drink. As soon as Virgil touched the reins to draw Jack out of the water, the cattle, seeing the movement, bolted.

"Guess it would be like the old days trying to round them up. 'Bulldogging' would be the word for it."

"What are you talking about, Virgil?"

Virgil told Marian about Billy Three Hats along with some other Indian kids watching the roundups long ago. "Billy said it was some show."

"He was right," Marian said. "Straight out of a John Wayne movie. Saw it so many times, I can close my eyes even now, see the dust clouds, hear the wranglers yelling, see the whites of their eyes as the cattle tried to escape. Didn't think of it before, but that's part of what ties me so strongly to this land. The wildness of it."

"Then why did you leave?"

"It's a long story, Virgil. Haven't spoken of it in a long time."

Virgil undid Jack's girth till it hung loose under his belly, then threw the reins over his head, draping them around the pommel of his saddle. There was enough slack so Jack could drop his head and nibble some bunch grass growing along the creek even with the bit in his mouth. Virgil sat down on the ground, pushed his hat back on his forehead, and looked up at Marian.

"Well, since we're taking a little downtime here, I guess we got time for a story." Marian cocked her head, then sighed. Then she followed Virgil's example with Ringo. When she was done, she came and sat next to him.

"It's not a warm fuzzy." She picked up a stick that she had almost sat on and started scratching the ground with it. "Before, you were asking about my brothers. Vernon's the younger, Calvin's the older by about five years."

"Calvin? No Charles junior?"

"No. That would have been even worse. He was named after my mom's brother who was killed when she was carrying him. My uncle was an airplane mechanic in the air force. Mom told me he was working on a jet engine with two other guys when it blew up. So that's how Cal got his name. Anyway, Pop got two sons. Guess I was an afterthought. Pop wasn't easy, but he was always fair. Wouldn't ask you to do something he wouldn't do himself. But this life was all he knew and he grew up in a different time. He was born to it, like four or five generations before him, but that was okay. He loved it. It suited him right down to the ground. Figured his boys were next in line, and raised them that way. Cal never fell in love with the idea, but it got a lot worse when he got into high school and started hanging out with some kids who didn't share his life experience. He didn't want to come home, muck out stalls, or bale hay. They started knocking heads. Along about that time Cal was diagnosed with juvenile diabetes. That just became another complication and made matters worse. He wasn't supposed to drink. Pop didn't want him hanging out with the kids from school. Guess he was trying to protect him, but Cal didn't see it that way. Their relationship went from bad to worse. Meanwhile, Vernon had pretty much fallen through the cracks. By the time Cal escaped to college, Vernon had been living the life Cal had wanted. Drugs, drinking, the whole enchilada. He was pretty much out of control by the time Dad tried to get him in line, and Cal of course was egging Vernon on in his rebellion. All this was going on while Dad was trying to stay on top of everything on the ranch. But he kept trying with the boys. He still is. Can't accept that it's never going to happen."

"But that still doesn't explain why you left." Marian had dug a pretty good hole in the ground with the stick. She stopped abruptly, then snapped it in half before chucking it into the water. She watched as the two pieces floated toward the outlet.

"There was no reason for me to stay. Dad was old school. I was never on the radar, never would be. When I finally realized that, I went away to college. I didn't come back. It hurt too much. I had worked harder and more willingly than either Cal or Vernon. I loved the ranch, the life, but I was a girl. Couldn't change that."

"What did you do after college?"

"Got a job. Went back, got a master's, met a guy, got married, moved to the suburbs, and had two kids. Now they're in college. My husband died of cancer two years ago. I'm pretty much on my own."

Virgil stood up, looked down the canyon where the creek disappeared around the bend.

"Guess we're both a little at odds in our lives right now. But like this stream up there. You never know what's around the bend."

He reached down, offered Marian his hand, then pulled her to her feet.

"I know you're right, Virgil. It's just that I don't know how I'm going to handle what's around the bend when I find out."

For the next couple of hours they crisscrossed the landscape within the half- to three-quarter-mile boundary of the reservation land. Twice they came upon evidence of a rider, but there was no way of telling who it might have been. There was no sighting of Charlie Thompson or his horse. The terrain was definitely higher and more barren along the boundary line. Cacti were more in evidence, along with scrub trees and an occasional cottonwood. Virgil pulled up his collar. The cooler air was driven by a steady breeze because of the openness. He hadn't seen Marian for at least twenty minutes. He would have been a little concerned, but it had become fairly obvious that she knew her way around this part of the world better than he did. Periodically he paused, then stood in the stirrups for a better vantage point. Once he saw a rattler sunning on a rock. Virgil was surprised it hadn't already gone to ground for the winter, but he knew that a couple more cold nights would send it underground. He listened for a call from Marian, but all he heard were Jack's shoes scraping and scattering the shale along the embankment he was crossing. When he got to the other side, he saw Marian in the distance. He put his heels lightly to Jack. They scrambled down the side, small pieces of shale stirring a dust cloud in his wake. By the time he reached Marian, she had dismounted, taken a hoof pick from her saddlebag, and was working on Ringo's right-front hoof.

"Forgot just how rocky it was up on this mesa," she said.

"Yeah, not much in the way of topsoil or ground cover up here. Nothing to fatten a steer unless they like cactus or shale."

Virgil sat in his saddle waiting for Marian to finish. He glanced at the sky. The sun had passed its zenith and was starting its downward slide. Slanted light started to bounce off flat surfaces. Straight lines and angles softened as the shadows grew. Marian stood up to replace the hoof pick in her pack when Virgil noticed a more concentrated light at some distance.

"Stay here," Virgil said. "I'll be right back."

Marian watched as Virgil urged Jack a little farther down the rimrock. She saw him crest a rise about a quarter mile away, pull Jack up, and dismount. He crouched down, then reached toward the earth. When he stood up, she could see that he was holding something in his hand, but she couldn't make it out. Then Virgil got back into the saddle, turned Jack, and headed back to where Marian stood.

"What have you got there, Virgil?"

He had pulled Jack to a halt alongside her, then he held out his hand.

"Looks like a small hand pick. Guess some prospector passing through must have dropped it."

He handed it to Marian.

"Doubt if it was from somebody looking for the mother lode up here," she said. "I'm no expert, but this doesn't seem like a likely place for a prospector. Besides, this looks almost new. Hasn't been out here in the elements too long."

"Well, what would anyone be looking for up here if not gold?"

"I know paleontologists use a small pickax to dig for fossils."

Marian handed the tool back to Virgil, who put it in his saddlebag.

They stopped two more times as the day and their search progressed. It was late afternoon when they had stopped the second time. They were close to the reservation line and within an hour to the next line cabin. Virgil abruptly pulled Jack up. Marian, who was a little farther down the trail, caught up to him. He was looking up at the sky.

"What is it, Virgil?"

"Maybe you ought to wait here," Virgil said.

"What do you mean? Why?"

He didn't answer. Instead he raised his eyes to the sky again. Marian followed his gaze. High on the thermals she saw them. Flying in circles, almost like they were caught in a vortex, pulling them closer to the earth. The circles became tighter as they spiraled down. Black with outstretched wings, they marked their target as they closed in on the prize. Virgil turned again to Marian.

"Why don't you stay here? Let me check it out."

Marian swallowed hard.

"No, Virgil. I came with you to find my father. It didn't seem right to me that I should sit back. Let someone else absolve me of my responsibility. It wasn't right then. It's not right now. Let's go."

Without waiting for Virgil's reply, Marian put her heels to Ringo's flanks. Virgil caught up with her as they crested the last rise. The carrion birds were still circling lower. The nearest couple issued raucous insults at the suspected intruders. When Virgil pulled to a halt, he heard Marian's intake of breath. They were near the edge of a steep ravine.

"Jupiter."

That was all she said. Then she moved Ringo forward at a slow walk. Virgil followed. They looked down on the bloated carcass.

"Jupiter," she said again. "Dad's horse."

Two of the birds had settled near the body. Virgil reached in his saddlebag, drew out his sidearm, firing two shots in the air. The cloud of rebellious black flew into the air, loudly protesting the interruption of their anticipated feast. Then Virgil and Marian carefully made their way down the embankment to reach the dead horse. Marian sat in the saddle while Virgil dismounted. He bent over the dead animal. The bloating told Virgil that he was looking at an event that had taken place a couple of days before. The horse carried no rigging. Virgil walked around the animal twice, a little surprised at the absence of blowflies. He attributed that to the cold weather along with the persistent wind, which even now caused him to turn up his collar a little more. The wind also blew away the scent of death. Finally, he returned to stand by Ringo's side. Marian's face was devoid of emotion, giving no hint of her suspicions.

"Obviously, no sign of your father, but this was no accident. The horse took a round squarely in the chest about two or three days ago. I'm not sure whether Charlie walked away, but someone took the saddle and any other gear the horse was carrying. I just don't know what became of Charlie."

Marian's body language showed little change except for the tightness in her face, which caused her cheekbones to become more prominent.

"Guess our search isn't over," Virgil said. We've just got to keep on looking."

"Looks that way," Marian said as she looked at the sky. "At least until we find another flock of vultures."

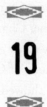

19

Doctor Arthur Kincaid was a little surprised when he called the sheriff's office on the day after Thanksgiving and Jimmy Tillman answered the phone.

"Hey, Doc."

"Hey, yourself. What are you doing there, Jimmy? Thought you would still be home nursing your wounds or eating leftovers. Where's Virgil or Rosie?"

"Hold on just a second, Doc. The other phone is ringing."

The second lasted over two minutes, and Art Kincaid was tempted to hang up the phone.

"Sorry about that. It was Alex Rankin down in Redbud just checking in. He knows I'm alone here, like he is down there."

"So, it's a little thin as far as personnel in the sheriff's department this holiday."

"Yeah, well, things are usually pretty quiet this weekend. Most folks sitting around feeling guilty about eating too much. Then of course, there's football. I got nothing happening in my life right now, 'cept physical therapy, which ain't exactly what I'd call much of an ingredient for an exciting social life."

"What about that Simpson girl?"

There was a momentary hesitation before Jimmy responded.

"Guess nothing's secret in this town."

"C'mon, Jimmy. We only got a weekly newspaper. This is news of the day."

"Well, it ain't no more. That water hole is just about dried up. She met some guy who drives a Corvette. Guess she thinks he's got a little more potential for excitement than a deputy who lives in a double-wide with his mother and twelve-year-old sister, whose only means of transportation has a divider separating the front seat from the back. Hell, I ever pick up a girl in that, everybody in town will spread the word I'm dating a criminal."

Jimmy couldn't see the smile on Art Kincaid's face.

"Jimmy, from where I sit, your life is pretty exciting. More to the point, I've never had a lady fall out of the sky on top of me."

"Yeah, I could've passed on that."

"Anyway, Jimmy, where's your boss? It's that lady I'm calling about."

"Well, Doc, can't exactly say. He's somewhere up on the High Lonesome looking for Charlie Thompson. Been gone two days now."

"Do you think there's any chance of cell phone service up there?"

"No way. He's probably thirty miles away and up over three thousand feet. Is it something real important? I could maybe get word to somebody at the ranch if he shows up."

"No, it'll keep. I just wanted to find out if he remembered anything about the logo on that truck that lady was driving when he met her."

"I'm sorry, Doc. You're digging a dry well here. I have no idea what you're talking about."

"Sorry, Jimmy, I thought you boys shared everything except your women."

Art explained about his last conversation with Virgil.

"So the sheriff actually did meet that lady before?"

"Seems like, but that's all we got," Ark said.

"Maybe, if we could find out where she was working?"

"Yeah, but how are we going to go about that?"

"Well, I haven't figured that part out. But you know how nothing's a secret in this town. I bet somebody knows."

"You know, Jimmy, you might be onto something. Think you've just given yourself a job. Good luck with your search."

Jimmy sat back in his chair after he hung up the phone, trying to figure out what had just happened and what job he had actually taken on. He was still sitting in his chair wondering when the phone rang a few minutes later.

"Jimmy, you want me to come in?"

"No, Dif. I've got it covered, unless you're looking to escape your relatives."

"Jimmy, I do believe you're a mind reader. I'll be there in ten minutes."

Dif was as good as his word. Jimmy had just come out of the bathroom when Dif walked through the door.

"How was your Thanksgiving, Dif?"

"Oh, it was good, particularly as far as the eats go. I'm still trying to recover from that overindulgence. You know, I promised myself I wasn't going to eat like one of those starving Armenians. Decided I was just going to take a little of everything. But there was so much of everything that it didn't make no difference. Edna put out all these appetizers. Then her sisters come along adding more, insisting I had to try this one or that. Course to be honest, I didn't put up much of a fight. By the time we sat down for the main event, I'd already let my belt out two notches. You know what they say, Jimmy—the road to hell is paved with good intentions."

"Yeah. I guess a lot of people are feeling like you today."

"Not that brother-in-law of mine from Alamogordo. He got up today like yesterday never happened. My God, eating everything in sight. Couldn't watch anymore. For a second, thought he'd eat the plate. Wouldn't mind, if he was three hundred pounds, but my right leg weighs more than him. Go figure. There I am, trying to cut down. He's got a gleam in his eye like a cannibal at a Weight Watchers convention. Anyway, that's why I'm here—so you can take off."

"Actually, I realized after you called I could squeeze in my last PT appointment in a half an hour, so I'm outta here." Fifteen minutes later, Jimmy was sitting outside the physical therapy room at Hayward Hospital when he heard someone call his name.

"Hey, Deputy Tillman, we've got to stop meeting like this."

When Jimmy looked up from the magazine he was reading, Virginia Dalton was standing next to his chair. There was a quick response hiding in his brain somewhere, but he couldn't find it.

"Hello." It was the best he could do. She sat in the chair next to him.

"How are you feeling?"

He looked into the warm smile he saw in her blue eyes and felt like he was drowning. He mumbled a response. He could hear the words coming out of his mouth, but he had no idea what he was saying.

"That's good. So do you think this will be your last session?"

"I think so. I'll know in a little while." He was finally getting a grasp on language.

"Hey, I have a great idea. I'm going upstairs to visit a friend. I'll stop back later. If you're done, why don't we grab some lunch at Margie's to celebrate your recovery?"

"Okay, sounds good. Actually I'm starving."

He didn't say that if she asked him to walk hand in hand with her to the train station, to step in front of a fast-moving freight, he would have obliged with a stupid grin on his face.

Margie's place was like a church after a funeral. Not a soul in sight.

"Hope you have a reservation," Margie yelled from in back of the counter when they walked through the door.

"We can always do takeout if you haven't got room," Jimmy yelled back. Jimmy had found his voice.

They sat in one of the booths that looked out on Main Street. "Deader than a graveyard," Jimmy said.

"Guess the day after a big holiday is always a bit of a letdown. Christmas is the worst," Virginia said. "You work up to it for weeks, even months, then it's over in the blink of an eye."

"Guess that's why a lot of people get depressed at that time of the year. All that expectation of something. Then they wake up the next day and realize nothing's really changed, except they have a boatload of bills they didn't have before."

"So, you all done with PT?" Virginia asked.

"Seems so. They gave me a printout of exercises for my arm that I can do at home."

"Pretty soon you'll be back to a hundred percent."

"Don't know that I was ever a hundred percent. I'll settle for anything above eighty."

Margie was standing next to the booth.

"So, you better get your order in before we run out of food."

"Yeah, guess you could have stayed home today, Margie."

"Well, you know how that works. If I had, I'd have gotten a call that they were lined up down Main Street. That's what they call Murphy's Law. So what can I get you?" Virginia and Jimmy each ordered the Southwestern burger and fries. Margie left only to return in a few minutes with a couple of lemonades. They each immediately took a long drink.

"I was so thirsty," Virginia said.

"It's the hospital. Every time I come out of there, the first thing I do is get a drink. They keep that place so hot."

"So, where's your boss? Still looking for Mr. Thompson?"

"Far as I know. Haven't heard a word."

"So, who's minding the store?"

"I was, then Dif came in, so I was able to get to that last PT session."

"Guess our meeting was meant to be," Virginia said. "Kismet."

"Kismet?" Jimmy said. "Like the word, but don't think I ever heard it before."

When Virginia offered an explanation, he suddenly felt out of his depth. He had experienced the feeling many times, but never was it as painful as it was at that moment. Margie put plates of food in front of them. He immediately picked up his sandwich and took a bite. He felt Virginia's eyes on him. If he could have snapped his fingers and been a thousand miles away, he would have done it in a heartbeat. Instead, he ate quietly while her eyes burned a hole right through him.

"Margie sure knows how to cook a burger."

Jimmy didn't respond.

"So, what are you going to do with the rest of your day?"

Jimmy had just put his glass on the table. "Oh, I'm going to try to track down something about that lady that landed on my car."

"Can you tell me about it?"

Jimmy related his earlier conversation with Dr. Kincaid.

"I think that's a great idea you had. Find out where she was working. Nobody else thought of that. Way to go, Jimmy. Where are you going to begin looking?"

"Well, it'll take forever if I start door to door," he said. "I've been thinking if there's some common connector. A place where she might have gone while she was in the area often enough that someone might have noticed her."

"Like a gas station or a restaurant, you mean."

Jimmy's eyes seemed to come alive.

"That's it," he said. "Even if she was working on her own, she had to stay somewhere, eat somewhere. Maybe someone noticed her."

He looked around the restaurant. One other person had come in while they were eating. He was sitting over a cup of coffee at the counter. Jimmy spied Carmella, one of Margie's longtime waitresses. She saw him wave to her.

"What can I get you, Jimmy?"

"Carmella, do you remember a woman who might have come in here alone a couple of times a few weeks ago? Mid to late thirties, maybe wearing a kind of uniform? A jumpsuit?"

Carmella shook her head. "Sorry, Jimmy. I missed a week a while back, but you should ask Margie. Even though she doesn't wait on that many people, she doesn't miss a trick. Anybody new, she would know. I'll send her over as soon as she comes out of the kitchen."

While they waited, they finished their food. When Margie came over, they put the same question to her that they had put to Carmella. She leaned on the corner of the booth for a moment, looking out onto Main Street.

"There was someone who came in by herself a couple of weeks ago. I'd never seen her before, but because she was alone I noticed her. I didn't speak to her or wait on her."

"Was there anything about her that you noticed? Something different?"

Margie stepped back from the booth. "Sorry, Jimmy. Drawing a blank."

"Thanks anyway, Margie."

Margie turned, then walked back to the kitchen.

"Well, we can try some other places, like gas stations," Virginia said.

"Yeah, I guess."

They stood up from the booth after paying their bill, then started for the door. They had it opened when Margie yelled to them. She came out from in back of the counter.

"I just remembered. There was one thing, Jimmy. It was because she was parked right outside the door. I noticed when I went outside to sign for a delivery. Her truck, she was driving a pickup. It had a cool logo. A wave. It said 'Coastal' underneath."

"Great. Thanks, Margie."

"A wave and a word. That's a good start. Your instincts were right on target." Virginia made the comment as they stepped onto the sidewalk.

"Well, it's only a part of the puzzle, but it's something. More than we had. Now I've just got to figure out how that piece fits."

They walked down the street, around the corner to the parking lot outside the office, where they had left their cars.

"That was fun." They were standing next to Virginia's car. "Like being a detective. I'm sure your boss will be impressed."

Jimmy's mind was going in another direction. "I was wondering if, maybe you would like to do this again. I mean, maybe you and I could . . ."

She was looking at him in a different way. "You mean like a date?"

Virginia wasn't making it any easier. Jimmy had that drowning feeling again as he looked at her. He felt his tongue start to swell in his throat.

"Well, I just thought . . ."

Virginia reached up, putting her index finger to his lips.

"Relax, Jimmy. We just had a date. I asked you out, now you're asking me. That's the way it works, if the first date is a success. I just said it was fun, so the answer is an unequivocal yes. I would like a second date with you. Of course, maybe you might want to tell your boss when he returns."

"Why should I tell the sheriff?" he said. "I mean, I don't tell him everything I do."

"Oh. I thought you knew."

"Knew? Knew what?"

"It's just, I guess it's still not out there."

The look on Jimmy's face told her he didn't have a clue.

"Jimmy, the sheriff . . . Virgil is my father. I thought you knew. My real name is Virginia Dalton, not Hayward. I haven't changed it. Legally, I mean, because I only just found out. For that matter so did Virgil. He's my father. I thought you should know. I don't want you to feel uncomfortable." Jimmy couldn't have stood more rigid if he were carved from stone.

"Virgil is your dad."

Virginia nodded. "I guess it's a bit of a surprise."

"I'm sorry," he said. "I didn't know."

"I thought maybe he had told you," she said.

For a long moment they looked at each other. The stillness in the world around them underlined the awkward moment.

"Think about it for a while, then if you still want that second date we can talk."

She opened her car door, then got in and started the engine. She gave a slight wave. Before she turned onto the street she looked in her rearview mirror. Jimmy hadn't moved. He stood in that same spot awhile after she had gone. At last, he turned, then walked into the office.

Dif was sitting behind one of the desks. He had turned on the television, which was mounted on the opposite wall. He was watching a football game. He hardly looked up at Jimmy when he came through the door.

"Hey," was all he said.

When Jimmy didn't acknowledge, he turned slightly in his chair to face him. "How did it go? Any problems?"

Jimmy looked at him without comprehension. "Huh," he said. "What?"

"I said, how did PT go? Any problems? Any questions for me?"

"Oh, it was fine. No problems. I'm finished."

"Good. Any questions?"

"Questions?" Jimmy said. "Yeah. What does 'unequivocal' mean?"

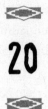

20

They were less than a quarter mile from the next cabin when Virgil pulled Jack to a halt. They had not seen or heard anything since they had found Jupiter's carcass.

"What is it, Virgil? Do you see something?"

They had turned away from the fence bordering the reservation land. Now they were at the bottom of the ridge. Once again they were among the conifers that were interspersed throughout the rugged grassland. It was in a cluster of them that Virgil had stopped.

"What do you see?" Marian said again.

"I don't see anything, but I smell something. Wood burning." He stood in the stirrups, looked about, then settled back down into the saddle. "Can't see anything. How far do you think the cabin is?"

"It's been a long time, but I smell the wood smoke, too."

Virgil got down from Jack. He handed the reins to Marian.

"Wait here. Hold the horses." He slipped his rifle out of the scab-bard.

She watched him disappear in a copse of trees up ahead. After a few minutes, her anxiety began to build. She bit her lip, then toyed with the idea of dismounting and tying up the horses to follow Virgil on foot. Every movement of a branch, even the prick of Jack's ears, caused her to tighten her grip on the reins till her knuckles showed white and the nails of her fingers bit into her palms. Finally, when she couldn't stand it a minute longer, she got down off Ringo, still holding the reins of both horses. Then she heard the crack of a branch underfoot. She gasped, slid her own rifle from its nest as she looped the reins around a low-hanging branch. Then she put the rifle to her shoulder, squinted through the sight as she aimed it at the sound. A slight drip of blood oozed from her lip. She held her breath. Then Virgil stepped from behind a tree.

"Oh." It was all she could say.

"Sorry I was so long, but I think we might have a problem. Are you okay?"

"You were gone so long . . . I thought maybe . . ."

"It's okay, Marian. Take a deep breath. Here, let me have that."

He took her rifle, slipping it back in the scabbard, doing the same thing with his. Then he came over to her, held her a little awkwardly, then had her sit down.

"I think we might have a problem. That smoke is coming from the cabin."

"Maybe Dad . . ." She didn't complete the thought.

"I thought of that, too, but I didn't want to chance it. I waited to see if I could spot anyone, but no one came outside. It was too light to chance getting closer, especially with you waiting for me.

Besides, if it is him, he was able to build a fire. That tells us something."

"But I don't understand. What are you saying?"

"I'm thinking because we don't know who is in there, that maybe we should wait until dark before we go in. If it is your father, no problem. But if it isn't, it just might be the person who put the hole in Jupiter."

Virgil checked the reins where Marian had tied them. He unsaddled each of them, placing the saddles on the ground. Marian got up from where she had been sitting. She took a currycomb and a brush from her saddlebag, then began grooming Ringo. Virgil spread the saddle blankets out, got some energy bars from his saddlebag along with a thermos. By the time Marian had finished with both horses, he was sitting on one of the blankets, munching on one of the bars. She came over, sat on the other blanket, took the energy bar he offered, and bit into it. They passed the thermos back and forth a couple of times before Marian spoke.

"Damn. Damn, I hate this waiting, not knowing."

"I understand, but I think this is the smart thing to do."

After a few minutes, Virgil lay back. He pulled his Stetson down, shading his eyes. Marian got up, walked around for a few minutes, then returned and stretched out on her own blanket. A faint breeze moved the branches overhead in a constant rhythm. Angled sunlight filtered through. She could tell from Virgil's regular breathing that he was dozing off. She had become suddenly anxious. The last couple of days were taking their toll. She had truly expected her father to turn up at the ranch like he had done all her life. The unexpected loss of her mother had hit her hard. The agonizing moment when her father showed up and she had to break the news was all she thought about. Then when

Virgil turned up everything changed. After his narrative, she had to confront the possibility of losing her father, also. Now, when the answer was within reach, she was lying on a blanket under some swaying conifers, and it was killing her.

When Virgil shook her into consciousness, she could not believe she had actually fallen asleep. She felt out of sync, that feeling like everything was just beyond her grasp. Sunlight had gone, long shadows had crawled across the land. Virgil helped her to her feet. She saw that he had already saddled Jack. He took the blanket she had been lying on. After shaking it out a couple of times, he threw it on Ringo's back. When he turned around, Marian was holding the saddle. Within moments, both saddles were cinched up and ready to go. Virgil suggested that they lead the horses rather than ride.

"Won't they call to a strange horse in the corral?"

"I didn't see any horses when I scouted the cabin out earlier. Follow me. Try to make as little noise as possible."

He untied the reins of both horses, handing Ringo's to Marian. They moved through the trees until they came within sight of the cabin. Faint light showed through the windows. Wood smoke was coming from the chimney. With the loss of sunlight the air had noticeably chilled. Breath from the horses condensed in small puffs, rising on the nighttime air. Marian and Virgil each buttoned up their jackets, then turned their collars up.

"Stay here," Virgil said. "I'll go in alone. You hear shooting, get out of here. Don't hesitate."

"No, Virgil. I have a rifle and I know how to use it. We go together. You lead the way, but I'll be right in back of you."

Virgil could see from the look on Marian's face that it would be useless to argue. They tied both horses up to a corral post. Then, each carrying a carbine, they started for the cabin.

There was only a sliver of a moon showing from a cloud. Virgil was sure a glancing look out of one of the cabin's windows would not reveal their presence. Within a couple of minutes they were hugging the cabin's walls. When Virgil attempted to look in one of the windows, he realized that it was so smoke stained and clouded that all their precautions were unnecessary. They could have walked boldly right up to the cabin. He motioned to Marian to stand to one side as they reached the door. Rifle in hand and remembering how the door from the cabin of the previous night was stuck fast, he drew in a deep breath, then threw his full weight against it. The door flew open as he broke in, his rifle aimed to meet any threat. He could hear Marian right behind him.

A young man who had been placing a log on the fire leaped to his feet. When he saw the rifle in Virgil's hands, he threw his hands over his head.

"*¡Lo siento! ¡Lo siento!*" he shouted.

Virgil never took his eyes off him or lowered his rifle. "What's he sorry about?" Virgil said.

"Virgil," Marian said, pointing to the bed in the corner of the cabin. "Look."

They had found Charlie Thompson.

21

His name was Ernesto. He was sixteen and terrified. Marian had immediately gone to her father while Virgil tried to get a handle on what had happened. In mixed English and Spanish, the boy told Virgil how he had been up on the ridge when he heard the shots. At first he thought somebody was shooting at him. Then, he said, he heard the death scream of Jupiter on the other side of the rise from where he had taken cover. By the time the shooting had stopped there was no sign of anyone, so he climbed over the rise. He found Charlie Thompson with his horse in the bottom of a steep ravine. He saw that he also had been shot. Blood was streaming from a scalp wound. It was only after he reached his body that he realized Charlie had been shot a second time. Whoever had done it, Ernesto said, had come and gone. More than likely they saw Charlie along with the dead horse, all the blood in the bottom of the gully, thought they were both dead, decided to leave them both for the vultures. Ernesto also thought Charlie was dead. He had only realized he was still alive when he got up close. He managed to pull him out from under his horse, then carried him to the cabin. He went back then to see if there was anything in Charlie's saddlebags that he could use to help him. Ernesto pointed to the opposite corner of the room from where Charlie lay. The saddlebags along with Jupiter's tack were neatly piled there. He also said he had found a first aid kit, which was what he had used to dress his wounds. Virgil went over to the bed. Marian looked up at him.

"The boy did the best he could, Virgil, but Dad's in a bad way. His pulse is irregular. He's lost a lot of blood. As far as I can tell, the bullet that grazed him didn't probably do more than knock him unconscious. That along with the fall into that gulch. Maybe he's got a concussion."

"That scalp wound might have saved his life," Virgil said.

"What do you mean?"

"Scalp wounds bleed profusely. Whoever shot him probably saw all that blood, reckoned he was dead, didn't want to climb down into that ditch. If they had, they would have seen that he was alive. They would have taken the time to finish what they started."

"The bullet that hit him in the abdomen is the one I'm worried about."

Marian lifted up Charlie's shirt, exposing the area.

"I didn't find an exit wound. It's still inside. What are we going to do?"

Virgil crouched down. Charlie was ashen.

"I'm going to see if we can get him out of here." Virgil held up his cell phone.

"There's no cell phone service up here," Marian said.

"I'm sure you're right, but maybe if I'm up on that ridge I

could send a text. I think it's worth a try." He stood up. "I'll be back as soon as I can. Keep him warm—see if you can rouse him enough to get some liquid into him."

"But Virgil, it's dark out. You don't know the terrain. I should go."

"I'm sure you are a much better nurse than I could ever be. Stay here. Take care of your dad."

Virgil called Ernesto over, told him to keep feeding the fire, then left the cabin.

He caught Jack up after he put Ringo into the corral. He leaped into the saddle, then immediately headed for the high ground up near the boundary line. It was full-on dark. For the most part he had to pick his way. The moon was skirting in and out of clouds, so he was constantly getting whipped by low-lying branches when its face was hidden. Finally, he reached open ground. When he put his heels into Jack's side, the horse responded with a burst of speed. He didn't slow until they hit the grade leading up to the high line. When Virgil touched him again, Jack gave a snort, then plunged up the grade. Virgil could feel his strength as he dug in without any hesitation. Virgil didn't have the luxury of picking the easiest trail. Sometimes he could barely see. Jack was scrambling up an almost-vertical ascent. Shale and loose rock cascaded down the slide in back of him. Virgil didn't have to urge Jack. He dug in even harder. After a quarter of a mile or so of straight up, he could hear Jack blowing hard. Jack's neck was glistening and soaked with the effort. A couple of times, Virgil could actually feel his front legs buckle as he climbed. Once he felt him go down on his knees, but he dug in even deeper. Virgil knew it was a dangerous situation, but he had no choice. Jack was now grunting with each lurch forward. Virgil knew he couldn't last much longer. Suddenly, a fresh breeze struck him in the face as Jack cleared the top. Virgil jumped off immediately. Clouds of Jack's expelled breath rose in the night air. Virgil loosened the saddle as quickly as he could. Jack's sides were heaving as he gulped in the night breeze. Virgil stood next to him, then he took out his cell phone. He held his breath as he punched in a text to Billy Three Hats. He had sent the text to him because he knew geographically he was closest. His phone was lit so he knew it held a charge. He was about to try again when to his delight and surprise he got a response. Three texts later, he breathed a sigh of relief. Then he turned to Jack.

"Great effort, son."

Jack's breathing had become more regular. He raised his head at Virgil's touch. Virgil walked him around the plateau for five minutes to make sure he wasn't lame. He ran his hands up and down his legs, checking for any injury. Miraculously, he found only one significant gash on his right-rear leg just above the hock. He took the piece of terry cloth that he had used to wipe Jack down, then tied it around the cut. Then he started leading Jack down, carefully crisscrossing the hogback, letting him pick his own pace. The trip was five times as long, taking over an hour before they reached the grassland. The three-quarter moon had broken free of the clouds. Virgil was thankful for the light. By the time he reached the cabin, he had been gone almost two hours. When he walked through the door, Marian took one look at his scratched and sweat-stained face, hoping for a positive sign. He leaned against the cabin door, then gave a slight nod.

"I got through. They're sending a chopper."

Tears of relief rolled down her cheeks. The young boy came away from the fire when Virgil gestured to him.

"We've got to build another fire. *Venga*," he said.

The two of them, boy and man, left the cabin. Virgil explained that they had to build a signal bonfire near a clearing for the helicopter that would soon be coming for Charlie. They walked only a few hundred feet before they found a likely spot.

"*Rurales*. Border patrol. They come here?"

Virgil could see the fear come into Ernesto's eyes. In an instant he knew history was repeating itself. In Ernesto's eyes, he saw the same look that his father must have seen in Cesar's eyes over fifty years before when he had pulled him from the river. The boy was looking around like he was expecting someone to jump from behind one of the large pines. Virgil reached out to him, placing a hand on his shoulder.

"Easy, boy. Nothing to worry about. They are only coming for the man inside." He gestured toward the cabin. "No one is coming for you."

Virgil wasn't sure if Ernesto got everything he said, but the boy seemed to grow calmer. Virgil told him to scout around, gather as much deadfall as he could find, then bring it to the clearing where they had stopped. Within a half hour, they managed to accumulate almost half a cord of wood. Virgil got some dry tinder, then started to build a pyramid of wood on top of it. By the time he finished, the stack was so high, he had to throw the last couple of pieces on top. Then he went into the cabin, returning with a burning brand from the fireplace. He reckoned it had been more than two hours since his communication with Billy, so he decided to light the fire. The tinder caught right away. Within minutes, flames were shooting high into the night sky. Virgil sat down on the ground, the boy alongside him. They waited in the quiet of the night as the warmth of the fire layered over them. Shadows danced against the pines at the perimeter of the clearing. Virgil thought of the nights he had spent long ago, sitting around a much smaller fire with his father while they spoke of the hunt they were on or the history of the place and the people who had gone before them. They were timeless memories that he planned to hold on to till he died. He looked at the face of the boy sitting next to him, hoping that he had memories that would sustain him throughout his life. They sat in the afterglow a long time. Marian came out of the cabin for a moment to join them.

"Do you think it will be much longer? His breathing seems to be getting shallow." The words were hardly out of her mouth when Ernesto jumped to his feet.

"Listen," Virgil said.

A faraway sound that could have been mistaken for a high wind, except for the regular pulsations, grew louder and louder. They were all on their feet now, looking at the night sky. At last over the treetops they saw it, lights flashing, blades turning. It came over the clearing, poised, then started to lower. As it got closer to the ground, air currents buffeted them. Embers from the fire blew out from its center. Virgil and Ernesto ran about, stomping on them. Finally on the ground the rotors stopped, the fire settled, then the door of the helicopter opened. Two EMTs got out. Marian went inside with Ernesto while Virgil went to greet them. He gave them a quick assessment, then they followed him to the cabin with a stretcher. In less than ten minutes Charlie was loaded into the chopper, given oxygen, hooked up to an IV, then prepped for takeoff.

"Virgil, I hate to leave you here."

"Don't worry. Go with your father. The boy and I will get down to the ranch. I'll catch up with you there. We'll get Ringo home."

Virgil and Ernesto stood watching as the helicopter rose above the trees, then disappeared from view. They listened till they could no longer hear the whirling blades, then they turned their attention to the fire. They sat for over an hour watching it, till it reached a point where Virgil could push all the wood to the center. At last there was more glow than flame and they finally turned their backs on it to walk to the cabin.

There was nothing but glowing cinders when Virgil stirred the ashes in the fireplace in the morning. He threw in a couple of small logs, just enough to take off the chill that had settled in as the fire died. By the time he and Ernesto had finished breakfast, the sun was well above the horizon. He went outside to check on Jack. Virgil was relieved to see that there was no swelling in his rear leg. The Fura ointment that he had packed on the gash had done its job. Jack was moving freely around the corral with Ringo. He gave each of them the last of the grain that he and Marian had packed. Then he took everything out of the saddlebags while the horses were grazing. Anything he could dispose of he did, anything that wasn't perishable he brought inside to store for the next person who came this way. Then he took Charlie's saddle with the rest of the tack from Jupiter, to load on the two horses. Charlie's saddle he decided he would load on Ringo so that the injured Jack wouldn't have to carry any extra weight. He was about to start the process of loading up when he saw Ernesto watching him.

"We've got to get going. It's going to be a long day."

"¿Dónde?" Ernesto asked.

"Down to the ranchero, off this mesa. It will be a long ride."

"No," Ernesto said. "No go back."

Virgil saw the panic in his eyes.

"No *policía*."

Virgil reached in his shirt pocket. Ernesto's eyes widened when he saw the badge that Virgil held up. He looked around, wild-eyed. Virgil ran to him, fearing he was going to make a break for it.

"Ernesto, *mi amigo, amigo. Está bien.*"

For the next few minutes, Virgil talked to Ernesto till the fear left his eyes. Then he saddled both horses, took their hobbles off, and led them to the front of the cabin. He spent some time trying to load Charlie's saddle and gear onto Ringo, but finally came to the conclusion that there was just too much bulk. He hated the idea of leaving it all behind. While he was standing there trying to puzzle it out, Ernesto went to Marian's horse. He took Ringo's saddle off, then replaced it with Charlie's much bigger saddle. Virgil watched as he picked up the smaller saddle, placed it on Charlie's saddle, then used the leathers on the aprons to tie the two saddles together. They looked incongruous, but Virgil realized it could work. Ernesto climbed up into the saddle. He was slight of build, not more than five foot eight. When Virgil climbed onto Jack, because of Ernesto's added height, they were eyeball to eyeball.

"*Muy bien, muy bien*, Ernesto."

The flash of white in the boy's dark face told Virgil all he needed to know. Marian had quickly scratched out a map for Virgil, telling him that the route back to the ranch would be much easier. A pair of pines identified as the Twin Sisters marked the entrance to an arroyo that led off the top of the plateau to the flatland. It had been the way cattle had been driven off the mesa for over a hundred years. According to the map, the Sisters were within two miles of the cabin. Glancing once more at the cabin, Virgil spurred Jack forward. There was a definite change in the weather. Morning chills were lasting longer and coming earlier. He knew it wouldn't be long before that morning flurry would become something more in this high country. It was the cycle of seasons reflecting the cycle of life. The year was winding down. Virgil rarely reflected on where he was in that arc before, but this had been a significant year of change for him. He had found a daughter he never knew he had, brushed death a couple of times, been renewed in the arms of a woman who might be lost. Through it all the common thread that was his anchor was his ability to roll with the punches life had thrown at him. After all, he had long since learned, life doesn't go in a straight line.

22

Sam Harris was waiting outside the hospital with one of the ER interns when Charlie Thompson was brought to them. He had known Charlie all his life. When he was young, he had looked at Charlie and Virgil's father as relics of another age. A time when life was more one-dimensional. Good and evil, not so much gray. But then as he matured he came to the realization that the gray was always there. He could only wonder what could be the story behind Charlie being shot and left for dead while his wife lay downstairs in the morgue of the hospital. Marian was first out of the helicopter. Then the two EMTs took Charlie out. Sam gave him a quick check, then ushered them into the hospital.

Two hours later, Dr. Sam Harris stepped out of surgery, still in his scrubs, and found Marian Thompson waiting for him.

"Breathe easier. Your father is going to walk out of this hospital in a week or two. The scalp wound was easy, the fragment inside a little tricky. It would have been a lot worse, but I think he was hit by a ricochet, which is why there was no exit wound. The bullet had lost a lot of its velocity. He lost his spleen, has four fractured ribs, which near as I can tell were fractured once or twice before, lost a lot of blood, but all of that will heal. He won't be conscious for a while. Those rib fractures are going to remind him of his rodeo days every time he breathes, but other than pain meds, there's not much we can do for broken ribs. Fortunately, they were lower ribs so there was no lung puncture. But don't be surprised when he wakes up if he has no memory of how he got here or what happened to him. That knock on the head might have stalled his short-term memory for a while. It'll come back to him. Rest and more rest, that's what he needs. He's tough as rawhide, but I'm glad Virgil found him when he did and he had that boy looking after him. Don't think he would have lasted another day. After you look in on him, you ought to get back to the ranch and get some rest yourself."

"Thank you, Doctor."

Sam Harris started to walk away, then stopped. "I'm real sorry about your mom. But I'd hold off as long as I could, telling Charlie. They were joined at the hip a long time. He's going to take it hard."

Marian nodded in response. Then she walked to her father's room to sit with him for a little while. He was pretty much in a drug-induced coma. After a little while sitting there in the quiet, her eyelids started to feel heavy. She left the hospital a little before midnight. A cold breeze was waiting for her when she stepped into the parking lot. Manuel was waiting there. She had called him when she first got to the hospital to update him. It was his suggestion that he come to get her when she was ready to leave the hospital, otherwise she would have no way of getting back to High Lonesome ranch.

"How is Señor Charlie?"

"He seems to be resting comfortably, but he's in and out of consciousness. I don't know if he realizes what happened to him, where he is, or even if I was there."

"He is a strong man," Manuel said.

"Yes, I know, but he's not a young man anymore. I just wish I could have been there more for him and Mom."

"You are here now. That is good."

Marian laid her head back against the headrest as she listened to the rhythm of the tires on the pavement. They drove through town without seeing another car or any evidence of life. She fought to stay awake. By the time they turned onto the ranch road, she had almost lost the fight, but the first few ruts jarred her back to wakefulness. Manuel drove her right up to the walkway, then hopped out of the truck while the engine was still running. By the time she opened the door he was standing there waiting. She swung her legs around, readily taking his extended hand for support.

"Thank you, Manuel."

"*De nada*. A night's sleep, you will feel better."

"*Sí*," Marian said as she let go of his hand. "Tomorrow will be a better day." He smiled, then went around to the driver's side, got in, then drove away. She stood looking at the darkened house, feeling for just an instant like the little girl she used to be.

Sunlight was streaming through the windows of her bedroom when she awoke. She glanced at the clock on the night table, blinked, then looked again. She couldn't believe she had slept for almost twelve hours. It took her more than a few moments to shake off the coma she had been in since her head had first hit the pillow. At last she dragged herself to the bathroom. By the time she had washed off the last three days, she was beginning to think she was fit for company. The emptiness in the pit of her stomach was a reminder that she really had little or nothing to eat during the last twenty-four hours, so she went downstairs. As she expected, the pantry and refrigerator were stocked full. Her mother had lived a hardscrabble existence before she met her father. Fallout from that life was that there was always enough food on hand to feed a small army. Marian's mother had told her that there were many nights when she had gone to bed hungry. Marian ate way more than a normal-sized breakfast. She was sitting over a second cup of coffee when she saw a car pull up to the fence outside that marked the perimeter of her mother's garden. Even from a distance, she recognized the two men who got out of the car. Taking her cup she went out onto the front porch. She was sitting in her mother's chair when they reached her.

"Hello, Marian."

"Hello, Calvin, Vernon. I had wondered whether or not you were coming when I didn't get a response from either one of you. But then, what's it been, eight, ten years?"

"Yeah, well, we just kind of hooked up with one another and decided to come ahead, been busy." Marian didn't acknowledge the comment. "So, what are the arrangements?" Calvin asked.

"That's still to be worked out. Mom is down at Simpson's. She was just brought over yesterday, far as I know."

Vernon, who had been standing on the path, stepped up alongside of Calvin.

"Don't understand . . ." He started to frame a question, but Calvin interrupted.

"We thought we'd be too late to see Mom. It's been what? Five, six days."

"Well, it took so long because as it turns out Mom didn't die a natural death."

"What? You didn't say. I mean in your message."

"I didn't know. It was a surprise to me, too."

"So you're saying, what?"

"I'm not saying. The coroner, the evidence, is saying Mom was murdered."

The two men looked at each other before Calvin spoke.

"That's crazy. Mom and Dad were old. These backwoods medical people are probably just covering up for the fact that they can't come up with a real medical explanation."

"Obviously, you haven't been to Hayward Memorial. It's a long way from backwoods, Calvin. But then you haven't been around to visit or look in on Mom and Dad. But what about you, Vernon? I understand you stopped by a couple of times. Was that just to visit or maybe you wanted something."

"What do you mean?" Vernon blinked his eyes in rapid succession.

"Still got that nervous habit, Vernon. Did I hit a nerve? I know you sure didn't stop by to help Dad on the ranch. So my other thought is, maybe you wanted something. Maybe money. Wouldn't that be about right?" Vernon stepped back. "What about you, Cal? What do you want? Since you thought Mom was buried already, you must have returned for some other reason. What do you want?"

Calvin glared at Marian. "Pretty full of yourself, aren't you, Marian? I didn't notice you hanging around here after you graduated from college."

"That's because Dad thought his boys were going to stay on, run this place with him. I never got that invitation."

"Yeah, well, I guess with him gone, that's as good an excuse as any."

"Well. With luck we might all get a second chance with Dad."

"How's that?" Calvin asked.

"Well, I mean, when he gets out of the hospital. The doctor suggested I wait before telling him about Mom."

Vernon stepped back alongside Calvin again. "Did you say he was in the hospital? I mean, now?"

"I thought you knew. I thought you both knew. Virgil Dalton, the sheriff, and I found him up on that plateau. You know, the High Lonesome country, as he always called it. The name of the ranch. He'd been shot. A helicopter brought him out. He's in Hayward Memorial right now. Going to be there for a couple of weeks, but they say he's going to walk out. You know, Dad is tough."

Once again, Calvin and Vernon looked at each other.

"Always was, always was," Cal said. "Is he conscious? I mean, should we go see him?"

"No," Marian said. "The doctor said he'll be in the twilight zone for a while. Probably doesn't even know what happened. He wouldn't even know if you were there, so you might as well hold off for a few days. Guess we'll have to bury Mom without him."

"Oh, yeah, guess we'd better," Calvin said. "Vernon, maybe we could stop at Simpson's, check on the arrangements. Give Marian a break. Sounds like she has had a rough couple of days."

Vernon didn't react to Cal's suggestion.

"Vernon . . ." Calvin said in a louder voice.

"Oh, okay, whatever you think, Cal."

"Boys, I'm sorry. Maybe I was a little harsh a few minutes ago."

"It's okay, Marian." Cal gestured with his hand. "Guess we all got a bit of a shock."

"Where are you staying? There's plenty of room in the house."

"No, we already took a place. A cabin on the other side of the river by a roadhouse called the Branding Iron. We're fine. Don't worry about us, we'll make out. By the way, is the sheriff in town? Maybe we should stop by and thank him."

"No. He's still up in the high country. I expect he'll be coming down much later today or first thing tomorrow. He had to bring Pop's gear down and the horses. He insisted I go with Dad in the helicopter. I'm sure he'd like to meet you. He was asking about you. I'll tell him what you said when he gets here."

"That'll be fine. Okay, Vernon, we better get going, take care of business. See you soon, Marian." Calvin turned, then stepped off the porch. "C'mon, Vernon."

Vernon followed him to the car. Marian watched them. Deep in conversation, they never looked back. When they were out of sight, she set her empty coffee cup on the table next to her mother's rocker. She had a strange feeling, like an actor missing a cue. She lingered, looking out on the scene from the front porch that she had known all of her life, but which in a strange way she felt like she had never really seen until now. In a sense it had taken her absence to appreciate how much this place meant to her. Since her husband's death and her children going off to college, she had been at sixes and sevens. There was no sense of direction, only the nagging feeling that for the last two years she had been basically treading water. Only now, brought back to the place of her youth, did she find a kind of peace. She didn't fully understand why this was, especially when the instrument for her return was the death of her mother. But she felt good in this place for the first time in a long time, in a way, looking at her past through new eyes.

The landscape before her was timeless. The path bisecting

her mother's gardens held only the barest hint of the vibrant beauty they had displayed throughout the last months of her life. She noted the horse trough along with the two hitching posts beyond the white picket fence that her mother had insisted on, though her father thought it clashed with the Southwestern homestead. Beyond the area that had been pounded into hardpan by horse's hooves and truck tires over decades, she saw the string of corrals, which fronted the huge barns that now showed age and neglect from lack of use. All of it framing a view into her past that had somehow renewed itself in her. She saw a shadowy figure against one of the barn walls, then saw it disappear through an opened door. Finally, she stood up, took a couple of deep breaths of the chilled morning air, stepped off the porch, and started walking to the barns to see if she could be of any help to Manuel.

23

By midday, Virgil and Ernesto were well off the mesa and on the semidesert flatland where bunch grass or any other graze was a much rarer commodity. It was the kind of range-land where a cow-and-calf unit needed about ten acres. Typical of a huge area in the Southwest, it made Virgil appreciate the lush bottomland of his own ranch. Remembering the trek up to the High Lonesome, Virgil also appreciated how much easier it had been to return, although he knew the distance to the ranch was going to be more than they could accomplish in a day's ride, particularly with Ernesto sitting atop two saddles lashed together. Even a gentle canter was a stretch to make up time. At least it was not a trip made in the one-hundred-degree heat of summer. Virgil was certain that journey had been done many times over the years. Cold, clear, late November worked for him. Looking over at the boy on Ringo, he smiled at the caricature of a nomad on a camel. Completing the image, Ernesto had wrapped a scarf across his face to protect against a windburn.

Virgil knew a dilemma where the boy was concerned awaited him once he got down to High Lonesome ranch. He was conflicted because he knew as sheriff there was one way to go, but there was a history with this boy that would be hard to ignore.

They had ridden steadily into late afternoon, stopping only occasionally so Ernesto could adjust or reset the saddles, checking for any friction marks or saddle sores on Ringo. During their last stop at the base of a wash where a small pool had formed, they watered the horses and ate. As Virgil was replacing Jack's saddle, he saw the rolling thunderheads on the horizon, felt the dampness in the wind. It made the decision to take shelter for the night much easier. He saw little sense in pushing the animals for the ranch in a cold, dark rain over ground that he had never ridden in daylight. They rode for another hour until Virgil spotted a rock overhang a little way up a slope. He explained to Ernesto his plan for the overnight, then together they climbed up toward the mesa, leading the horses on foot to the overhanging rock. By the time Virgil had built a pit fire with some dead cottonwood they had scavenged along with dry grass for tinder, the sky had filled with gunmetal-gray clouds broken only by streaks of lightning. From under the escarpment Virgil and Ernesto and the two horses watched while rolling thunder accompanied the bolts that lit up the panorama. At last the rains came with an intensity that Virgil knew would soon turn the almost-dry wash where they had not long before watered their horses into a raging torrent. These were the kind of gully washers that many times had caught unsuspecting animals and people, robbing them of their lives. Secure in the choice of shelter, they spread out the saddle blankets and ate what food they had while they watched the storm spend its fury over the land. At one point before they turned in for the night, Virgil prodded Ernesto for some of his history.

"*Mi madre está muerta*," Ernesto said in response to Virgil's inquiry. "No one, *hermanos* or *hermanas*, in Mexico. *Todo en Estados Unidos*," he added.

"*¿Dónde?*" Virgil asked.

"*¿Quién sabe?*"

"You have no idea where?"

"Maybe California, maybe Florida," the boy answered. "Me, the last. The youngest."

Virgil listened to his words, realizing it was an immigrant story as old as time. When all familial ties are gone, the search for a new life begins. Ernesto was the latest in an unending line. Before long, while Virgil looked out on a landscape he could barely see, he could hear in the intermittent moments of silence Ernesto's regular breathing and he knew he had drifted off.

As the storm released its energy he felt a kind of calm. The last couple of days had been therapeutic for him. He went looking for Charlie Thompson to displace an overload of anxiety and it had worked. It had always been that way for him—a step or two back so he could move forward again. When he got down to the Thompson ranch and Hayward, what he had left behind would still be there, waiting for him. He was ready.

24

Cesar picked up the phone on the third ring. He was relieved to hear Virgil's voice. Virgil had never been an open book, but Cesar had the closeness born of their years together. He knew about the lost plane in the Superstitions along with the deepening mystery of High Lonesome. So the timbre of Virgil's voice told him something he was anxious to hear.

"Hey, old-timer, if you can get off your rocking chair, you can come up to High Lonesome and get me and Jack."

"Well, I was gonna take a nap, but I guess if I have to . . ."

A little more than a half an hour later, Virgil was standing outside the Thompson ranch house waiting for Cesar when Marian joined him.

"How are you, Virgil?" She had seen him stretching, then rubbing his lower back as she looked out the kitchen window.

"Stiffer then a fence post," he answered. "Been riding that desk chair in my office a lot more than Jack lately. Three serious days in the saddle, I feel like my backbone is ready to pop through my skin."

"You could come back in the house, strip down, then I could rub your lower back. We're well past the formal stage in our relationship."

They traded glances, each offering the other a hint of a smile.

"That's a mighty tempting offer, Marian. Probably the best I'll get today, but if I was to take you up on that, I might start to get achy in other parts and Cesar's going to be pulling into the place soon. I do appreciate the offer though."

"Well, if you don't get any relief, I'll be here. Looks like your ride is coming."

Before Virgil could respond, he saw a cloud of dust on the ranch road. In another moment, he heard the sound of the pickup and the horse trailer.

"Yep. Looks like my Mexican father is coming."

"Virgil, what about the boy?"

"I been wrestling with that for two days," Virgil said.

"Why couldn't he just stay here?"

"What do you mean?"

"We owe him something, my family. The doctor told me Dad wouldn't have made it without him. Let him stay. We could use the help. He needs a family."

Virgil looked toward the barns. He saw Ernesto lugging a bale of hay toward the corral. "Okay, but what happens when you leave in another week or two? I'm only postponing the inevitable."

"I don't think I'm leaving. Oh, maybe for a brief time to take care of some loose ends, but I think my life is going to go in a different direction now. Since I've been here, I realize how much this place means to me. It's my anchor point."

"But what about San Francisco?"

"Well, my husband is gone, my kids are in college, like I told you. They're going to start living their own lives. I've decided to start living mine, doing what I want to do. That's here, this place. I belong here. If Dad will consider it, I'd like to see this ranch become a going concern again. Think I could do it. Bring it back. At least, I'd like to try. Maybe that young boy could find a future here."

Virgil looked at Marian. A slight breeze tugged at a few loose strands of her uncombed hair. He saw a look of determination that he hadn't seen before.

"You know, Marian, you really are a good-looking woman."

"Why thank you, Virgil. There isn't a woman alive who wouldn't like to hear that. That's nice, but it sounds almost like a revelation."

"It is," Virgil said. "I mean, maybe I don't always say something I should, in the moment."

She could sense his unease. "You mean, like the other night in the cabin."

"Yes. But I wanted to say it now. Maybe the other night it would have got lost. But now, here, in the clear light of day I want you to know how I feel. You weren't just a moment for me. I want you to know that and I'm really glad you're staying. Whatever else, I'll be there if you need me. Hope I'm saying this right. I . . ."

Cesar had pulled the truck alongside the corral fence, shut off the engine, and was leaning against the front fender waiting for Virgil. Virgil raised his hand in a half wave, then turned to Marian. He could see tears in her eyes. She took a couple of steps toward him, then reached up and brushed his cheek with her lips.

"Virgil, you said it just right. You weren't just a moment for me, either."

She reached up again this time, kissing him on the lips. In the next moment, she turned and ran toward the house. Virgil watched until she disappeared inside, then he put his hand to his face, touched a dab of moisture, wondering for a moment whether it was his or Marian's. When he turned toward the truck, he saw that Cesar had not moved. Virgil walked across the broad open area to meet the older man.

It was early afternoon by the time they reached the ranch. The dull ache in Virgil's back had eased some, but when he stepped out of the cab of the truck, he felt stiff all over.

"Who's the old-timer now?" Cesar said.

Virgil winced at the well-aimed jab. "Been a long time since I spent that much time in the saddle."

Cesar gave a little snort.

"What?" Virgil asked.

"I noticed you were walking a little bit bowlegged. Reckoned it was from riding one thing or another." He threw a knowing look at Virgil. "Nice-looking woman we left back there."

Virgil took a couple of steps forward, accompanied by a grunt. Cesar had come around the cab.

"Well, you're always at me to get out, be more social."

"Absolutely, but you got to pace yourself. You're not twenty-one anymore. Remember old bull, young bull. You can still get there, but you just don't have to be in a hurry."

"Thanks for the philosophy. Yeah, well, ninety percent of this ache is from Jack. The other ten percent, well, let's just say you're right. She is a nice-looking woman. Now, since you got what you were after, do me a favor, unload Jack while I go inside and soak in the tub for about two hours."

Cesar nodded, then walked to the rear of the trailer. He let down the ramp, then Jack backed out. He glanced at Virgil, stiffly going up the stairs to the porch, and a little smile crossed his face.

Virgil couldn't resist the lure of the bed when he climbed out of the tub. He was asleep in less than five minutes. When he awoke almost two hours later, he realized he was in the exact same position as when he first lay down. He swung his legs around, resting his feet on the floor. When he stood, he was pleasantly surprised that much of the ache was gone. He was taking inventory of the contents of his refrigerator a half hour later when Cesar walked through the kitchen door.

"You're pretty much wasting your time. A starving man wouldn't last more than a day with what's in there."

"Guess that means I'm eating at Margie's."

"You could actually go to a food store. Then watch one of those cooking shows to figure out what to do with the stuff you bought."

"I can cook," Virgil said as he took a box of cereal out of the cabinet over the dryer.

"Pouring out-of-date milk over a bowl of raisin bran don't exactly qualify as cooking. Me, I just had a burrito filled with leftover steak, chili, a little hot sauce, and a scoop of sour cream. Oh, and some rice and beans on the side." Cesar patted his stomach. "Real tasty."

"That don't show much culinary imagination. Hell, you'd have rice and beans with pancakes."

"Maybe, but it tasted better than anything you're going to find to eat here."

Virgil just scowled at that. Cesar left him standing in front of the mostly empty fridge along with an even emptier stomach.

It had gotten to that time of the year when the light begins to fade early. Virgil stood on the porch awhile noting the shadows in places where they hadn't been a couple of weeks earlier. He hadn't put on his uniform when he got up. Instead, he was wearing jeans that showed some wear and a new blue chambray shirt. There were times when he didn't want to be just a uniform. His matching denim jacket lay on one of the porch chairs. As yet the evening winds hadn't picked up, so he left his jacket there when he walked down the stairs toward the barns. Jack wasn't in the corral. He reckoned Cesar had bedded him down early in his stall, probably after giving him a thorough going-over. Checking his feet, working out any small stones with a hoof pick, maybe even painting his hooves to avoid any cracking. Probably also hosed him down, then gave him a good rubdown, combing his mane and tail, then currycombing and brushing him nose to butt. It was the kind of thing Cesar did because it was just the right thing to do. It was hard for Virgil to think of him as anything other than family. They had been so close so long that Virgil couldn't even remember a time when it hadn't been that way. First of the month, he always cut a check for Pedro and José, but there wasn't one for Cesar. When Cesar needed money he just wrote out a check for cash on the ranch account, but he always insisted Virgil sign it. He was no forger.

By the time he got down to the barn, Cesar was well into his end-of-day routine. Virgil watched him move down the aisle between the stalls with the wheelbarrow, checking each stall before he brought the horses in to feed. While the weather held, the horses were still left out at night. Most of the time Jack was with them, but Virgil figured tonight he'd probably stay in the corral, a little downtime for him after the workout he'd had during the last few days.

The cattle were out almost year-round, unless the weather turned rank. In winter that could be on the heels of a Blue Norther, which could drop temperatures forty degrees overnight and bring blowing snow creating deep drifts on the range. The driven snow along with the bitter cold could be disastrous. Over the years, as begun by his father before him, Virgil, along with the men, built loafing sheds out on the range, where the cattle could shelter from the extremes in winter or in summer. Virgil could remember only three times in his life when the winter weather had been so severe that the cattle had been rounded up and brought down to the home pasture. Winter kill occurred occasionally, but it more than likely was the result of a freak accident, a steer slipping on ice or predation by a mountain lion. Other than that, most of the losses were the result of the natural cycle. A cow with a prolapsed uterus undiscovered, after giving birth out in some arroyo where she had gone for seclusion, or a too-large bull calf wrong way in a cow. These were the events every cowman did everything he could to avoid, but on some level were unavoidable, no matter how much oversight was given.

Virgil followed Cesar down the aisle, scooping up grain from a filled wheelbarrow used for that purpose. He gave each horse the required allotment in the heavy, rubber feed pail that hung in the corner of each stall. Cesar had come up with the idea of hanging a feeding sheet on the door of each stall in the new barn, so anyone could check it to make sure they had given the correct ration. Virgil also checked the water buckets in the opposite corner from the feed buckets, filling them when it was required. When he and Cesar were finished with their routine, they met at the end of the barn, then opened the doors to the corral on the far side, where the horses had gathered and were impatiently waiting. Not a word had been spoken. They stood in the half-light as the horses entered, each going automatically to their assigned stall. The last box stall was reserved for Star and her yet-to-be weaned colt.

"You know," Cesar said when Virgil came alongside, "he could use some work if your appetite hasn't got the better of you yet."

Virgil looked at the colt as he sidled up to nurse from his mother while she buried her nose in the grain bucket.

"He looks good," Virgil said as he and Cesar stood leaning over the top rail of the stall. "Got some size to him, good straight legs."

The colt finished nursing, then ambled over closer to where they were standing. Virgil extended his right arm between the rails, his hand palm up. The colt, ears forward, stood his ground.

Virgil started talking to him in a low voice. "Hey, son, easy."

The colt watched, then after a few moments took a hesitant step forward, then another, until he reached a point where he could stretch his neck out so he could make contact with Virgil's outstretched hand. The soft velvet of his muzzle brushed Virgil's fingers. Virgil continued his monotone. The colt took a step closer, began to nibble, then suck on Virgil's fingers. Virgil reached his left hand inside the stall slowly, then while the colt worked the fingers of his right hand, he ran his left hand along the colt's neck. The process continued until Virgil could run either hand over the colt's head.

"Good start," Cesar said as he handed Virgil a small halter and a brush.

Virgil stepped inside the stall, then spent the next ten minutes brushing the mare while incidentally stroking the colt. Finally, after rubbing the halter over the mare's body to pick up her scent, he began rubbing it on the colt, letting him smell it, even at one point nibble at it until he no longer showed interest in it. At last, Virgil slipped it over his head. The colt balked a little so Virgil continued talking to him in a soothing voice. The colt settled after a couple of minutes. By the time Virgil left the stall, he had haltered the colt numerous times. Cesar smiled as he stepped out.

"*Bueno.*"

Virgil nodded.

"Next time, I'll halter him in the corral. Maybe try a lead rope, drop a come-along over his rear end, then get a little more serious."

On the way into Hayward a little later, Virgil reflected on how much he had enjoyed the experience with the colt. In a way he knew that part of his life offered a balance that down deep sustained him. His stomach was growling, but before he headed to Margie's there was something he had to know. Rosita and Dif were in the office.

"Didn't expect to see you today," Rosie said. "Figured, after all that time on horseback, you'd be sitting in a bucket of Sloan's Liniment."

"Hell, that was just a light jaunt," Virgil lied as he sat down behind his desk.

"So, I guess that wince when you sat down was just for show," Rosie said.

Virgil glanced around the room, choosing not to engage.

"Yeah, well, it's nice to see this place didn't go to wrack and ruin while I was gone. Sure is a comfort."

"There you go, thinking you're indispensable," Rosie said. "This place runs like a well-oiled clock whether you're here or not."

Dif gave a snort. "Guess you ain't going to tell him about that mix-up at the Lazy Dog or about that Travis woman shooting her husband when she found him in the wrong bed or . . ."

"A well-oiled clock," Virgil interrupted as Rosie glared at Dif. "So, what's the body count?" Virgil nodded in the direction of the holding cells on the other side of the closed door on the far wall.

"We are full up," Dif said.

"Full up?"

"Yep, we're stacking them up in there like cordwood. We even got them in transit."

Rosita never said a word.

"We sent two lightweight offenders down to Redbud with Dave to work off some time and to make some space for any new arrivals."

Virgil couldn't resist a smile. "So, it's nice to know you got everything under control."

Suddenly, the door opened and Deputy Jimmy Tillman came in. When he saw Virgil, he stopped in his tracks.

"Well now, it looks like we got the whole Hayward police force on duty," Virgil said. "Guess things got a little busy around here over Thanksgiving weekend. Hello, Jimmy."

"Sheriff."

Jimmy didn't add to his one-word response.

"Okay, Virgil," Rosie said. "So, maybe we're glad you're back. Virgil, we need another deputy. Things got crazy here last night. Dave had to come up from Redbud."

"I guess," Virgil said. "Looks like I'm going to have to make a case. In a way, this looks like pretty good justification. I might even bring the council in here to see this place full up."

Jimmy started for the door.

"Where are you going, Jimmy?"

"Oh, I just got to see someone, Sheriff."

Before Virgil could respond, he was out the door.

"Kinda closemouthed today," Virgil said. Rosie and Dif looked at each other, but said nothing. "Well, I'm going over to Margie's, but before I go, did Kyle Harrison call with any news?"

"Nothing, Virgil. They haven't found any trace of the plane. He said it could be at the bottom of one of those canyons in the Superstitions. If the weather holds they are going in there to do a ground search. He said maybe they'd try to enlist some volunteers from the reservation to help in the search. Virgil, I think you got to accept the real possibility that they won't find anything." After Rosie's plea Virgil looked out the window from his desk for a long time. Then he stood up.

"I'll stop back later."

"Virgil?" Rosie said.

He glanced again out the window. "Yes. There's a lot of country out there to get lost in."

25

When Virgil walked through the door at Margie's he was surprised to see Marian Thompson sitting at one of the tables.

"Hey, Marian."

"Sit with me, Virgil. Don't like to eat alone. Too many stares when you're a woman eating by yourself in a restaurant."

"Didn't need the invite, Marian. Not a big fan of eating by myself, either. Do it too much. But for me the stares come from a different place. Maybe I've had a negative interaction with them or someone in their family. Sheriffs aren't universally well liked. That's why I'm here in disguise, hoping no one will notice me."

"I noticed. Not even carrying a gun. If I didn't know better, I'd think you were just another working cowhand. I almost think I can smell the barn on you."

"There's no almost about it." Virgil explained how he'd spent the last hour on his ranch.

"Working with a new colt. I'd like that. That was one job Pop always gave me, like Ringo. Pop always said a lot of women had a natural intimacy with horses. I always gentled the babies."

Margie came over to their table. "That tapeworm acting up again, Virgil?"

"Big-time, Margie. My stomach feels like my throat's been cut. Was going to try to rustle up something at home, but like the old lady said, the cupboard was bare. So I figured I'd come in here to stimulate the local economy."

"Thanks for thinking of us, Virgil. Need all the help we can get. So what'll it be?"

"I'm thinking that rib eye sitting on Marian's plate looks good for starters."

"You got it. I'll get it working."

A minute or two after Margie left, another waitress came over with a cup of chili and a tall glass of lemonade.

"Margie said, while you're waiting."

"Thank you," Virgil responded as he reached for a spoon. "So, Marian, why are you in town?"

"I came in to bring some flowers from Mom's garden over to Simpson's. Going to be a wake tomorrow, then a funeral on Tuesday."

"How's your dad?"

"He's stable as far as his vitals are concerned, but he's pretty much out of it. Doctor says it will probably be another day before he's fully conscious. Doc says they got him just in time. But we've got to go ahead with Mom's funeral without him."

"Good thing we were able to get that helicopter," Virgil said.

"Yes. You know an interesting thing about that. I mentioned to the pilot about how he was able to find us at night. I mean, obviously the fire helped, but still there's a lot of country up there. He told me that he was pretty familiar with the general area because he's made a few trips up there in the last six months."

"I must be missing something. Don't get it. Why would he be going up there?" Virgil asked.

"That's the way I felt, but I didn't get the chance to follow up, because we were getting ready to set down at the hospital. Anyway, just thought it kind of strange, which is why I mentioned it." As Marian finished, Margie set a steak down in front of Virgil that overflowed the plate, then she set down a couple of sides in separate dishes.

"You look like you need a little nourishment, Virgil."

"If I manage to get through this, I won't need any more for the rest of the week. I'll give it my best effort, Margie."

She smiled as she stepped away from the table. "I'm sure you will, Virgil."

"So, Virgil, do you think that's odd or strange about the helicopter making those trips up to that ridge?"

Virgil stopped cutting his steak, looked around the room, then at Marian.

"Strange? Yeah, I'd say so. But the way things have been going in my life lately, I'm beginning to think strange is the new normal."

26

Virgil had planned to head back to the ranch after eating, but instead chose to walk Marian over to Simpson's.

"Do you want to come in with me?" she asked on the sidewalk outside the funeral home.

"No. I'll wait here if you don't mind, unless you feel the need for a little support."

"No, I'm fine. I won't be long, but if you want to take off I'm okay with that."

"I've got no plans. I'll wait for you. By the way, those flowers look nice. I'm sure your mom would like them."

Marian looked down at the flowers she had taken from the car after they left the restaurant. "I was afraid they'd seem a little skimpy. Not much more than a bouquet."

"But they'll mean more than any other flower arrangement in there. Her flowers picked by her daughter."

"You know, Virgil, you are developing a knack for saying just the right thing at just the right time."

Virgil watched as Marian walked to the front door, then disappeared inside. While he waited for her return a few cars passed, then after a couple of minutes he saw Jimmy in the patrol car, probably going out for his first run of the night. Virgil stepped off the curb, then waved, but the car never slowed and Jimmy gave no indication that he even saw Virgil. Virgil stepped back on the sidewalk, shaking his head.

"What's the matter?" Marian asked when she came up to him.

Virgil didn't respond right away. "Probably nothing," he finally said. "Everything okay with you?"

"I guess. It's just . . ." She didn't have to say anything else.

"Listen, I was going to head back to the ranch, but it's still early. How about we walk down to the Lazy Dog, listen to some music over a beer or two?"

"Oh, I don't know. I should get back, get ready for tomorrow."

"C'mon. You need it. We both need it—a little diversion. We'll go chug a few, listen to some music. If we really get lucky, maybe Florence will whack some out-of-line customer with that hockey stick of hers."

"She's still doing that? My God, she must be close to eighty."

"Yep, and her aim is still pretty good. No one complains. Guess they don't want to admit to being toasted by a senior citizen."

Virgil and Marian walked through the door of the Lazy Dog ten minutes later. The décor was strictly saloon. One of those places that could have been found in most cow towns throughout the Southwest, fifty, sixty years earlier, but were becoming an endangered species. On the left was a bar that went on to eternity while the space to the right of it was taken up by a mixed assortment of tables and chairs. Any thought of some uniform decorating theme was given up long ago. Some of the chairs that had met their end in disturbances over the years were replaced by new ones. The rest looked like they had been there since the Flood. Along the right wall was a line of booths that seemed to have escaped most of the carnage over the years. They stretched almost all the way to the back. The place in the way back where maybe another table or booth could have filled the space was instead given over to a raised platform. This was for entertainers who could range from paid to amateurs. Most of them had lost their inhibitions after a couple of hours and more than a few drinks. Some had become convinced that they had something to offer in the vast area of the performing arts. This could encompass anything from rope tricks to rap. The Lazy Dog had evolved through the years from what in an earlier time might have been described as a bucket of blood to a place that now seemed intimidating to no one and open to all comers. The change was not lost on Marian.

"My God, I never realized there was an end to this place. Last time I was here there was a cloud of smoke so dense you couldn't see the rear. It was weird. I kinda got the feeling that if you walked through it, you'd drop off the end of the earth." She made her reflection as they slid into the first unoccupied booth they came to, which was about halfway down the room.

"Yeah, well, a lot of places have become gentrified since 'no smoking' became the eleventh commandment. You can actually breathe now."

"You know, Virgil, I remember there was a singer I'd heard of who was called the Velvet Fog. I often wondered if he got his start here because you could never see the singer so the music and lyrics seemed to be coming out of the fog which hung in the center of the room. It was kind of cool."

Virgil could see that coming here had been a good call. Marian was obviously enjoying the step back into her past.

"Well, Virgil, what'll it be?"

He looked up at Florence standing next to the booth. "Maybe you thought I wouldn't recognize you in your disguise. I look beyond the uniform."

"Most people don't, Florence."

"Yeah, well, they're the same people life passes by and they don't even realize it."

"A little too much philosophy for me this late in the day. All I can think of is a kick back and a cold one. How about a Coors and a slice of lime?"

"And the lady . . . Wait, I know you. You're . . . you're Charlie and Velma's girl. You look a lot like your mom, God rest her."

"I can't believe you recognized me after all these years."

Next thing they both knew, Florence was sitting in the booth with them. She waved to a barman. For the next half hour they talked. At one point they were laughing so hard at one of Florence's stories, the tears came.

"Your father and yours," she said, pointing to Virgil. "They were a pair. I remember that story of your father and Charlie going over the pass, pulling that horse trailer, when it come loose on the downhill, then tried passing them by, because one of them had forgot to snap it on the ball of the hitch. Only thing keeping it attached was the umbilical chain. Your father looked at Charlie when that trailer come alongside. 'What are we gonna do, Charlie?' he says. Charlie looks at him and says, 'Don't rightly know. I ain't never been in this situation before, but I know one thing, Sam. When we get to the bottom of this here grade, we better be in front.' They was something, those two. Matter of fact, if I remember correctly, they was each on top, in the first go-round in their events at that rodeo they was going to. Charlie come in here the next day, told that story. I said to him that was amazing that you could sit that bull till you heard that buzzer after that. He looked me dead in the eye and he said, 'Florence, that bull was nothing. Hell, I'd already had the shit scared out of me coming down that mountain.'"

By the time Florence left the booth each of them was nursing their third beer.

"That was fun," Marian said. "Even if most of it was fiction."

"Don't know that I'd go there, Marian. Found out a lot about my father that I didn't know from other people. Guess it has to do with not wanting their kids to learn from their horrible example. Maybe, since your father's a little more vulnerable in the hospital right now, you might ask him about some of those old lies. Tell him it would be a good way to test his memory. Bet you'll be surprised."

She didn't respond, but Virgil could see a kind of faraway look come into her eyes. Then the sound of a guitar infiltrated the silence, followed by the low voice of a woman who joined in, then strengthened, filling the room. They sat there in the lull of conversation, sipping their beers while they listened.

"It's a heartache, nothing but a heartache . . ."

A song from another time. The singer's voice took on a decidedly Kim Carnes kind of raspy, throaty sound. The room noise noticeably subsided. At the conclusion of the song there was a burst of applause.

"'Nothing but a heartache, nothing but a heartache.' Kind of fits the scenario," Marian said.

"Yeah, well, if you look around this room, right now there's probably more than one or two people having that thought."

"You're right, Virgil. I'm starting to wallow."

"Wallow?"

"Feeling sorry for myself. It's something Dad used to say whenever I'd go to the dark side over something that went wrong in my teenage life. Can't stand people feeling sorry for themselves, wallowing in their grief, most of the time over nothing. Everybody's got problems. Put your head down, plow through."

"You know, I really didn't know your father that well except from occasional tales, but I'm liking him more and more. When he gets out of the hospital, I'd like to sit with him a stretch, get to know him better."

"I'm sure he would like that, Virgil."

"Hey, Sheriff, didn't know you got out in the world."

Virgil looked up into the smiling face of one-eyed Chet Harris.

"Shh," Virgil said, raising his finger to his lips. "I'm undercover, trying to see if I can blend in like a regular person."

"Well, why don't you and the lady come on over and join us? See if the disguise works."

Virgil looked over at Marian. She nodded slightly.

"Sure, why not, but only if you call me Virgil."

"You got it," Chet said.

They got out of the booth, then followed Chet back to the rear of the bar to the last table by the upraised platform. Sitting at the table were a man and a woman. The man stood up as they approached.

"Virgil, you know Karen. And this is a really good friend, Simon Levine. Simon and I, you could say, shared a foxhole once upon a time. We were both in the same unit." Virgil extended his hand.

"Thank you for your service," he said.

"Hope you're not put off by a back hand. Lots of people get a little shaky when I extend the claw right off the bat."

He held up his right hand, showing his prosthesis. "I think it would take a little more than that to throw Virgil off his game, Simon."

"Oh, you a vet?" Simon asked.

"In a different kind of war," Virgil responded. "Maybe I'll tell you about that sometime. Right now, we just want to hear some more of that good entertainment and sit over a beer. This is Marian Thompson, a really good friend, by the way. Guess you could say we shared the same foxhole, too. Now where's that singer?"

"What about it, Karen?" Chet asked. "You up for more?"

"Maybe, after we visit awhile."

Marian picked up on the cue. "Was that you singing?"

"Guilty as charged," Karen replied.

"Wait a second, you're a nurse," Virgil said. "Never sang to me once, the whole time I was in the hospital."

"What can I say? I'm a woman of many talents and you weren't a paying customer. My mother told me never give it away for nothing."

Virgil laughed out loud. "I'll be damned," he said. "Your mother. There's another person I'd like to meet."

For the next hour or so they sat talking. Light banter going back and forth like a Ping-Pong ball. Virgil kept drinking beer with the boys long after Marian had switched to soda. He was over his limit and he knew it. Finally, after Karen's last set of the night, the place was starting to empty. Florence came over one last time.

"You did good, Karen. See you Friday night?"

"I might have to work, Flo. I'll find out tomorrow."

"Well, you let me know. If not Friday, we'll set another date. Looks like you had a good time, Virgil."

"I did, Florence, I really did. First time in a long time."

"You got to get out more, Virgil."

Virgil regarded her comment with a silly smile on his face. "Florence, you're right, but I didn't get to see you whack anyone with that stick of yours."

"Well, I'm trying to save my arm for special occasions. You know, Virgil, I'm on the yonder side of seventy."

"Yeah, well, if I'm any judge, you'll still be swinging it on the yonder side of eighty, if someone doesn't sue you first."

"That'll never happen," Karen piped up.

"How so?" Virgil asked.

"There are guys who act up just so they can say they've been whacked by Flo. Some of them come here from out of town. All this time I thought it was for my singing, but no, just to get whacked by Flo."

Chet leaned over and gave Karen a hug. "It's the singing," he said.

Karen gave him a quick kiss.

"So I guess they're starting to pull in the sidewalks," Chet said.

"Yeah, about that time," Virgil said. "Nice meeting you, Simon. Where are you off to after your visit here?"

"One place or another. Someplace I haven't been. Maybe a place where I can pick up the pieces, start all over."

"What about home?" Virgil asked.

"Well, home is New York. Lower Hudson River Valley. Right now, with this . . ."—he held up his prosthesis—"the competition is pretty tight for my work skills."

"What are they?"

"Well, my original goal was law enforcement. I was an MP and sniper at different times in my career, but don't think there's much of a market for those skills, considering this." He raised his artificial hand again.

"Can you fire a gun?"

"Rifle, shotgun—no problem. Revolver, I'd need to work on. Other than that, physically I'm probably in the best shape I've ever been in, courtesy of the rehab at the VA." Virgil sat back in his chair, not saying anything while Simon finished the last of his beer. Simon then turned to ask Chet something. Virgil stood up from the table to join Marian.

"I really enjoyed meeting you all," she said.

"So, Chet, did I pass the test?"

"Flying colors, Virgil. Just like a regular person."

Simon, standing next to Chet, was obviously puzzled.

"Simon, nice meeting you. By the way, if you aren't in a rush to put Hayward in your rearview mirror, I'd kind of like to talk to you."

Simon had reached out to shake hands. Virgil took note of the taut muscles that drew his shirt tight across his chest.

"I'm not sure. Staying with Chet, but you know what they say about fish and visitors after three days. What did you want to talk about?"

"That different kind of war I mentioned. Simon, I'm the sheriff of Hayward County."

"Oh, I didn't know. Chet never said."

Chet, who had been listening to their exchange, joined them and spoke up. "See, Simon, like I always said, I'd keep an eye out for you."

They both turned and looked at Chet.

"That just might be the lamest joke I've heard all night," Virgil said.

27

They could see their breath as they walked to Marian's car.

"Hope the weather holds for the next few days," she said. "At least until after Mom's—"

"I think it will," Virgil interrupted. "Sky is clear and the night has a thousand eyes."

"That's nice. A thousand eyes."

"Not original with me. A line from an old Edward G. Robinson movie. Liked the image. It just stuck with me."

"So what were you talking to Chet's friend about when we were getting ready to leave?"

"Nothing too specific. He seemed like someone I might find some common ground with that could have the possibility of benefiting each of us. Just a gut feeling." They had reached Marian's car.

"Funny how that is, about gut feelings. I've had a couple of them lately, kind of disturbing," Marian said.

Virgil wasn't sure in the dim light by her car, but he thought for an instant he saw a look of sadness come into her eyes.

"Thanks for talking me into this night, Virgil. It was good medicine."

"For me, too."

"You going home?"

Virgil looked again at the sky. Then pulled the collar of his denim jacket up. "No, don't think so. Heard the click."

"Heard the click?"

"I think it was after the third beer. Knew if I went beyond that, I wouldn't be driving home tonight. Made my choice, 'cause I was having a good time. Wouldn't look good in the community if the headline read DWI for Sheriff Dalton after he runs into a tree."

"You don't look to me like you would have any trouble driving."

"Looks can be deceiving. Guess I hold my liquor fairly well. I might be able to get away with it, but I know if I was to blow into a Breathalyzer, the numbers wouldn't lie. I'll stay in town tonight."

He opened the car door for Marian.

"It was a good night, wasn't it? We'll have to do it again."

"I won't refuse the invitation," she said as she got behind the wheel.

Virgil watched as Marian drove away. Then he walked the couple of blocks over to the office. He could hear Dif snoring through the closed door, but as soon as he pushed it open the snoring stopped.

"What are you doing here, Virgil?"

"Trying to catch one of my deputies sleeping on the job."

Dif pointed to the clock. "Yeah, well, I'm on unpaid overtime. Jimmy's late. Should have been in my own bed over an hour ago."

"Have you heard from him?"

"Yeah. He'll be along soon. Got a flat when he was on his way back, over on the River Road. Called in. I said I'd wait."

"Thank you, Dif. You're a good man. Any calls?"

"Nope, quiet as a tomb. But you haven't told me what you are doing here."

"Closed the Lazy Dog tonight, got a snoot full. Thought maybe I shouldn't drive."

"Good for you, Virgil. Got to do that once in a while. Let a little steam out of the pressure cooker."

Dif got up, then poured a couple of cups of coffee. He placed one in front of Virgil. "Let's sit awhile. Drink up."

Virgil eyed Dif, then did as he was told. After a second cup, Virgil said, "Dif, you can take off now. I'll cover any calls. Wait until Jimmy shows up."

"Okay, Virgil, see you tomorrow. Won't put in for the overtime."

"Don't know that it would make much difference if you did."

After Dif left, Virgil went to the cell block. The symphony of snores coming from the occupants suggested an uneventful night. He counted seven—one unoccupied cell. He recognized everyone, which wasn't much of a surprise. Most of the time his was a repeat business. The rollaway was just inside the door, so on his return from inspection, he pushed it into the office, then over to the corner between where the coffee urn was set up and the far wall. He had just opened it up when Jimmy came into the office.

"Hey, Jimmy."

Virgil could tell immediately that he was an unpleasant surprise.

"Sheriff, where's Dif?"

"I sent him home before Edna came looking for him. Don't

want her to get the notion that he's tomcatting. Can't afford to lose a trusted employee like Dif. Heard you had a little car trouble."

Jimmy looked down at his hands, which were dirt covered and grease stained.

"Got a flat out on River Road. Had a hard time loosening some of the lug nuts. It was dark even with my spot."

"Guess that wasn't fun."

"No, sir. No, it wasn't."

"Well, get yourself cleaned up, then you can go home. I'm staying over tonight, but before you take off, I think we need to clear the air."

Jimmy didn't say anything, but turned and went into the bathroom. He came out about ten minutes later. Virgil was still sitting at his desk looking over some incident reports concerning his cellmates on the other side of the door. The most serious infraction appeared to be the damage done to a car belonging to the new boyfriend of a girl by her previous boyfriend.

"Have a seat, Jimmy. Be with you in a second."

Jimmy sat down while Virgil finished the last report. "Some people have a hard time with rejection."

He placed the report on the stack on the side of his desk. Then he pushed his chair back.

"You want to tell me what the problem is?" Virgil said. "My take is you've got a burr under your saddle about something. Let's have it."

At first Jimmy didn't say anything. It was obvious he was a little uncomfortable in the hot seat. Virgil was getting ready to prod him again when he blurted out one word.

"Virginia."

"I don't understand. What has Virginia got to do with this?"

"Is she your daughter?" Jimmy asked.

Virgil sat up in his chair, then stood up and walked around the room.

"So that's it." He stopped and looked at his young deputy. "I'm sorry, Jimmy. I should have told you but, well, I guess you'd have to say I didn't become a father in the traditional way."

He walked over to his desk, pulled his chair around until it was next to Jimmy's, then sat down. For the next ten minutes he explained the circumstances surrounding the revelation of his fatherhood.

"There it is. I guess it's time for it to become public knowledge. Secrets are rarely kept. In this case obviously it has already caused a problem. I didn't mean to leave you in the dark. Guess it just took time for me to grasp all the nuance."

Virgil stood up, pushed his chair back to its place behind the desk. "Go home, Jimmy. I need to get some sleep. Tomorrow is probably going to be another long day."

He walked over to the rollaway, sat down, and untied his shoes.

"Okay, Virgil. Glad we had this talk. I feel a lot better."

"Me, too," Virgil replied as Jimmy stood at the door.

"Oh, Virgil. There's just one more thing."

Virgil looked up from the edge of his bed. "Do you have any objection to me asking your daughter for a date?"

Virgil just stared at Jimmy, standing in the open doorway.

"Is this what being a father is all about?" he said.

Jimmy smiled and walked out the door, leaving Virgil sitting there in his new role.

Sunlight came streaming through the office window much too soon for Virgil.

"Paying the price for your night on the town, aren't you?"

Rosie was standing over him with a cup of orange juice in her hand. "Drink this—it'll help."

Virgil sat up, swung his legs over the side, resting his bare feet on the floor as he reached out and took the cup. He drained it in one gulp. "Dry mouth always follows a night of drinking."

"I'm not even going to ask how you know," Virgil said as he stood up. "I make no apologies. It was fun."

"Okay, sport. Get cleaned up and I'll get an extra breakfast for you and the other inmates."

When Virgil emerged from the bathroom twenty minutes later, a plate of sausage, eggs, and toast was on his desk alongside a cup of hot, black coffee.

"That was good, just what I needed to kick-start my day. By the way, you might like to know it wasn't just about fun last night. I might have a prospect for that vacancy you want me to fill."

Virgil went on to tell Rosie about Simon Levine. "Well, what about that?"

"You did good, Virgil. If he walks through that door and is fool enough to want to stay, I'm not letting him out till he's in uniform and his name is on the contract. Sounds like what we need. A Jewish boy from New York. He'll blend right in with a Baptist, a Catholic, and what are you again? . . . an agnostic. Now, if he fits, all you got to do is sell it to them born-again Christians on the town council. He ain't by any chance gay, is he?"

"Never thought to ask the question, but we can live in hope. After all, we're striving for diversity, right?"

Virgil spent the next few hours taking care of some paperwork, his least favorite part of the job. About ten minutes after eleven, Simon Levine came into the office, much to Virgil's surprise.

"Simon, good to see you."

"Chet dropped me off. Think he wants to get me out of the house."

"That could be a good thing. Have a seat."

Simon reached for a nearby chair.

"Let me ask you a quick question," Virgil said. "If everything were to fall into place, could you see yourself working as a deputy in Hayward County? I'm about ready to hit them with a request for a new deputy and I'm not going to give them much wiggle room."

Simon looked like someone had just thrown a bucket of water on him.

"You don't waste much time, do you?"

"Only when I absolutely have to, but you haven't answered my question."

An hour later, after Simon had left, with the prospect of a new deputy looking a lot more favorable, Virgil got up from his desk, ready to leave the office. "What did you think of Simon?"

"I liked him," Rosie said. "He looks you straight in the eye when he talks to you. Easy to look at and he isn't afraid to speak up. I think he's a keeper. I got a good vibe."

Virgil picked up his hat. "Me, too." Then he started for the door.

"Where are you heading, Virgil?"

"Going down to Sky High to see a man about a helicopter ride."

"This about Velma and Charlie?"

"We'll see."

"Say hello to Margaret and Eustace for me."

"Will do."

"Any closer, Virgil?"

"Well, I'm thinking if I can find out the why, then there's a chance I can find out the who. Maybe this pilot can give me something in that direction, because I'm afraid if the who is desperate enough, he or they might not just stop with Velma and Charlie."

28

Virgil hadn't been down to the real desert part of the county, south of Redbud, since they had found two headless murder victims, a brother and a sister, the previous summer. The farther south you traveled, the more barren the landscape, the more scattered the inhabitants. It was a region of earth tones and right angles. Any green areas were mostly the result of irrigation. The growing season here was well over four-fifths of the year, but the problem was water. The area had become drought stricken the last four or five years. Water had become an expensive commodity. The Southwest had become a mecca for many escaping from cold and snow. Their refusal to recognize that much of it was desert and their reluctance to leave green lawns behind contributed heavily to the stress on the water table. Serious farmers had to go deep to tap into an aquifer. They could no longer depend on nature to meet their needs. Virgil saw the desert beauty, but knew it could be unforgiving. People who lived here also knew to respect the desert. People who didn't could lose their lives. There wasn't a lot of wiggle room.

Virgil's destination, Sky High Airfield, was a bit of an anachronism. On one level it could be considered something of an aeronautical dinosaur, but that hadn't always been the case. Throughout the early part of the twentieth century, it was in the mainstream, even cutting-edge. This was the age of wing walkers and flying acrobats. A time when the people were enthralled by airmen. Curtiss, Lindbergh, Wiley Post: they were the names in the headlines, the heroes of the day. Sky High got its name then. Everybody looked to the sky. As with all innovations since the discovery of the wheel, when flying became routine, the awe and wonder faded away. It became a casualty of commerce and business. Places like Sky High faded from the landscape in the wake of huge metro airports.

Coming down off a ridge, Virgil could see the airfield in the valley below. As if to draw attention to itself, one small, private plane was doing circles in the sky overhead. As he reached level ground and got closer, he could see ten or twelve similar planes sitting in the grass facing the runway. The runway was nothing more than hardpan. A desert airport like this didn't need the expense of a paved runway when dirt that had been rolled over for decades became as hard as concrete. Unlike the ribbons of interlaced tracks at the airport in Phoenix, it never had to be hosed down when the temperature climbed above one hundred to keep the runway from buckling. There were four separate buildings that served as hangars. In the first of these was what amounted to an office. Virgil pulled up to it, noting as he stepped out of his car the sign above, which indicated its purpose. Like everything else it did not seem to wear its age lightly. The name

SKY HIGH, along with any other information it offered, was so faded as to be unreadable by anyone with anything less than 20/20 vision and farther than ten feet away. Virgil, squinting in the glare of midday, barely fit the first category. It was another of those imperfections of aging he was trying to ignore. When he walked to the door, he saw peeking out from this building and its nearest companion the drooping rotor blades of a helicopter. The door of the office was slightly ajar, so he walked right in without knocking.

Everything inside, matching the sign, provided ample evidence that Sky High was stuck in a time warp of long ago. There was what could be loosely referred to as a reception area. Assorted chairs lined the walls, separated by similarly mismatched tables on which sat piles of indiscriminate magazines for waiting customers. Most showed heavy wear, with ripped covers or dog-eared pages. The majority of them were related to flying. Virgil had a suspicion that none of them had been published within the current year. At the far end of the room opposite the door was a desk that sat outside of a windowed, closed-off area that served as an inner office. In contrast to everything else about the room, the top of the desk held a neat assortment of papers stacked to one side on a desk-set pad. On the other side stood a computer. Between them both sat a woman.

"Hello, Margaret."

On hearing her name, the woman looked up from a paper she had been reading. She sat ramrod straight, had piercing blue eyes, not a hair out of place, and a smile that spread a continuous web of wrinkles across her face.

"Virgil." She jumped from her chair, came around the desk, then fell into Virgil's arms. "Oh, my," was all she could muster.

Virgil could feel her thinness through her dress. It had always been that way. He knew he could have lifted her off her feet with one arm. The lightness of a hummingbird. "Eustace!" She shouted "Eustace" in a voice belying both her age and her size.

On the other side of the glass in back of her desk, a man of similar chronology looked up from a desk that was the antithesis of hers. Piles of papers stacked randomly on top, held in place by some invisible cousin of gravity. Only his face showed above the mound nearest to him. With his bald head and smiling eyes, Virgil thought of the moon coming over a mountain. With great effort, he got to his feet, then came stumbling out into the outer room, where Virgil still stood wrapped in the clutches of Margaret.

"Virgil . . . Virgil." Like his wife, it was all he could say. Bent almost in half from a long-ago flying accident, he barely reached above Virgil's waist. Finally, Margaret disentangled them one from the other, then led them through the inner office on to their living quarters.

It was a different world. Margaret's hand showed everywhere. The room was large enough to hold a biplane, which in fact it had, as it was the first hangar built at Sky High almost a hundred years earlier. Margaret and Eustace had converted it to living quarters over sixty years before when they had come to Sky High as newlyweds. At one end of the large, open room was a modern kitchen. A long harvest table separated that from a living area with comfortable furnishings placed strategically about to create an intimate atmosphere. Margaret led Virgil by the hand to one of the groupings. After placing him in a center chair she and Eustace sat on either side of him. A low, octagonal table with a vase full of fresh flowers sat in front of Virgil. He glanced about the room. Nothing had changed. The walls were literally covered with aviation history. He wondered if someday it would all end up in a museum. Photographs of flying Jennys, some with wing walkers, were interspersed with head shots, many of them autographed, showing the likes of Rickenbacker, Earhart, and Jacqueline Cochran, along with a host of other aviators who had challenged the skies as their domain. Some were unknowns or lost in the history of the spectacular achievements of a few others, but were nevertheless important.

"Virgil, why don't you come down more often?" Eustace asked. "It must be over a year."

Virgil immediately felt the weight of guilt, especially since he knew he had not come merely for a social visit, but instead had an ulterior motive.

"I apologize. A weak excuse, but I've had, let's say, an unusually busy year."

Margaret reached over and patted his hand. "We know we're just being selfish, but you are just about all the family we have left."

Virgil knew there was no blood relationship to back up that comment, but something just as strong, maybe even stronger. Aunt Margaret and Uncle Eustace had been in Virgil's life well before he drew his first breath. They, so to speak, came with the furniture that is the flowering of long, intimate relationships. He was probably in his late teens before he figured out that they shared no blood relationship. Margaret was his aunt Clara's closest and dearest friend. When Eustace signed on for a future with her, he eventually introduced Clara to his closest friend, Clyde. Then nature took its course. They had become then and forever his aunt Margaret and uncle Eustace. When Virgil's parents were killed and Clara down in El Paso was so far away, it was Margaret who moved into the house and helped Virgil with all of the arrangements. It was Eustace who suggested Virgil to other members of the town council as the likely candidate to take over the job as sheriff, replacing his father in that role. Truth be told, it was easier convincing them than it was Virgil, who had set his sights on parts unknown and new adventures that had little to do with the sleepy outpost of Hayward in the Southwest. This coming on the heels of his own personal tragedy in the loss of Rusty, for whom he would have stayed in Hayward until the last tooth fell out of his head. Once she was lost to him, so also, he thought, was Hayward. He was ready to pack his bags. Eustace somehow held sway. Convinced him to take the job for a year, catch his breath after the devastation of two personal tragedies. It was good advice. All these years later, it was impossible, sitting in a room with these two, not to wonder how he got here or what his life would have been if he had not listened to Uncle Eustace.

"How's Clara?" Margaret said, interrupting his fleeting reverie. "She told me you spent some time with her after you got out of the hospital."

"Good. She's good."

"Still making her special lemonade?"

"Oh, yeah. Maybe more potent than ever."

"Good for her," Eustace said. "Always look forward to our visits down there. Margaret gets mad at me when I try to duplicate her recipe."

"That's because he never knows when to stop pouring the tequila. The last batch he made had me seeing double for a couple of hours."

"That's just because you forgot to put on your glasses."

Virgil smiled at the light banter. "Anyhow, I've got to fess up to an ulterior motive for this visit."

Margaret and Eustace leaned forward a little.

"I need to talk to the guy who runs the helicopter service."

"That's no problem," Eustace said. "They're both out in one of the hangars now."

"Both?"

"Well, they're brothers. Nice fellas. Jake and Cory Lassiter. One of them is always on call, but they work on maintenance together when they have downtime. That's why they are both here today. C'mon, Virgil. I'll walk you over, introduce you." Eustace got up from his chair. Virgil did the same.

"When you boys come back lunch will be sitting on the table waiting for you."

While Eustace and Virgil walked toward the hangar, Eustace told Virgil how pleased he and Margaret were with the success of the helicopter operation.

"Guess this is the good fallout from growth," Eustace said. "These boys are pretty busy. Beside the contract with Hayward Memorial and a couple of other clients, they do private flights, even sightseers. Don't mind telling you, Virgil, they came along at just the right time for Sky High. Margaret and I were wondering if we could stay afloat with just the private planes that stay here. Matter of fact, down the line maybe Hayward ought to consider an arrangement with them as a supplement to EMT services and other policing. Those birds can cover a lot of ground faster than cruisers or horseback. They can also get to country that you can only get to on mule or horse. Look how they got Charlie Thompson out."

"No argument, Eustace. Anything that helps. They saved Charlie's life."

Virgil stayed longer with Margaret and Eustace than he had planned. That was initially the result of his guilt, but in the final analysis it was because he plain just enjoyed their company. He loved their stories. There was always a new one. He belly laughed for the first time in a long time when Eustace told the story of the lady wing walker who went up on a brutally hot day dressed in shorts and a halter. She became the victim of a sudden drop in altitude and some unpredictable air currents. As the pilot did the last loop, she lost her halter. Needless to say, for the male audience, she became the hit of the afternoon. Eustace said that for years after, whenever it was announced that act was performing, they always had sellout crowds. Margaret insisted that the wardrobe misstep was no accident.

Virgil decided to bypass Hayward when he left Sky High and take a different route to the ranch. He didn't want to go to Velma's wake in his uniform. It wasn't as late as it looked. The sky showed leaden and gray. There was a distinctive bite to the air. Mile after mile of desert sameness had a kind of numbing effect. The occasional vehicle, the only thing to break up the monotony. One flew by in the opposite direction at least twenty-five miles over the limit. Virgil just wasn't in the mood. Out here, speed wasn't much of an issue. If a driver went off the road on either side, the biggest obstacle in his path might be a barrel cactus. The terrain was flat and endless. Rarely was anyone seriously hurt from one of these incidents. Usually the biggest complaint from a driver if they had a blowout or got mired in loose sand was that cell phone service was at best spotty. The country was so remote that they could wait an hour or more, depending on the time of day, for a car to come along. For Virgil, it was the perfect ride to reflect on what the Lassiter brothers had told him.

Each of them had made multiple trips in the last few weeks to the high plateau that bordered the reservation and High Lonesome ranch. Their clients in all instances had been less than talkative. The one exception was the woman who seemed enthused by the landscape and happy, as she put it, "to be out in the field." Cory Lassiter, the older brother, said she hadn't returned on either of the last two flights. He said when he inquired of the men, they said she had decided to remain behind and would be hiking out. He thought that more than a little strange, but was quickly rebuffed when he tried to inquire further.

Jake, the younger brother, told Virgil that on one of the earlier flights in, before the flight to bring Charlie Thompson out, he had dropped off another man. He had gone in two days before he got the call for Charlie and brought the man out. He saw no sign of the woman. The man was gruff and uncommunicative. His gear, Jake was sure, included a case for a high-powered rifle.

29

Marian stood looking down on the unsmiling face of her mother. A face she didn't recognize without that smile. Too late, she wished she had opted for a closed casket. This was not the image of her mother she wanted to remember. The viewing had just begun. She looked around the room for Mr. Simpson, wondering for an instant if it was too late to act on her initial response, then silently acquiesced when she saw no sign of him. They had always been close, she and her mother, living in a male-dominated environment. The irony was that Marian thrived on High Lonesome. From day one, she had always been thrilled to be part of it all. She wasn't interested in dolls or fancy clothes and makeup. She was one of those storied ranch kids who learned to ride almost before she could walk. Way earlier than either of her brothers. She was caught in a stereotypical dilemma. No matter how many times she impressed her father with her natural physical skills or accomplishments, whether it was roping a steer or gentling a broncy colt, she couldn't break out of the mold. Her father loved her, but the boys were the heirs apparent. It was her mother who brought that reality home to her time and time again, beginning when she was no more than four or five. She asked Marian one day what she would like to be when she grew up.

Marian responded, "A boy."

"Well, that ain't likely to happen, honey, especially on High Lonesome."

Nevertheless, Marian kept trying, waiting for that day when her father would recognize what she had to offer. Now, almost forty years later, she was still waiting.

She looked about the room as more people started to file in, recognizing most, noting how some were beginning to show the wear and tear of life. Standing at her mother's side, she greeted the first few, wondering where her brothers had got to, hoping she wouldn't have to play the role of sole mourner. After three or four old family friends passed by, she looked up into the smiling faces of her son and daughter. For the first time that night, she cried.

Virgil stepped out onto the porch to be greeted by the screech of an owl, probably on the hunt for his evening meal. He spent so much time in his uniform that he felt almost unfinished without a sidearm at his waist.

"Well, it's either a wedding or a wake. I'm guessing a wake." Virgil hadn't seen Cesar sitting in the dark.

"Little cold to be sitting out here, isn't it? I was thinking the other day that it was time to move this outdoor furniture to the barn. Anyhow, it's Velma tonight, in answer to your comment."

"I figured it was most likely. Thought I'd ride along with

you. Nice people, the Thompsons. Manuel always tells me how sad it will be for him if he has to leave the ranch."

"Well, maybe he won't have to worry about that no more. Marian tells me she's staying on. Wants to help her father breathe new life into the place when he gets back on his feet."

"*Bueno, bueno.* Manuel always said she never should have left. The boys couldn't hold a candle alongside her, but her father never saw it."

"Yeah, that's pretty much what she told me. Charlie was fairly typical of his generation. Guess I was lucky to be born the right sex."

"Wouldn't have mattered either way in your case. Your mother was the ramrod here and your father knew it. Sam might have been the top dog in town, but not on this place."

Virgil couldn't remember the last time Cesar had called his father by his first name.

"Those boys of Charlie's . . ."

Cesar never finished. Virgil knew Cesar well enough to read between the lines.

"Anyway, let's get going before I freeze to this chair." Cesar got to his feet. "Guess we won't be sitting out here until sometime next spring."

Virgil remembered the leaden sky he had driven home under from Sky High.

"Maybe when we put these chairs away, we ought to bring back a couple of snow shovels."

Simpson's was fairly typical of most funeral homes, particularly in small towns. It stood out like a sore thumb—all white with that almost-colonial look that went with nothing else on the street. It didn't need the sign out front. No one would have taken it for anything other than what it was. Virgil was happy to see the parking lot full. Velma deserved a good send-off. One of the Simpsons was the greeter at the door.

"Evening, Sheriff."

He ignored Cesar. Virgil just nodded.

"Still invisible to a lot of folks," Cesar said as they stepped inside.

"Invisible isn't always a bad thing," Virgil said.

They joined the line to the casket. When they got to the front Marian greeted them both warmly, then introduced each of them to her children. Virgil took one look at the boy and the girl and knew Marian and her late husband had done a good job. Each of them stood on either side of Marian, holding on to her hand. Virgil and Cesar joined Manuel, who was sitting in the back of the room. There was hardly anyone who came through the door that either of them didn't recognize. In some cases, Virgil was sure he knew more about them than they would have liked, but that again was life in a relatively small town when you had been the sheriff for almost fifteen years.

"Well, Virgil, guess you've been busy lately." Mayor Bob "Ears" Jamison had just sat down next to him.

"Little bit, Bob." Virgil had caught himself just in time, although Bob didn't really mind the nickname, as he had told Virgil more than once.

"Velma didn't deserve this," Bob said.

"Few people do," Virgil said. "The ones that do—well, let's just say I'm looking for them."

"Any luck with that? What about that unidentified girl that's been lying on a slab in the morgue for almost two weeks? Anything there?"

"Not sure. Let's just say I'm plodding along. It's kind of like a puzzle. Think I've got some of the pieces."

Virgil sat for a while with Bob, spending most of the time lobbying for a new deputy. He told him about Simon Levine. After a few minutes Virgil got to his feet.

"Let me see what I can do, Virgil. You know Lester has been asking if we could find something for his nephew Elroy."

"Well, don't point him in my direction, Bob. That kid has been in my care three times. He's mean down to the bone and a bully to boot. He's about the last person in Hayward I'd hand a gun to."

"Lester says he's changed."

"Yeah, well, if he stays out of jail for six months maybe you can get him a job down at the town dump collecting tickets from folks who are dropping off their garbage."

"Okay, okay, Virgil. Like I said, I'll see what I can do. One hand, that's rough. Would kinda like to give him a shot if you think he could handle it. Excuse the pun."

"Thanks, Bob. I'd like to move on it. Really need more personnel. I'll try to avoid siccing Rosie on you."

"Speak of the devil." Virgil saw Rosie walking toward them.

"I won't tell her you said that." Bob got up to stand alongside Virgil.

"Hey, Rosita, thought you'd be here sooner," Virgil said.

Rosie nodded, then came close to Virgil and whispered in his ear. Cesar noticed Virgil stiffen slightly, his teeth clench. Then Virgil turned to Cesar.

"Listen, can you get a ride back to the ranch? Got something that needs my attention."

"No problem. Might even stay in town tonight. Go out first thing in the morning."

"Good," Virgil said. Then he excused himself from the group to walk to where Marian was standing.

"Virgil." He had placed his hand on her arm.

"Marian, I've got to leave."

"Oh, I understand. I'll be fine, especially now." She glanced at her son and daughter, who were introducing themselves to people who had just reached the casket.

"No, it's not that."

"What is it, Virgil?" She could see the concern in his eyes. "My father—something with my father?"

"No, no. I hate to tell you this. Here. At this time. It's your brother Vernon. He was found in his vehicle outside of town. Looks like an accident. He's dead, Marian. I'm sorry, he's dead. No easy way to tell you this."

She sunk into a nearby chair. Virgil felt like he had just sucked the oxygen out of the room.

"I don't get it," Virgil said as he stood by the side of the road looking down the embankment. "What caused him to go clear across the road from the opposite side? It makes no sense. It's a straightaway. Not even a dip or a turn in the road."

"That's what I was wondering, too," Jimmy said. "Another ten feet, he would have been in the river. Then we might never have found him. River's pretty deep here."

"How did you even spot him? I mean, it's really dark, not even a trace of a moon."

"His one headlight wasn't broken, but twisted out of its mounting. It's so dark along this stretch that I had to stop when I saw a light shooting up into the sky from down below. At first I thought somebody was doing some night fishing from a boat on the river, but I thought that would be pretty odd. Too cold to be out on the river at night this time of the year. Actually, in daylight I probably wouldn't have noticed the light. By tomorrow night that battery would most likely be done, the light gone. He would have been down there a long time before anyone would have spotted him. There's a lot of underbrush so it would have been from the river—not likely the road. Like I said, there's not much traffic out there."

"Think you're probably right about that, Jimmy. Must have been tricky getting down there."

"Surely was."

Jimmy turned around. In the glare of the headlights, Virgil could see Jimmy's rear end was covered in dirt and his pants ripped in multiple places.

"Looks like the county is going to have to spring for a new uniform."

"Yeah, well, I didn't have much choice about going down there. Figured I'd find what I found, but I had to be sure. Felt bad, but I think he was dead on impact. Felt worse when I realized who it was. That family has been taking some hits lately."

Virgil took note of the slump in Jimmy's shoulders.

"You did your best, Jimmy. Couldn't have done more. I wouldn't have done anything different." Virgil saw a look in Jimmy's eyes that caused him to ask, "Something else, Jimmy?"

"No."

"C'mon, what is it?" Virgil prodded.

Jimmy looked down the ravine before responding. "I was just thinking. It was kind of what happened to me, but I survived. Guess there's just no figuring."

"Don't dwell on that, Jimmy. Life is too random. Accept that and move on."

"Yeah, I guess."

While they were talking the EMTs pulled up in the ambulance. Virgil went to speak to them. He gave them an assessment of the situation, then returned to where Jimmy was standing.

"You're sure he was dead, Jimmy?"

"No doubt, Sheriff." The tone of voice said it all. Virgil went back to the EMTs, then returned.

"They're going to wait until the tow truck hauls the car up. Since there's no rescue, they say it's too dangerous going down there in the dark. Why don't you head back to the office? I'll stay here until everything is done."

"I don't mind, Virgil."

"I know you don't, but you've done more than enough. Go back, get cleaned up, then go home."

"Okay," Jimmy said.

He turned and started walking toward his vehicle. His walk told Virgil it was more than just fatigue he saw.

"Jimmy!" he shouted after him as Jimmy stood by the opened door of the cruiser. "You did all you could do. It was his time."

After Jimmy left, Virgil went to his car and got a flashlight. He spent the next few minutes walking the stretch of road leading to where the car went over the embankment. He did this a couple of times, stopping finally when the tow truck showed up.

"What are you looking for, Sheriff?" Toby Sweets asked as he exited the cab.

"Toby, I'm looking for a reason why that car down by the river with a dead man inside ended up there. So far, I've got nothing."

30

Charlie Thompson wasn't a college graduate, but that was only because he had found out early in life what his skill set was. He recalled on more than one occasion his father telling him he was born about a hundred years too late. He was a primitive. His father was right. Never happier than when he was sitting on Jupiter or any of the long string of mounts that had come before him. Born to the life he led, he couldn't have been happier if he had a choice. Velma, Marian, and the two boys had completed his circle. As the years had unfolded, his boys' lack of interest in the ranch brought bitter disappointment.

The cold light of an almost-winter's day was filtering through the window and falling on his hospital bed. Falling on a wide-awake, fully aware Charlie Thompson. He'd been in and out of consciousness for the last two days. It was the pain of broken ribs that had awoken him. He had resisted at first because the lull of the coma had allowed him to exist in the twilight world of non-involvement. In the end, he was as he had always been, a realist.

He had spent too much time as a witness to the natural world to deny participation now. Over the last twenty-four hours, even though he had not engaged, he knew that Marian had been at his side. Only last night was she absent. More ominously, Velma had not been there. That coupled with Marian's absence told him that there could be only one reason for her absence. Although he didn't know how he had come to be in this hospital, he knew where he was. There could be only one reason why Velma was not at his side. It was a reality he accepted, but something he did not want to think about. Beyond that, he also knew there had been no sign of Calvin or Vernon at his bedside. That was no surprise. He held on to his dream of them, what he had hoped for, until it became ashes in his mouth. The realization that High Lonesome would die with him had finally been accepted. Almost two hundred years of sweat and hard work that made up the history of the Thompson family and built High Lonesome would vanish like the dust in a desert windstorm. That realization for him was a pain almost too much to bear. On top of the loss of the woman that shared his life every step of the way. Way beyond the sharp knife pain he felt in his ribs every time he took a breath.

It was a little after seven when Marian came in to his room. To her astonishment he was sitting up in bed.

"Dad! Dad, I can't believe it. When I was here yesterday you—you were still out of it."

"Knew you were here. Just wasn't ready to talk. Knew you weren't here last night. Kept looking for you, but you didn't come. Then I knew you had things to do."

Marian's eyes glistened, a tear ran down one cheek. "Dad, I . . ."

Charlie reached over to where Marian was sitting, then brushed away the tear that was rolling down her cheek. "You don't need to say it. I know. Only one thing could keep your mother away. I figure I've lost more than a few days here. But you're next to me. That makes me feel good. Can't recollect all that's happened. Guess you are going to have to connect some of the dots for me. Want you to take your time."

An aide came into the room to collect his breakfast tray. "You did real good, Mr. Thompson. Ate everything but the tray. The nurse called your doctor, told him how much better you were. He'll be along later this morning." She smiled, then left.

Over the course of the next half hour, Marian told the story of the previous week. Charlie took in every word. He drew in a deep breath when she told him about Velma, gripping the bed rail until his knuckles showed white. He pressed her for additional details only once or twice. After the news about Velma his head sunk a little deeper into his pillow. Marian poured him a glass of water, then held it to his lips. He drank deeply, emptying the glass. She filled it again, placing it on the night table next to his bed.

"You drink it," he said.

She nodded, then did as she was told.

"Too bad there isn't something a bit stronger here. Guess that'll have to wait. A lot to think about, take in," he said.

Marian didn't respond, but sat in silence.

"There's something more, isn't there?"

She nodded in affirmation.

"Let's have it. Let's have it all."

Marian sat up in her chair. "It's Vernon. He was killed last night in a car accident out on River Road. Virgil Dalton had to tell me while I was with Mom."

Charlie glanced about the room, then out the window at the cold sunlight before he spoke. "Guess when it rains, it pours. Poor Vernon. He was lost a long time ago. Hadn't hardly spent any time with your mother in years. Now he's gonna get to spend a lot of time with her."

Neither of them spoke for a while. The silence grew while the light from the window stretched farther into the room. Hospital sounds, the intercom, people walking down the hall, became background noise they hardly heard. At last the spell was broken when Charlie's doctor came into the room.

"Looks like you've made a sharp right turn, Mr. Thompson. Let me have a listen."

He took the stethoscope, adjusted it on his ears, then placed it first on Charlie's chest then on his back. "Take a deep breath."

Charlie did, wincing a little.

"Boy, you old cowboys don't give up easy. I know you're still hurting and you will be because of those ribs for quite a while, so even after you leave here continue to take the pain medication as needed. Couple of days, we'll be ready to chase you out of here."

"Got a different timeline, Doc. Want to say good-bye to my wife and boy. Leaving here today."

"No, Dad, no."

"Marian, I've been hurt worse than this when I didn't make go-round money. Then I signed up for another event. I plan to see your mother one more time, see her buried next to the little one we lost young, while she waits for Vernon to join her."

Marian knew there was no point to arguing.

Charlie's doctor spoke up. "Mr. Thompson, how about this. I know what you want to do and I understand. I'll go along if you promise to come back here after the funeral. Give us another day or two just to be on the safe side."

Charlie, who was never hardheaded for the sake of being hardheaded, agreed.

Virgil Dalton walked into Simpson's funeral home two hours later to be stunned like all the other mourners at the sight of Charlie Thompson standing alongside his wife's casket. Rosita said it best.

"When they were handing out grit that old cowboy got a double helping."

31

In a place like Hayward, if you live there long enough, your passing doesn't go unnoticed. Virgil looked down on the good-sized crowd of people who had come to say good-bye to Velma. He was standing apart up on a knoll at some distance where his own mother and father lay. He didn't hold much with wakes, or funerals, for that matter. It wasn't that he didn't have the courage of his convictions. He just didn't have a lot of convictions. The notion that it all didn't end with a hole in the ground was something he wished he could sign on to, but like he had said to Jimmy the night before, standing out in the dark on River Road, life was just too random. Maybe his attitude was fallout from spending most of his life as a governmental representative of the concept of justice. It was an irony that was not lost on him. In any event, he had long since accepted that he was doomed to go through life always wrestling with the eternal question.

Looking down now on the collection of people starting to

move slowly away from the grave site he thought of something his father said when Virgil first posed the dilemma of him as sheriff reconciling the concept of justice with the injustices in the world, which more often than not seemed to go unchecked and unpunished.

Sam hesitated for a moment. They had pulled up their horses. Sam looked out over the prairie on the bluff where they had paused. Then he turned to answer Virgil. "'Sheriff' is just a label. I don't think of myself as meting out justice. In the old days they called someone like me a peace officer. Yep, that's what I'm doing. Just trying to keep the peace in our little corner of the world."

Virgil thought of that whenever, like now, he found himself getting caught up in those thoughts for which he knew he would never have an answer.

"Guess cemeteries are not the places to come to for answers." He tipped his hat to the marker on which his mother's and father's names were chiseled, then walked down the hill to his car.

"How were things at the cemetery?"

"Pretty quiet, Jimmy, but then they usually are there. What about here?"

"About the same, quiet. There was something I meant to tell you last night."

Virgil could almost hear the wheels turning.

"Sorry, Virgil, I lost it."

"Well, maybe it'll pop up later. I'm heading over to the hospital, then I'll stop back. Maybe it will come to you while I'm gone. That's the way it usually works."

Virgil gave a short wave, then left Jimmy scratching his head.

*   *   *

"Figured I'd be seeing you sometime today." Dr. Arthur R. Kincaid, the coroner, made the comment as Virgil stepped through his office door.

"Yep, we sure have been seeing a lot of one another lately."

"Well, don't be getting your hopes up. We're not buying furniture together. I'm already spoken for."

"Never crossed my mind, Ark. Don't take this too personal, but you ain't exactly my type. But that's a discussion for another day. What have you got for me on Vernon Thompson?"

"Let's take a little walk, Virgil. Been cooped up in here all morning. Need some fresh air."

A couple of minutes later, Virgil found himself back out in the parking lot where he had just parked his cruiser.

"Looks like we're moving into a new season," Ark said. "Cold air feels good for a change. Terry and I plan on getting the kids into the snow for a week or so up in one of those ski resorts north of Santa Fe. Never get much of it down here. When we do it doesn't last long. I was thinking I might even do some skiing again."

"Again?"

"Virgil, you forget. I'm not a native. Grew up in Vermont. I was put on skis about the same time you were put on your first horse."

"You're right. Did forget. Feels like I've known you forever."

Virgil looked at Ark like he was seeing him for the first time. He was on the north side of fifty, but could have passed for much younger. Had hardly any gray hair and all his teeth. Not everyone in his age grouping who Virgil knew could say that.

"You probably feel that way because of Terry. You guys have known each other practically your whole life."

Virgil nodded. He and Terry had lost track of each other. Virgil had left Hayward for school. When he returned, she had gone. She didn't return until Hayward had opened up a regional hospital. She had become a nurse. A couple of years later, she hung up her nurse's uniform when she married Ark, who many thought would never jump the broom. Terry and Rusty had been in school together. She was Rusty's best friend. Virgil remembered how hard she had taken Rusty's loss. Ark had gotten a late start on the marital state, but jumped in with both feet. He and Terry now had three children under ten, the last born on his fiftieth birthday.

"Before we talk about Vernon, Ark, I wanted to tell you something. Something I want you to share with Terry."

"You got my attention, Virgil. Shoot."

"Virginia Hayward is my daughter. Mine and Rusty's. Before it gets out there in the general public, I wanted you to know. She's Rusty's and mine, but I never knew until a few months ago. Tell Terry. She's taken to calling herself Virginia Dalton even though I don't think she's made it legal yet."

Ark didn't say anything right away. A few dead leaves got caught by the wind, eddying around the parking lot in a kind of frenzied dance. An exiting car drove right through them.

"Wow, Virgil. That is news. Not what I was expecting. Never knew Rusty, but felt like I did because Terry talks about her often. Wait until she hears this. Matter of fact, I'm going to make a special trip home for lunch. Terry is going to be thrilled to hear this. She actually said on more than one occasion how she thought it would have been great if you and Rusty had the chance to have a baby. Boy, life sure does take some unexpected turns, doesn't it?"

"Yep, sometimes takes your breath away. Now, what have you got for me on Vernon?"

Ten minutes later, at the tail end of their exchange, Dr. Art Kincaid walked Virgil over to his vehicle.

"I'll have a more definitive analysis when I get those lab reports back, Virgil. Call you when I do, but I don't think they are going to contradict what I just told you. Feel bad for the Thompsons. Seems like they have gotten more than their share lately." Virgil got in the car and rolled down the window.

"Thanks, Ark."

"By the way, Virgil, you know Terry is going to want you to bring Virginia over."

"I figured as much," Virgil said. "I think she would probably enjoy it. Terry could tell her things about Rusty that I didn't know. They were pretty much joined at the hip."

"We'll arrange it. Virgil, you know I've always thought of you as a friend. You know that. Now, well, I just want to say that I'm glad for you, that you have her in your life."

"Thanks, Ark. We'll talk about Vernon."

"Again, feel bad for the Thompsons."

"Yeah. Just wonder if it's over," Virgil said as he rolled up the window and turned the key in the ignition.

"Rosie, what are you doing here? Didn't expect you to come in—Jimmy's here, holding down the fort." Virgil had just come out of the office bathroom.

"Guess I wasn't in the mood for socializing. Dave headed right back down to Redbud after the service. I didn't feel like going to the reception by myself. You didn't go."

"Got too much on my plate. Wanted to see Ark about Vernon. Did Charlie get back to the hospital?"

"That was how I was able to skip the reception. Marian was going to bring him back, but I volunteered. He was pretty beat. I think he was actually happy to get back in that hospital bed. They gave him a shot for pain. Got him settled in the bed. He was asleep in five minutes."

"Good. Would have thought his son would have wanted to do that."

"He's a strange one, that Calvin," Rosita said. "I mean, he hardly said a word to me at the wake or the funeral. Figured he might want to ask me something, you know, about finding Velma or even something about Vernon's accident since I work for the sheriff. Never said a word. Dave said he never liked him. When they were in school he said he used to trash-talk his father and he was always with a tough crowd. Velma hardly ever talked about him. She'd refer to Vernon once in a while. She agonized over his drug use, but she knew he was way beyond her reach by then. I do remember her saying Calvin had more sway over him than anyone. Ever since they were kids. Guess Vernon idolized him. When Calvin took off after college, Vernon did the same. Marian told me she hadn't seen either of them in years."

"Well, I gave our guests lunch." Jimmy had come through the door to the holding area. "Always makes me hungry seeing other people eat."

"C'mon, Jimmy," Rosie said. "You get hungry looking at road-kill."

"There you go. You're always at me 'cause you're going to those meetings all the time."

Rosita winced. "They're about healthy eating. You can't just eat anything you want."

Virgil smiled at the ongoing give-and-take. "You can if you're twenty-five, six feet tall, and dress out at a hundred and sixty pounds. Don't think Jimmy has to go to any Weight Watchers meetings for a long time, Rosie."

"Thanks for the vote of confidence, Virgil. All this talk about food, now I'm hungry."

"Tell you what. I'll amble over to Margie's, get us some lunch. Jimmy, I'll get you and me a couple of shakes, a mess of fries, and some cheeseburgers. Rosie, I'll get you some greens with a light dressing and a bottle of H2O."

Rosie picked up a paperback she'd been reading off and on and chucked it across the room at Virgil. Virgil caught it in midair right over his desk.

"*The Lock Artist,*" Virgil said. "Reading those bondage books again. You and Dave getting kinky with the handcuffs?"

"You ought to try reading, Virgil. Good book for you to start with. Give you some insight into life beyond Hayward."

Virgil stood up, walked over, dropped the book on Rosie's desk, then started for the door. "Enough going on in Hayward right now to take up my free time, keep me busy. Anyhow, be back in a little while with some grub."

"Bring me one of Margie's burgers and one of those shakes, too," Rosie said. "I'll graze on the greens tonight at home since I'm eating alone."

"You got it. A Margie's special coming up."

"That's it."

Virgil and Rosie both turned and looked at Jimmy.

"I remember what it was I wanted to tell you. Virginia and I were eating at Margie's. Margie told us about that lady that got killed on the interstate who is over at Dr. Kincaid's. Said she came in a couple of times a while back. Margie said she was driving a vehicle that said 'Coastal' on the side. It had a picture of a wave underneath the name."

"Coastal," Rosie said. "That name rings a bell." She looked at Jimmy and Virgil. "Coastal." She said the name again. "Velma mentioned a while back one of the boys had some kind of a connection there. Coastal, yes, that was the name. I'm sure of it. By the way, Virgil, what did Doc Kincaid say to you about Vernon?"

"Well, for one thing, he said he never should have been behind the wheel. He said the tox screen will be more definitive, but he said his alcohol content was off the charts and if drugs were factored in, well, he said he probably didn't even know he was driving. Which kind of explains what I found or should say didn't find."

"What was that, Sheriff?" Jimmy asked.

"Well, after you left, I went up and down that piece of road with my flashlight a half a dozen times or so until Toby Sweets showed up with his tow truck. There wasn't so much as a hint of a skid mark. Nothing. Don't think Vernon ever hit the brake, not even once. I think that car was on autopilot when it headed for the river."

"What are you saying, Virgil? You thinking suicide?"

All this time Virgil was standing by the door. He opened it, looking outside into the bright sunlight, mulling over Rosita's question.

"I don't know," Virgil said. "Maybe Vernon had some demons he let out of the jar and he just couldn't put them back in. Maybe he just couldn't deal with them anymore. In any event, think I'm going to have to look into the possibility. Listen, while I'm over at Margie's, see what you can dig up on Coastal. Pretty sure they most likely have a website—everybody does these days."

"Will do, Sheriff," Jimmy said.

"Virgil, when you're looking into that possibility you mentioned, I'm guessing it's going to involve Marian and that old cowboy. Be easy on them. They've been through a lot this last week."

Virgil nodded. "I know they have, Rosie. I also know we all got our demons, but I think it's key that I find out what Vernon's were because they likely were bad enough to get him killed."

32

Virgil was right. There was a website. Coastal, according to what Jimmy and Rosie had learned while he was gone, was a Texas-based company down on the Gulf principally involved in oil and natural gas exploration. Beyond the site description there wasn't much other than the address of the corporate headquarters and some contact numbers. After lunch Virgil decided to put in a call. It was an exercise in frustration until he finally got connected with someone in human resources. Virgil explained the reason for his call, immediately getting what he figured was a typical response to anyone calling in regards to personal information about any company employee.

"I'm very sorry," the somewhat detached voice said. "There are privacy concerns here which I can't possibly abrogate."

Virgil knew immediately this was going to be an uphill battle.

"I fully understand your privacy concerns, but I'm not really looking for personal information. I just really want to find out whether this particular person is one of your employees."

"I'm sorry, even that is protected under privacy law. Beyond that, I have no way of knowing that you are even who you say you are."

"If I could validate my identity, would that help?"

There was a slight hesitancy on the other end. Virgil jumped on it. "Listen, I'm going to explain the whole situation to you. Then I'm going to offer verification of who I am. No commitment on your part."

Over the course of the next few minutes, Virgil acquainted the voice that had become a little less detached with the circumstances that led to an unidentified woman lying on a slab in the basement of Hayward Memorial Hospital for the last couple of weeks. At certain parts of his narrative, Virgil picked up on a veiled emotional reaction. When he had finished, he told the woman on the other end of the phone that he was faxing her verification of who he was along with the photo of the woman in question. He even went so far as to tell her he would Skype her if she thought it necessary. She could then speak to him as he was sitting at his desk in uniform. By the end of the conversation, Janet Turner, who it turned out was an assistant to the head of HR, had become much more compliant. She told Virgil she would look at everything and get back to him promptly. It turned out she was as good as her word.

Virgil had decided it might be a good idea if he headed out to High Lonesome. He put in a call, but got no response. Then he thought maybe Marian was at the hospital. He was about to pursue that possibility when the phone rang.

"Sheriff Dalton, how can I help you?"

"I'm hoping I might be able to help you, Sheriff. This is Janet Turner."

The voice on the other end was much different from the

voice that had responded to his initial inquiry. "To begin with, the woman in the photo is Linda Murchison, home address 155 Skyline Drive, Colorado Springs, Colorado."

Janet Turner went on to explain that Linda Murchison was a geologist who had worked for Coastal on a contract basis from time to time. Approximately ten years earlier, she had been an employee, but then had decided to go out on her own.

"Do you have any record of her working for Coastal in the last year or so?"

"Yes. About a year ago. We had a contract with her, but nothing within the last six months."

"Would you have any idea why she would have been in this area and probably working or, as they say, out in the field?"

There was a momentary hesitation.

"I'm not trying to put you on the spot here, Janet, but if there's anything that you could give me to help me understand why she got killed in our neck of the woods it would be huge. I told you in our earlier conversation that she was killed in a road accident, but it's looking more and more like she was trying to escape from someone whose intent was to kill her."

"Oh, I didn't realize."

A momentary silence followed. "Well, I think I can share this with you because it's generally well known in the industry. There is a lot of speculation that there are significant untapped oil and gas reserves in the Southwest. Kind of like what's been discovered in North Dakota in the last couple of years. Well, as I said, there is a lot of evidence that the same kinds of discoveries are going to be made there. Are you familiar with the expression 'Where there is shale there's oil'? Some companies including ours are making a stab at negotiations with some Native American tribes to explore for oil and gas reserves on reservation lands. If Linda Murchison had a contract with some of these interests, that could explain why she would have been in your area."

"Janet, could you give me a general idea of how this all works? I mean, I don't know anything about the process. I'm way in over my head here."

"Well, as you already know, I'm in human resources, HR. I'm hardly an expert on the technical aspects of what we do, but I guess I could give you a general idea. If you want something more detailed or precise, I could have someone from engineering call you."

"I don't think that will be necessary. Like I said, I'm just trying to get a handle on how she would fit into the overall process."

"Well, she would be part of a team. Before going out in the field, members of the team spend time trying to assess whether or not a particular area looks like it might be worth investigation. From what I gather that means spending a lot of time poring over topographical maps, analyzing information, sharing what they know or suspect with geologists, hydrologists . . . other members of the team, to see if there is a consensus that might suggest further exploration of a region is warranted. If that seems to be the case, then the fieldwork begins. Test samples, core samples from the area, things like that. Then a field survey is written, reporting all their findings. Based on all of these things, a decision is made as to how to proceed. I guess if it's a thumbs-up then offers are made to owners of sites and the lawyers get involved. End result, if everything gels, a calendar for drilling on the site is drawn up and the ball starts rolling. Like I said, I'm not a technician, but I think that's generally the way it works."

"So, Linda Murchison would be part of the team that actually went out into the area to determine whether it was worth going forward?"

"Yes. She wouldn't likely be alone, but she would be integral. Her assessment in the report submitted would be looked at very closely. In her case, even more so, because she has an established track record. That's probably why she went out on her own, working as an independent. The fact that the company continued working with her long after she left suggests to me that she was held in very high regard."

"Thank you, Janet. This has been great. At the very least we've given this poor woman a name. By the way, if you have any next-of-kin information . . . If not, I'm sure I can get something from the local police in Colorado Springs."

"I'll see what we have and I'll send it to you."

"One last thing. Could you tell me if you have or have had a Calvin or Vernon Thompson on your employee list?"

"I'll have to get back to you on that. Particularly if you want me to go beyond current employees."

"Okay, whatever you can do. Again, I really appreciate the cooperation along with the fact that you made a judgment call in my favor. I know that's not so easy in the light of privacy restrictions. Seems everything has gotten a lot more literal these days."

"Absolutely. I'm afraid the genie is out of the bottle in that regard. It's going to be a lot harder to keep private things private from now on. Another fallout of technology. On the other hand the information that you and I just shared would have taken at least a week to get in a less-technological world. Good luck with your investigation, Sheriff. Glad I could help."

Virgil sat back from his desk, mulling over everything he'd just found out. He knew he was a couple of steps behind in terms of new technology. He also knew this was because of the psychological roadblock he'd built in his own mind. Virgil knew the lesson of the dinosaurs.

"Well? Well?" Rosie's voice interrupted his internal dialogue. "What did you find out?"

"Her name is Linda Murchison, from Colorado Springs. That HR person, Janet Turner, said she would try to get more for me, but it might take a little while."

"I'll work on it from this end—see what I can find out," Rosie said.

"What do you mean? I mean, how are you going to find out about her?"

Rosita gave Virgil a strange look. "Duh, Virgil. I'm going to begin by Googling her, then follow up with Facebook or Twitter."

Virgil looked at Rosita without responding. He wondered if the dinosaurs ever had an epiphany like he just had.

33

"Hey, Mom, what are you thinking about? Here, I brought you a cup of tea." Marian's daughter, Holly, set the cup on the table next to Marian, who was sitting in the kitchen.

Virgil was right. Marian had been at the hospital. She had gone there after the reception she had hosted following her mother's funeral. In some way, seeing people she had known all throughout her childhood had made her feel like she had never left Hayward. It was not that in any way she regretted her years away. She'd had a good marriage, a good career, and she only had to look at her son and daughter to know those years away had been a personal success. But each day that passed made her sure of her decision to return.

"Oh, I guess I've been reminiscing. You know, a lot of those people at your grandmother's funeral I hadn't seen in years. It kind of got me to thinking about my past. Growing up here on the ranch, what it was like, how I felt. Now, I guess it's time to be thinking about what comes next."

"Me, too," Holly said. "I've been meaning to tell you I applied for a master's degree program for next year. Just before I came down here, I found out I was accepted. So, I know maybe this is a rough time to tell you, but after I graduate I won't be coming back home."

"Where are you going?" Marian asked. "What school? Where?"

"I'm going to New York. I've been accepted into a master's program at Ithaca College. So not only won't I be going home, but I might as well tell you that Oren told me that after he graduates next year, he's planning on trying to get into law school, so he won't be going back home, either."

Marian took a sip from her cup, then smiled at her daughter. "Well, I guess that makes it unanimous. I won't be going home, either—that is, once I sell the house. After I do that, then I'm coming back here to High Lonesome. I was waiting for the right time to tell both of you. I guess that's now."

"Mom, you don't have to do that. There are agencies. You can hire a caregiver for Granddad."

"No, your grandfather is not going to need a caregiver for a long time. He just needs to get back on his feet. I'm coming back to High Lonesome because I love it here. Being here, this last little while, has convinced me how much. I've always loved it, never wanted to leave. Only did when I saw no future. Now, that's changed, so I'm coming back."

"But I don't understand. What are you going to do here?"

"Well, for openers, I'm going to help that old cowboy in the hospital so the two of us can work to get High Lonesome back to where it used to be. It's what I always wanted to do, but he didn't see me in that role. Only this time I'm going to tell him and I'm not taking no for an answer. So, if you and your brother are looking for a home to come to, this will be it. But be warned, when you come you won't be sitting on your honkers. You might be stacking hay or mucking out stalls, because this is going to be a working outfit again. But it will always be home for you both."

The next morning, Marian was still standing in the driveway after waving good-bye to her children when she saw the cruiser with the dome light coming down the ranch road.

"Virgil, didn't figure to see you today."

"Hope I'm not interrupting your plans."

"No, nothing like that. I was going to hunt up Manuel, go over a few things, then go into Hayward, see how Dad's doing. I'm going to talk to him about the ranch and my plans. What I spoke to you about. Once that's settled, after I get him home and on his feet, I'm going to head up to San Francisco and pack up my other life. Then I'll be back here for good."

"Sounds like you got it all worked out."

"Well, let's just say I'm making a start. But I'm sure you didn't drive all the way out here to hear about my future life."

"No. I wanted to ask you about your brother."

"Which one? Although, like I told you, it's been years. Almost didn't recognize them when they first got out of the car."

"Well, to begin with, Art Kincaid told me that Vernon was pretty much non compos mentis when he went off the River Road the other night. Ark said he probably didn't even realize he was behind the wheel. Drugs and alcohol."

"I'm sorry for Vernon, but he started going down that road a long time ago. Tore the heart out of my folks, but we all make choices. That was his. The only person that maybe could have pushed him in another direction didn't."

"You mean your brother Calvin?"

"Calvin—Cal—could have nipped his weakness in the bud years ago. He didn't even try. He liked the hero worship. More than that I think he liked the total power it gave him over another person. Vernon was his introduction to manipulation. I think he's become a master of it ever since."

"What about Calvin? I mean, you never told me. Was he into the scene like Vernon?"

"You mean drugs? No. Remember, Calvin got an early scare with his diabetes. No, he never went there. But he did like nice things, fast cars, being in the life, as they say. My husband ran into him one time when he was in Las Vegas at a convention. He said everyone at the tables knew him. Dealers, that is. Guess Calvin liked to gamble. I often wondered where he got that kind of money. I suspect my father. Maybe it was his way of trying to lure Calvin back. I don't know. I never asked him. Probably never will. I expect Calvin will drift back into the shadows for another ten years."

"I wonder," Virgil said. "I wonder."

"What do you mean, Virgil?"

"Nothing, nothing. Just trying to connect some dots. Do you know where Calvin's at? I never got to really meet him or even offer condolences."

"Sorry, can't help you there. Maybe you can catch up with him tomorrow. The medical examiner said we could get Vernon in the morning. There's just going to be a small service, followed by the burial. Calvin said he'd take care of it. I know nothing about Vernon's immediate past life. All I had to notify him about Mom was a cell phone number. I don't even have an address for him. Calvin said he'd take care of whatever Vernon left behind, which I imagine isn't much. Calvin ought to be at

Simpson's tomorrow. After that I don't know. We really haven't had much time together or any significant interaction, for that matter."

"Okay, I'll see you in the morning."

Virgil tipped his hat, got in his vehicle, and left Marian standing in the driveway. She watched till the dust from his car rose and dissipated in the morning air. Then she turned and walked toward the barns.

Virgil had been gone about an hour. Marian had spent most of that time with Manuel, going over a schedule of sorts covering the next few days. She was particularly concerned with the time when she would be in San Francisco. Her father would be at the ranch on his own. Manuel said he would arrange to have his wife or one of his daughters stay at the house in Marian's absence.

"Don't worry about *su padre*," Manuel said.

Marian looked into the dark eyes set in the smiling face. "I don't know what we would do without you, Manuel. When I return to High Lonesome, I won't be leaving again. This is going to be my home. With your help we are going to work to bring this place back to what it once was." Marian saw the smile on Manuel's face grow.

"You stay? You going to live here with Señor Charlie?"

"That's right. I'm going into town to tell him that today. I'm telling you first because I want you to know how much I appreciate what you've done. I also want you to know you will have a place here for a long time to come."

"*Bueno, bueno.*" His joy was so obvious, it spread like a contagion to Marian.

"I'm thinking to hire some of the hands back. You'll handle that, of course, since you will be foreman."

Manuel's eyes lit up. In all his years on High Lonesome there had never been anything but an informal understanding of his role because Charlie had always been such a hands-on boss.

"I want you to be thinking about my plans for the ranch. I thought over the winter we'd get everything in working order—barns, fencing, anything that needs maintenance. Sometime during this time if the weather cooperates, I want to get back into the high country. Dad was right, there was some stock up there that was missed. The sheriff and I saw four or five cows with calves. I want to round them up, see what we got. Bring them down here, put them in with those Red Angus Dad held on to, so we won't lose any if it's a tough winter. Then in the spring we'll sort them all out. See what we want to keep, to start to rebuild the herd. Then maybe make a couple of trips down to Redbud to see what Luther's got for auction. I've got some other ideas I want to run by Dad, but I want your input all along the way."

"That is a good plan, but it will not be easy if there's cattle up there on that mesa catching them up. They by now mostly wild."

"That's why I need you to line up some good wranglers. I know it's going to be a little crazy, but it'll be fun. I'm already looking forward to it."

"You going up to that High Lonesome country yourself?"

"You bet I am. That's the other thing I want you to do for me. Pick out one or two good colts to work with when I return. Need to get my riding to where it used to be."

"This is good," Manuel said. "Gonna be like old days."

"No," Marian said. "It's going to be better."

Charlie Thompson was sitting in a chair by his bed, not watching the television even though it was on, when Marian came through the door.

"Hey, Dad."

Her smile was the first bright spot in his day. He had spent most of his morning considering his options. Though not one given to self-pity and pretty much intolerant of it in anyone else, he could not escape the notion that looking down the dark tunnel of what he saw as his future, he wondered if he wouldn't have been better off if that shooter up on the ridge had taken better aim. Always the realist, he knew time was catching up with him. Maybe his days of bulldogging a steer were long gone, but he could still sit a saddle, round up cattle, even clean out a stall, maybe not his favorite thing to do. But all this was slipping away from him. Sitting in that chair by the window with the nonsensical chatter from some talk show in the background, reveling in the gaffes of some so-called celebrity whom he didn't know or care to know, he knew he should accept his new reality, but he sure as hell didn't want to.

"What's the matter, Dad? You're looking kinda glum."

"There's a word you don't hear much anymore, 'glum.' Yeah, I reckon it fits. Guess when you see what you've spent your whole life doing coming to an end that can bring you down. Bit by bit, people, then parts of your life start to drift away. Guess I just wasn't ready, didn't see it coming. Then, of course, there's life's little ironies. You know I always hoped High Lonesome would be there for generations yet to come. While they were coming along, I hoped your brothers would take hold. That never happened. Now, your mother's gone along with one of your brothers and Cal shows up here this morning, says he wants to take High Lonesome off my hands. Says he has backers who'll buy it on speculation, then I can move to town. As he put it, sit on the front porch, put my feet up. Guess what he means is I sit there watching sunsets till I run out of them. That's not exactly what I had in mind for my last days."

Charlie slumped down in his chair, let out a sigh, then turned his face to look out the window. Marian grabbed the remote, clicking off the television.

"So Calvin's going to offer you a retirement package. Dad, you should have told him to stick it."

34

Virgil left the office as soon as Jimmy came in. Simon Levine had stopped by and was talking with Rosie when Virgil had returned from High Lonesome ranch. Simon wanted to know if Virgil had any word about the probability of him becoming a member of law enforcement in Hayward. Since Virgil knew the town council had their weekly meeting the night before, while Simon was sitting in front of him he put in a call to Mayor Bob Jamison.

"Mayor's office."

"Is he there, Hilda?"

"No, Virgil. You can probably reach him on his cell."

"I'm sure you can help me out. Everyone knows that secretaries are the real powers behind the throne. No doubt you've already typed up the minutes of last night's meeting. I want to know what happened about my request for a new deputy."

"Damn you, Virgil. I shouldn't even be talking to you. I am so . . . so pissed."

"Hilda, that you or has some evil twin taken over your body? Never heard you cuss before."

"You want to know if you can tell that Simon, Simon Levinson, whether or not he's got a job."

"Levine, Hilda. Simon Levine."

"Whatever. I'm so mad, if I could reach through this phone and grab you by the throat, I would in a heartbeat."

"Hilda, what did I do?"

"I'll tell you. You got your new deputy—Simon, Simon Levine or whatever his name is. You want to know what I got in this trade? I got Lester Smoot's nearsighted nephew as my assistant. Just what I need, some hormonal kid looking down my dress every time I bend over. You know Lester's had a hard-on for you ever since that night when Dif popped him in your office. Don't get me wrong. I think Dif should've got a medal for that. But no, he didn't and I got Elroy. That was the bargain so you could get your new deputy. You owe me big-time, Virgil."

"Thanks, Hilda, for the info along with keeping one of Lester's kin out of my office. A hard-on, pissed off. I didn't even know you knew about such things, Hilda." A low laugh followed Virgil's comment.

"I wasn't raised in a bubble, Virgil. Grew up on a farm like most everyone else around here. Remember, you owe me."

"Point taken. Thank you, Hilda."

Virgil hung up the phone. "Looks like you're going to be taking up residence in Hayward, Simon. You can tell Chet he's going to get his couch back as soon as you get a place of your own."

"Thank you, Sheriff. I really appreciate the opportunity. Hope I don't disappoint you."

"Don't worry—if you do I'll just take you out in the desert and shoot you."

Virgil smiled, then got up from his desk. He walked Simon to the door, then stood there watching him drive off. Virgil walked back into his office, collapsing into his chair.

"That's a good thing you did, Virgil," Rosie said. "I like him. We had a long talk before you came in. On the other hand, guess Hilda ain't going to be leading a parade down Main Street in your honor anytime soon."

"No, not likely. Remind me to stop by Kleman's and send some flowers over to Hilda."

"Forget the flowers, she ain't the type. A bottle of hooch takes the edge off quicker. Hilda likes vodka."

Virgil nodded, then stood up. "I'm beat. Heading home. Feel like I haven't spent any time there lately. Need a break. Jimmy's coming in now so you'll have company." Virgil waved as he opened the door for Jimmy, then left.

It was not just an idle comment. Virgil felt like he hadn't spent any time at home lately. During the last couple of weeks, it seemed like just a place to hang his hat, get some shut-eye, and change his clothes. He missed being there. Something about the rhythm of life that recharged his batteries.

Ark had been right. The weather had definitely made a right turn. The sun was setting earlier. Any wind that blew from the north packed more of a punch. He rolled his car window almost all the way up. Glancing at the dashboard, he saw the outside temperature was hovering around fifty. A little cool for the first week of December in this part of the Southwest. Ark was also correct about the snow. If and when they got any, unless it was above four thousand feet, it generally wasn't substantial. Usually it was gone in a couple of hours. Virgil actually liked snow. Maybe because it was a rare occurrence, but he liked how it transformed the world so quickly. All the sharp edges became blunted, softer. It became an impressionist painting.

He pulled into the driveway. The car rolled to a stop by the corral. He stepped out. Everything was quiet. He held his breath for a moment, joining the conspiracy of silence. No movement. Not a breeze or a leaf that clung stubbornly to a branch stirred. He could see horses in the distance, unmoving dots on the far hills. Time stood still. He breathed deeply, letting the quiet wash over him like a wave. It was what he needed. For a long time he stood there, reluctant to let time move on. At last he turned away. Then started for the house.

Fifteen minutes later, he was back outside in work clothes. He went through the barn methodically doing the daily chores that were saved for the end of the day. He knew Cesar would appreciate his efforts. The barns were still infused with new-wood smell from their recent construction. Mixed with the perfume of horse manure, leather, and hay it was not unpleasant. Only the evidence of age and past memories were missing but Virgil knew that to move forward you had to leave some things behind.

He didn't even realize he had broken a sweat until he got to the end of his work, then stepped outside into the chilled air. On his way to the house, he noticed a wood pile off to one side, which had grown in his absence, so he turned, then went back to the barn. A few minutes later, the rhythmic sound of logs being split broke the silence. Virgil stayed with the task for almost an hour. When at last he drove the ax into the heart of a large log to keep its edge, he stepped back, rewarded with close to a quarter of a cord of wood piled in a heap. He knew that the mound would continue to grow through Cesar's or Pedro's or José's efforts. The rest would fall victim to a mechanical log splitter. It didn't matter to Virgil. He was rewarded beyond that with an ache between his shoulders, along with sweat running freely from his pores. He felt good.

After he showered and changed he came downstairs, went into the kitchen, and took inventory of the refrigerator. He saw a freshly dismembered chicken, washed, plucked, and sitting on a plate. He did not dwell on the fact that the chicken population in the barn had been reduced by one. By the time Cesar came through the door a half hour later, the hapless fowl was frying in a pan.

"Looks like I'm done for the day. Somebody did my barn chores for me. They even split some wood. Must be that their life has become easier or it's a product of guilt."

"You're getting a little too profound for me. I guess when you get old, you just can't be thankful, you got to look for some kind of sinister motivation. A good deed can't just be a good deed."

"Who's getting profound now?" Cesar said.

"Just set the table and get a couple of cold ones."

"Yes, boss. Anything you say. By the way, if you want me to rub some horse liniment on your shoulders later . . . You know it's been a long time since you swung an ax."

"Keep it up, old man, and you'll end up like this chicken."

After dinner, Virgil took a walk outside to check on the horses. Jack whinnied when he stepped off the porch in greeting. Virgil went to him.

"Nice to be recognized," he said. Virgil ran his hand across Jack's neck, taking note of his thickening coat. "Guess you know winter's definitely coming. Putting on a winter layer already."

He stayed with Jack while the night shadows stretched

across the land. Cesar waved to him as he went toward his quarters in the adjacent barn. Then Virgil headed toward the well-lit house. A little while later he settled into a chair in front of the television. Before he turned it on, he punched a number into the phone. It rang and rang on the other end until a message prompt came on.

"Hey, Virginia, I've been pretty busy. Just wanted you to know, well, I've been thinking about you. Oh, it's Virgil."

He hung up the phone with that awkward feeling he had felt before whenever technology got in his way.

There wasn't much on the television that held his interest once he got past the latest global crisis. None of the so-called reality shows held his attention. He tried watching a guy who presented himself as some kind of survivalist making it in the wilderness with bare essentials. Virgil stayed with it until he showed viewers how to build a debris shelter where he was going to spend the night. This stretched the limits of Virgil's belief. He couldn't get past the notion that the entire experience was being filmed in this "wilderness" by a camera crew who were in all likelihood going to bunk down in some three-star motel in the nearest town. Virgil had an even harder time, when they turned off the camera getting ready to leave, accepting the notion that the survivalist wasn't going to crawl out of his superbly constructed shelter and head out with them for the adjoining room, a hot shower, and maybe even some room service.

The chicken had been good enough that after a couple of hours of uninspiring television he was curious enough to go see if there was anything left of it. Cesar had cleaned up after they ate. His disappointment was complete when all he could come up with was a leg that didn't offer much more than two mouthfuls. He started prowling the cabinets, looking for something to fill that empty space in the pit of his stomach, when he heard a knock at the door. Glancing out the window he saw the headlights of a car blink off. He wasn't in the mood for more policing tonight so he went to the door less than hopeful. His relief was apparent when he opened it and saw Virginia standing there.

"Sorry, if it's too late, but when I got in my car down in Redbud I heard your message. So when I was driving by I thought, why not stop."

"Glad you did. Come on in. Afraid it was going to be another late-night incident that I'd have to deal with."

"Do you get a lot of those?" she asked as she came into the kitchen.

"A lot more than I used to. Hayward's changing. I'm sure that's not news to you. Anyone that's been away for any length of time, like you at college, sees it more than anyone who is here every day."

"You're right. They even put in a traffic light down at that intersection by that motel they built in Redbud."

"Guess that's progress," Virgil said. "Anyway, I worked up more than my usual appetite doing a little work around here when I came home. I was trying to scare up a snack. Will you join me?"

"I could eat. Why don't you sit down and I'll see what I can come up with. You can get the beer."

"You got a deal," Virgil said. "That's the easy part."

Ten minutes later they were sitting on either side of a plate filled with crackers topped with cheese, olives, and sprinkled lightly with salt and pepper.

"That's a lot more inviting than anything I'd have come up with. Looks a lot nicer, too."

"A lot of chefs say the presentation is as important as the food itself."

"Well, I don't know about that," Virgil said. "Guess I've always started and ended with my appetite. Don't know if looking at something that looks good is going to satisfy me as much as eating it."

"I can't say I disagree," she said as she popped a fully loaded cracker into her mouth. "I like to eat."

Virgil smiled, watching her.

"So did your mother," he said. "She could eat two-thirds of a pizza after a movie, but it never showed. She was also willing to try anything. I remember her bringing me to this place that had just started serving Hawaiian pizza. I just couldn't wrap my head around the concept of pineapple on pizza, but she dove right in. That's the way she was with everything." Virgil averted his eyes, looking at the clock on the wall, but not really seeing the time. Virginia reached across the table, covering his hand with her own.

"Thanks for telling me that. I'd like to hear more about my mother from you." For the next hour while they cleaned the plate and sipped their beer Virgil talked. Virginia hung on every word.

"So you never said what you were doing down in Redbud."

"Oh, I've been working there since the pecan harvest. It's a busy time. The start of a new year."

"How's everything going? I mean with the business."

"Good. Caleb and Uncle Micah are working a lot more together. They're talking about more expansion, maybe getting into retail. I suggested maybe starting off with mail order. The harvest was better than expected this year."

"Is that something you would be interested in?" Virgil asked. "I mean, careerwise?"

"I'm not sure. Remember, I'm going back after Christmas

for one more semester. Guess it's time to start thinking about my future. Don't forget your promise. We're going to spend some time together around Christmas."

"Looking forward to it. By the way, I'd like you to meet your mother's best friend. She's married to Doc Kincaid. A real nice lady. I told Doc about you. About us. He said she's going to want to meet you."

Virginia had stood up from the table, then grabbed her jacket, which was hanging on the back of a chair. Virgil stood also. Then they both started for the door.

The air was much colder. They stood together on the porch, their breath rising into the night.

"I'd like to meet Mom's friend. How did you tell Dr. Kincaid?"

"What do you mean?" Virgil asked. "I just said you were my daughter."

Virginia smiled, looking at Virgil. "That's a coincidence. When I was in the office today, one of the drivers came in and we were talking for a while. Then he asked me my last name. I told him Dalton. Then he said that's the same name as the sheriff. I told him that was right because the sheriff is my dad."

She reached up, gave Virgil a kiss, then ran down the steps to her car, disappearing into the night. Virgil stood there a long time looking after her. He had never been called Dad before.

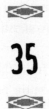

35

Virgil knew there had been a change before his eyes were half open. It could happen like that in these parts. It sounded like someone throwing pebbles against the window. He remembered how cold it had been the night before when he and Virginia were standing on the porch. He didn't recall seeing the moon or any stars, but beyond the cold, the recollection of other things warmed him. There were going to be a lot of stops along the way today he knew, but before he made any of them he began with a call. The phone rang only once before it was picked up.

"Reservation police, Sandra Redfern. How can I help you?"

"Sandra, Virgil Dalton here. Has Billy come in yet?"

"No, no, Virgil. That's why I'm here early. He wanted to go check on your grandfather first, before he started his day."

"Why, what's up?"

"Well, since he had the fall, Billy's been going there each morning to make sure he's set up for the day. Mrs. Hoya isn't coming back until tomorrow."

Virgil didn't want to advertise his lack of knowledge or neglect. "Okay, Sandra, thanks. I'll probably catch up with him there."

Virgil knew when he hung up the phone that another stop was added to his list. He jumped into the shower, then dressed in record time. Downstairs, he wolfed down an English muffin and a glass of juice, pausing only over a hot cup of coffee. He would have liked to sit over a second one to jump-start his engine, but knew that would have to wait. When he stepped outside onto the porch, the day effectively did what the second cup of coffee would have. A blast of the coldest air he'd felt since the previous winter hit him in the face, shaking him into full consciousness. When he reached the last of the five steps that led to the path, he almost took a header. Only his quick grab on the side rail kept him from going down. As he looked around he realized that a glaze of ice coated the landscape. He made his way a bit more carefully to his cruiser. When he got in he had to hit the defrost button, something that he hadn't done in a long time. The icy rain that had been pelting his window had stopped, but had left its residue. Within a couple of minutes the windshield wipers had cleared the last of the icy remnants from his field of vision. A little over a half hour later he had busted through Hayward, almost reaching his grandfather's turnoff. The roads down had been a little slick, but he knew that the ground still held on to its heat, so he didn't hesitate when he reached the road up to the mesa. Billy's car was still there, parked to the left of the double-wide. When he stepped inside the trailer, the two of them, Billy Three Hats and his grandfather, were sitting at the kitchen table drinking coffee.

"Virgil, what a nice surprise," his grandfather said.

"Not like the one I got this morning when I called Billy's office. What happened to you and why didn't you tell me?"

"I didn't want you to worry. It was just a little fall."

"Not so little. He tore a bunch of ligaments in his ankle when he fell climbing down off the tableland driving the sheep. He's lucky he didn't break it."

As Billy spoke, the old man glared at him.

"Just for the record, recall what you told me last summer, when I had the aneurysm. Well, that's a two-way street. It's my job to worry about you just as it's yours to worry about me."

"You're right, Virgil. I'm sorry, but I'm getting along fine now. Billy or one of his sons has been stopping by. Mrs. Hoya will be back from visiting her sister tomorrow. She will take care of me."

"Isn't it about time for you to stop calling her Mrs. Hoya?"

Grandfather gave a little wink. "I call her other names, but not when my relatives are around."

"Okay, I'm not going there," Virgil said.

"Sit, have some coffee. It is fresh. Billy made it right before you came."

Virgil went over to the cabinet above the sink, got a mug out, then filled it. "I'm sorry I haven't been up here sooner."

"We know you've been busy. Heard about Charlie and his wife," Billy said.

Virgil shook his head, then took a drink and set the mug down on the table. "Yeah, ain't had a lot of free time lately. Remember, Billy, when we used to watch late-night Saturdays, years ago? If it ain't one thing, it's another, like Roseannadanna said."

Billy laughed out loud at the reference. "Truer words were never spoken," he said while Virgil took another drink from his mug.

"By the way, long as I'm here I wanted to ask you something. Have you had any energy companies approach you about oil or gas exploration on the reservation?"

"Actually, we had a couple in recent months. They'd like to send teams of geologists in to assess the potential. There's one or two proposals that are being considered that are before the tribal council now. They haven't been put up for public debate yet. That ought to be interesting when it happens."

"Grandfather, how do you feel about that idea?" Virgil asked.

Chato sat back in his chair, looking into his empty cup before responding. "You know, back when they brought the Cherokee into Oklahoma, they kept pushing them off the good land until they figured the land they finally got them on was about the poorest. Only then was the government happy. But one day some poor Cherokee farmer who didn't give up on that land went out to dig a furrow to plant a crop. Instead, what he got was a puddle of oil. That poor land became the most valuable in the state. The Cherokees got rich. I call that payback. So, if this land wants to offer us something to make our lives a little easier, I sure don't object." Billy and Virgil exchanged glances.

"Grandpa, I don't know how true that story was but, Billy, when they hold that public forum, I think you ought to bring him there to tell it."

Billy shook his head.

"Where are you going in your new uniform?" Rosie asked Virgil.

"Well, I didn't want to wear it the first time on an ordinary day. So I figured I'd put it on going over to Simpson's. They're having a brief service for Vernon, then the burial. It was either going to be street clothes or the new uniform. I reckoned the uniform makes people take a little more notice."

"Who did you have in mind?"

"Well, I'm kind of looking forward to meeting Calvin Thompson. He's been pretty hard to come by and I have a few questions."

"That reminds me, that woman from that oil and gas company called. She said to tell you that Calvin and Vernon had worked for Coastal. Vernon in a fairly minor capacity, but Calvin worked in contracts. She said he more than likely worked with Linda Murchison on more than one occasion. She also left next-of-kin information on Linda Murchison. I wrote it all up. It's on your desk."

Virgil picked up the paper Rosie referred to, then let out a sigh.

"Guess there's no putting it off."

He picked up the phone and punched in the number listed on the paper for Linda Murchison's next of kin. The phone rang three or four times. Virgil was almost hoping that no one would pick up, but he knew if that happened, he was just postponing the inevitable. Finally, when he was expecting voice mail to pick up, a feminine voice obviously out of breath answered.

"Mrs. Taylor?" Virgil asked.

"Yes, sorry about that. Just came in from chasing the kids in the backyard. Out of breath."

It was more than Virgil wanted to hear. He was picturing now in his head a young housewife and mother, probably Linda Murchison's sister, who had no idea he was about to ruin her day. By the time he got off the phone about twenty minutes later, his own emotions were on knife edge. Rosita heard most of the conversation, noted the change in Virgil's face. When he set the phone down, she brought a glass of ice water to him.

"Here, Virgil. Take a couple of minutes. Drink this." He took the offering, then put it to his lips. "For what it's worth, after what I heard, if I ever had to get a phone call like that, I'd want it to come from someone like you. Virgil, you definitely raise the bar for members of your sex."

"You keep saying those kinds of things, I'm going to have to put you in for a raise."

He stood up, took his hat off the desk. "Well, now I'm really in the mood for a visit to a funeral home."

He wasn't expecting many people when he stepped inside Simpson's. There wasn't even the greeter at the door. For Velma, there had been the sound of conversation as soon as he and Cesar had stepped through, along with some muted laughter during the exchange of reminiscences between folks who had shared in Velma's life. For Vernon, just the sound of silence. He had been too long out of reach. A couple of people near enough Vernon's age that they might have been in school with him or played on a team with him. Other than that, there were Marian and Charlie sitting together across from the coffin, which was closed. A few other people mostly sitting, looking as though in some cases they might have been related. Virgil knew Charlie had a younger sister and brother. Velma grew up an only child after losing her brother. He scanned the room, looking for someone who might be Calvin, but came up empty. So he walked over to Marian and Charlie. Marian stood when she saw him approaching, then took a few steps toward him. Charlie, head bent, remained in his chair.

"Thanks for stopping, Virgil. I know you're busy."

"Not that busy, Marian, that I can't take a little time out for something like this. Like Rosie said, you've had more than your share lately."

"Guess life comes in bunches sometimes."

"Yeah, I've noticed that. How's your dad doing?"

"Believe it or not, I think some of the starch has finally been taken out of him. But I know he'll bounce back. The doctor told me I could take him home after the cemetery. He just needs some rest and quiet time. I think the ranch is best for that. I think he gets a lot of his strength just being there, if you know what I mean."

Virgil, thinking of his last twenty-four hours, nodded.

"Needs to recharge his batteries. We all do from time to time. I was wondering if your brother was going to be here." Virgil saw an immediate reaction to his inquiry. "Is there something wrong, Marian?"

She hesitated. "Wrong. No, not wrong. Odd. Strange, maybe."

"Anything you want to tell me?"

She sat down in the nearest chair after seeing that a couple had sat next to Charlie. "You are about the only one I can talk to about this. On some level I feel guilty about some of the things I told you, up on the mesa. I mean, you heard me saying things about my brothers, particularly Calvin, which now seem terrible. Maybe I was all wrong. I mean, oh, I don't know. I'm just confused."

"What's changed?" Virgil asked.

For the next few minutes she told Virgil about how Calvin went to the hospital, trying to talk Charlie into selling him the ranch.

"I was shocked when Dad told me. I mean, Calvin couldn't get away from High Lonesome quick enough. Now he wants it?

It made no sense. Dad of course at first thought maybe it meant his wildest dream of operating the place with a son was going to come true. But Calvin as much as told him there would be no place for him there. Dad was completely deflated when I came in. Guess he didn't see any other option. That's when I told him what I planned to do. Virgil, he lit up like a Christmas tree. Even the doctor saw it when he came in to check on him. Said whatever I told him was the best medicine he could have gotten. Today, when Calvin came in, I took him into another room. Then I told him what I had planned. How Dad was behind it one hundred percent. How there was no way he was going to get his hands on High Lonesome."

"Well, what happened? How did he take it?"

Again, Virgil saw her immediate reaction.

"That's what has me second-guessing about what I've thought all these years about him and Vernon. When I first told him, I thought he'd fly into a rage. Instead, he became real quiet. Didn't say anything at first. It was almost like he was contemplative. But there was no outburst. When he finally spoke, it was like it was coming from a different person, someone I didn't know. He even actually smiled. Then he said something odd. 'Guess we always have to plan for an alternative ending.' That was it. Then he said he had to leave for a little while, but he'd be back for the final act. Then he left. I don't know—it wasn't at all what I expected from him. Have I been wrong? Misjudging him all these years? Has he changed into someone I never knew?"

"Marian, I think you have pretty good instincts. There might be more at play here than you know. People don't all of a sudden go one-eighty. The person Calvin was all those years is still there. He's just decided to put on a different mask."

36

Rosie had come back from lunch when Virgil returned from the cemetery. Dif had been holding down the fort while she was gone. Virgil had hoped to meet Calvin in more than passing, but it wasn't going to happen in that scenario, he soon realized.

"How did everything go this morning?" Dif asked.

"About like you'd expect," Virgil said.

"How's Charlie holding up?"

"Considering everything, he's doing okay. They were heading back to High Lonesome. He needs to get back to the familiar routine."

"Yeah, there's nothing like sleeping in your own bed. Charlie will snap back. Hell, I bet he'll be throwing a rope before Christmas."

Dif made the comment as Rosie came through the door from the holding cells.

"Boy, Dif, I gotta say Edna trained you well." She was carrying the large rectangular rubber basin holding the lunch dishes from the cells. "You washed and stacked everything real nice."

"Here, let me take that, Rosie."

Virgil took the rubber container and set it by the door.

"Think I'll put that comment on my résumé if ever I start looking for a new wife."

"Don't waste your time. You got lucky once. Better hold on to Edna as long as she'll have you. Don't think there'll be a line of takers if ever you become available."

"Well, I got other talents besides washing and stacking that keeps that smile on Edna's face."

"Here we go, another fish story. All you men are the same— it gets bigger and bigger with every telling."

"Are we talking about fish here, Rosie?" Virgil asked.

"Might as well be. Don Juan over here actually thinks his amorous attempts with Edna are the reason for her smile. At your age, it's a wonder you can even raise the flag."

"You'd be surprised," Dif said.

"No, Edna would be," Rosie said. "Just keep doing the washing and stacking if you want to keep Edna smiling."

"I hate to get off the topic. No telling where this conversation is going to end up, but is there anything I should know regarding the affairs of this office?"

"It was quiet," Dif said.

Rosita nodded in agreement. "Oh, there was one thing, Virgil. First thing this morning, Kyle Harrison stopped by. He left this for you. Said he heard you were wondering why they hadn't brought in those helicopters from Sky High to help in the search for that plane in the Superstition Mountains."

"That's all he said."

"Well, Virgil, you know those federal guys aren't big on

small talk, but he did say one other thing. Let me see . . . Oh, yeah, he said to tell you to remember what he said to you that night in the parking lot of the Black Bull."

Rosita handed Virgil the envelope she had been holding. Virgil laid it on his desk.

"Well, are you going to open it?"

"Okay."

He picked it up, then ripped open the end of the envelope. A set of keys fell out onto the desk. Virgil picked them up, turning them over in his hand. Then he sat down heavily in his chair.

"Well?" Rosie said. "Keys? Keys to what?"

"Keys to the Black Bull," Virgil said.

"I don't understand. Why did he give you keys to the Black Bull? Where did he get them? What did he say to you that night in the parking lot?"

Virgil suddenly jumped out of his chair.

"What the hell?" Dif said as Virgil started heading for the door.

"Virgil? Virgil? What did he say? Where are you going?"

Virgil stopped at the door, then looked at each of them waiting for an answer. "I'm going to High Lonesome. Tell Jimmy to get out there pronto. I could be wrong but . . ."

He didn't finish.

"But what did Kyle Harrison say that's got you going out there?"

"He said, 'Things are not always what they seem.'"

37

Virgil was thinking about what he had said to Mayor Bob "Ears" Jamison at Velma's wake. Up until now truly everything had been like a puzzle to him, so many bits and pieces. He'd spent the last weeks since Linda Murchison got hit by the semi and thrown over the overpass trying to connect the dots, but he couldn't find a common thread. Where did she come from? Why was she on the highway in the middle of the night? Was she running from or to? How did she connect to Velma or Charlie or High Lonesome? Then when at last he thought he made a connection, it was not with either of them, but with their sons. Now with the death of Vernon, a man with more than his share of demons, that connection had become frayed.

It had taken the recollection of what Kyle Harrison had said to him that night outside the Black Bull, coming on the heels of his conversation with Marian only a little over an hour earlier, to know that the plane that was supposed to have crashed in the Superstition Mountains and the son who had calmly accepted that his sister and father were going to try to rebuild High Lonesome had something in common. Neither was what it seemed to be.

The day had never cleared. No sun had broken through. The world was gray. Now, in midafternoon, a surprising light snow had started to fall. The temperature readout on the dashboard was thirty-three degrees, cold for the end of the first week in December. Not unheard of, but very unusual. By tomorrow, the temperature would probably bounce back to sixty, and if the sun was shining this would be forgotten, an anomaly. As the cruiser climbed toward higher ground, he saw a couple of places where a hint of snow had collected. Virgil thought of when he had stepped out of the cabin he shared with Marian up on the mesa. How the nighttime snow for a moment had transformed the landscape. Another example of when things were not what they seemed. He came to the turnoff for the ranch road, never slowed, but gunned the engine to new speed. The tires spun on the hardscrabble, digging in, scattering stone and loose gravel in the car's wake. The brief snow flurry seemed to be losing its battle. Large raindrops instead began to splatter the windshield. Virgil turned on the wipers. Dirt that had flown up mixed with the rain streaking across his vision till he was forced to turn on the washer. The barns, corrals, and last the house came into view. Nothing seemed amiss or other than as it should be. He saw two cars parked by the house. He slowed his vehicle, then rolled to a stop alongside one of them. When he stepped out of the car, there was a moment of self-doubt. It was strictly instinct that had brought him here, nothing but an intuitive sense. That innate voice of premonition that he had learned long ago to heed, not to ignore.

He could see lights on in the house as he headed down the

walkway, past the gardens that would show no color for months to come. He stopped at the front door. It was the one moment when he hoped his instincts would prove wrong. He knocked loudly, then after a moment passed, he knocked again. The door opened. Marian stood in the perimeter of an overhead light.

"Oh, Virgil," was all she said as he stepped through. Then he felt another presence to his side, a sudden explosion in his head. The light and Marian faded from his view.

It could have been five minutes or five hours. All he knew was the pounding in his head was unrelenting. In a reflex move he put his hand to his head. He didn't need to look to know the sticky ooze was his blood.

"Oh, Virgil." They were the last words he had heard. Now they were the first. He opened his eyes wide, trying to follow the sound of her voice. Finally, Marian's face came into view. He realized at the same time he saw her above him that he was lying on the floor.

"Here, this will help." She raised his head so that she could reach his wound. He felt the sharp sensation of cold. A sigh escaped his lips. She took the cloth away, then replaced it with another. For the next few minutes, she kept repeating the process until at last the constant throb started to ebb. His vision became clearer. He saw Charlie sitting kind of slumped in a chair a few feet away. Then another figure overarching Marian as she knelt by his side.

"That's enough. You're wasting your time. It's not going to make much difference anyway. Get up."

Marian, with the bowl and cloths in her hand, rose in response to the command. The unfamiliar voice continued.

"So you're the sheriff I've heard so much about. Can say one thing for you, you got a hard head. You were only out for ten or fifteen minutes. Thought you'd be gone much longer." When he stopped talking, he reached down, roughly grabbing Virgil, dragging him to his feet. Then he literally threw him into a chair close by where Charlie sat. "What are you doing here?" Virgil looked up into the face he'd seen only in passing earlier in the day.

"So you're Calvin. Calvin Thompson. Out of the shadows, finally."

"You didn't answer my question, lawman. What are you doing here?"

"I came for you, Calvin. I came for you."

There was a momentary silence, then a sneer crossed Calvin's face. It was followed by the laugh of a madman.

"Well, you got me, but guess that's in reverse order. I got you." Another crazed, hollow laugh followed. "You're making my job a little harder."

"Oh, I don't know. You seem to be enjoying yourself. From what I know, you've been practicing for something like this for quite a while."

"What do you know?"

"Oh, it took me some time to put all the pieces together, but I think I've got it mostly figured out."

Virgil inadvertently glanced at Marian when he saw her move in back of Calvin. Calvin caught his misstep and swung around as Marian raised her arm. He grabbed her wrist, then smashed her in the face with a gun, which Virgil recognized only at the moment as his own. His hand automatically slipped to his empty holster as he saw the knife Marian held clatter harmlessly to the floor. He saw her reel back from the blow, grabbing for the table in back of her as blood gushed from her nose.

"Thanks for the heads-up, Sheriff. My sister almost got me."

Virgil tried getting to his feet. The room started spinning. "I'm sorry, Marian."

She had managed to steady herself on the table. Then she grabbed one of the cloths from the bowl that she had used when she was helping Virgil. She held it to her face.

"I'm all right, Virgil."

Calvin pushed her into another chair.

"No, no, Calvin. Why?"

Charlie stirred, pulled himself upright in his chair.

"Don't interrupt the sheriff. He was going to tell me how he's got me all figured out. Go on, Sheriff, continue."

Virgil glared at Calvin, but knew he needed time.

"Guess it began with the girl. You knew her from Coastal. Realized she knew her stuff. I guess you needed money. Maybe you owed some heavyweights in Vegas or you just flat out couldn't wait for your share of the inheritance. Probably a combination. Then you heard about the oil and gas reserves that Coastal and other companies were looking into in the Southwest. That's when you remembered all the shale up in that High Lonesome country that borders the reservation and you wondered. So I guess you somehow got Linda Murchison to go have a look. But something went wrong, didn't it?"

"Pretty good, so far," Calvin said. "She said it really looked good. As a matter of fact, she said the find could be huge. But then she told me she suspected most of it could be under reservation land. I asked her if it could be tapped on our land, then drawn out from there. She said she thought it could, but then she said she'd have to tell them on the reservation. I tried to talk her out of it, but the stupid bitch was adamant. That's when I knew she couldn't leave the top of that mesa. But she had a hard head like you. When I came back to finish her off she was gone. When I heard much later that a woman had been killed crossing the interstate I figured maybe I got lucky. Then I heard the old man had gone up there looking for some strays, I figured another opportunity had come my way. I knew I couldn't be there, had to have an alibi, so I contacted some people. The moron I got was a pretty good shot, but not too swift on the follow-up. He told me when he looked down into that arroyo the old man looked dead. Blood all over. I shoulda told him the old man wouldn't kill easy."

"So that's when everything began to head south?" Virgil asked.

"No, I figured I'd get lucky, get another chance. Here it is."

"But what about Vernon and your mother? That was all part of it?"

"Vernon . . . Vernon just fell apart. I got him to give her the barbiturates in her tea, but that's all. I had to finish it."

"An overdose of your insulin."

"Pretty good, Sheriff. The old lady just went to sleep. I probably did her a favor, avoiding a painful old age."

"But Vernon didn't agree with your rationalization, did he?"

"Vernon, he could have been part of all this, but he just kept getting shakier and shakier. I'd always been able to control him, but I couldn't take the chance anymore."

"So, what, you loaded him up on booze and tranquilizers?"

Calvin laughed a little. Virgil felt for the first time in his life like he was looking into the face of pure evil.

"He was higher than a kite. It was probably the best trip

Vernon ever had. When I loaded him in that car, he had no idea where he was. All it took was me following him down the road, then giving him a little nudge when he hit the right spot. Thought he'd end up in the river, but he didn't quite make it. No matter."

"So everything worked out until Marian."

Calvin looked at Marian, seated on the kitchen chair.

"She was always a pain in the ass, even when we were kids. 'Why don't you do what Dad wants?' 'High Lonesome can be yours someday.' Well, she was right about that. After today, it will be."

"So you figured she'd never come back here?"

"That was the plan. The old man could have lived out his days in some home. She could have sold me her share, gone on her merry way. What I have to do now is all her fault. You hear that, Marian? This is all your fault. Couldn't be content to stay in San Francisco. What was it you told me? 'I never should have left High Lonesome.' Well, you're getting your wish. You never will."

"What about me?" Virgil asked.

"You? Hell, you're just collateral damage."

"Calvin, whatever you have in mind . . . you'll be found out. How will you explain?"

Calvin's eyes lit up. "Nothing to explain. My sister and dad died in a fire. You tried to save them. Died trying. They're going to find you right inside the door. Yeah, that's good. That's exactly how it will look. Marian died trying to save the old man, getting him out of bed. You, trying to save both of them. It's perfect."

"No . . . No, Calvin." Charlie tried to get out of the chair as he spoke, but fell back down.

"That's it. It's perfect. Get on your feet, Sheriff."

He waved the gun in Virgil's face. Marian moved in her chair. "No, not you. Stay right there."

Virgil got to his feet. "Now, I want you to get him into the bedroom."

Calvin motioned with the gun toward the open door at the far end of the back wall. Virgil helped Charlie to his feet, then steadied him. Charlie leaned heavily on Virgil. Virgil placed Charlie's left arm around his shoulders, supporting him, with his right hand around Charlie's back. They took a couple of steps toward the open door.

"I'm feeling a little shaky," Virgil said.

"Marian, get around on the other side of him. Now."

She got up, then walked to support her father on the other side. She and Virgil exchanged glances, but said nothing. Slowly, they made their way to and then through the open door.

"Now, lay him on the bed." They brought him to the bed, then sat him on the edge. "Stretch him out. Then undress him, put him under the covers."

Virgil pulled off Charlie's boots while Marian undid his shirt. Together, they worked to get him out of his pants. All the while Virgil's mind was racing, trying to think of some kind of diversion, anything that would give him a chance at Calvin or the gun. But there was nothing. He was still breathing hard from carrying Charlie into the room. His head was pounding from the effort, while the nosebleed that Marian had managed to stop for a while was now running freely again, dripping on Charlie's shirt.

"That'll do just fine." Calvin was standing in the open doorway, gun in hand, the whole time.

"Calvin, you can't do this," Marian said.

"Sure I can." Calvin almost smiled. "You gave me no choice, Marian. Like I said, it's all your fault."

Charlie started moaning.

"What's his problem?"

"It's his broken ribs. When he lies down, they seem to hurt more."

Charlie tried shifting in the bed.

"What did they do for that in the hospital?"

"My pills, my pills," Charlie said, moaning louder.

"Get him to stop. Give him something." Calvin sounded agitated.

"I don't know," Marian started to respond. Charlie moaned louder.

"My pills, my pills," he said again, pointing to the night table next to Virgil. "Give me my pills," he said in a louder voice. "In the drawer."

Marian looked at Virgil, shaking her head while Charlie started moaning again. "In the drawer," he said again.

"Get the goddamn pills. Give him the goddamn pills. I don't want to have to listen to him while I'm finishing up here. Get them out of the drawer."

Virgil turned to the table, bent over it, then slid open the drawer.

"I don't see any pills in here, Charlie."

"In the back, Virgil. Way in the back." Virgil slid his hand in farther. Then he felt the familiar barrel of a pistol.

"I think I feel the bottle," he said. "Charlie, why did you put them so far back?"

"Safety, safety," Charlie said.

"Just get them, then give him a dozen," Calvin said.

Virgil slipped his hand to the grip, started to bring his arm out, flipping the safety on the gun as he did. He knew he'd only have one chance. He swung around, the gun gleaming in his hand. The look on Calvin's face was worth a thousand words. Virgil squeezed the trigger. The blast echoed, reverberating through the house. Calvin stood in the doorway, a puzzled expression on his face. He looked down at his chest. The red stain there got bigger and bigger. He opened his mouth as if to say something, but then sank wordlessly to the floor.

38

Virgil sat in his kitchen, staring down at the empty glass along with the set of keys he had given to Ruby as he was leaving the Black Bull that last day they were together. It seemed like a thousand years ago or a day. From his seat he glanced out the window into the darkness beyond. Again, he thought of his father, and the idea of trying to maintain the peace in his little corner of the world. Today, he had killed a man to do that. He knew he had no choice, even the man's sister and father told him that. It didn't make it any easier to swallow. A life is a life. It was a high price to pay. Sitting in the quiet of his own home, listening to the wind that blew in the night, he heard the voice of the old house. Creaks and sometimes whisperings as if the old house were rebelling against the wind-driven currents that were trying to find a way in. Virgil had heard the sounds before. He could hear the voice of his mother telling him as a small child that they were the voices of all the people who had come before and lived in this place. She had told him not to be afraid, because they were saying to the night that we are still here. There is life in this house.

In a way it was comforting to hear them now, remembering her words. He had been trying, not too successfully, to process what had happened at High Lonesome, along with what the key he was fingering on the table meant in the great scheme of things. He thought that in trying to understand the darkness that causes people to do the things that they do, the darkness that he was trying to confront, maybe it was important to understand the voice of the old house. That by doing what he did, he also was saying no, there is life here.

He got up from his seat at the table when he saw the headlights of a car pull in, then come to a stop by the corral. He slipped the keys into his pocket and walked to the door. It was biting cold standing out on the porch. The wind sounded like a coyote's howl. He walked down the stairs over to the car. A figure was standing by the corral fence.

"Hey, Jimmy."

"Hey, Virgil."

Like Virgil, Jimmy stood coatless. "That was something today. I mean, I just. His own mother, and brother. Virgil, I just don't . . . I don't understand."

"You know, Jimmy, neither do I. I've been sitting in my kitchen trying to figure it all out. But I'm thinking that's a mistake. No matter how hard we try, we'll probably never understand. Kind of like I said to you the other night when you were wrestling with why you walked away and Vernon didn't. Life is just too damn random. I guess when you are faced with something like this—death and dying—it's best just to walk away. That's what you and I are going to do right now. I'm going to get my coat. Then you and I are heading to the Lazy Dog for a couple of beers and burgers. Then we're going to talk about tomorrow and the day after that."